The Amish Quiltmaker's Unruly In-Law

JENNIFER BECKSTRAND

ZEBRA BOOKS
KENSINGTON PUBLISHING CORP.
www.kensingtonbooks.com

ZEBRA BOOKS are published by

Kensington Publishing Corp.
119 West 40th Street
New York, NY 10018

All Kensington titles, imprints, and distributed lines are available at special quantity discounts for bulk purchases for sales promotion, premiums, fund-raising, educational, or institutional use.

Special book excerpts or customized printings can also be created to fit specific needs. For details, write or phone the office of the Kensington Sales Manager: Attn.: Sales Department. Kensington Publishing Corp., 119 West 40th Street, New York, NY 10018. Phone: 1-800-221-2647.

Zebra and the Z logo Reg. U.S. Pat. & TM Off.
BOUQUET Reg. U.S. Pat. & TM Off.

First Printing: July 2021
ISBN-13: 978-1-4201-5201-2
ISBN-10: 1-4201-5201-7

ISBN-13: 978-1-4201-5202-9 (eBook)
ISBN-10: 1-4201-5202-5 (eBook)

10 9 8 7 6 5 4 3 2 1

Printed in the United States of America

A GOOD AMISH HEART

"One time, it was just Dat, me, and Levi camping, and Dat showed us all the biggest constellations. That was before he stopped loving me and before I stopped trying to make him love me."

Linda couldn't let that falsehood stand without a fight. "Of course your *dat* loves you. What a silly thing to say."

He didn't like it when she called him silly. She used the word purposefully in an attempt to light a fire under him. His anger was better than this self-inflicted hopelessness that he wore like a heavy winter coat.

He didn't take the bait. Instead, he sighed and slid his arm off her shoulder. "I've done too many bad things for anyone to love me. I know what I am. Might as well accept it."

Linda found herself getting angry at Ben's lack of emotion. "Accept it? And then what? Go on living in this tiny little world you've created for yourself?" She grabbed his hand. "You are not worthless, Ben. You have so much love to give. I've seen how you treat Winnie and your *mammi*. You good-naturedly put up with my essential oils and my snowshoes and my teasing."

"Not always so good-naturedly."

"You're fiercely loyal to Esther and Levi, and whether you want to admit it or not, you put yourself between me and that bear. You were more concerned for my life than your own. And no one who can sing like you can be all bad." Her voice cracked into a thousand pieces, but she pressed forward because she had to make him understand. "And because . . . *ach*, I love you, Ben. It's crazy and I can't believe I'm saying this, but I love you . . ."

Chapter One

Linda Eicher tightened her arm around her little sister, Nora, who was shivering uncontrollably. She rubbed her hand up and down Nora's arm in an attempt to generate some heat so Nora's teeth wouldn't crack from chattering so hard. "Cold day, ain't not?" she said, flashing Nora a grin.

Ten-year-old Nora sucked in her breath between her teeth. "We should move to Florida. There's lots of Amish in Florida. That's what Brittany Peeples says. And they never have bad weather."

"There's no such thing as bad weather," Linda said. "Only the wrong clothes."

Nora made a face. "What does that mean?"

"Sounds like a whole lot of nonsense," Mamm said.

Dat glanced back at Nora from the front seat of the buggy. "Isn't it nice to have a heater on days like this? The buggy will be warm in no time."

Mamm, as rigid and unyielding as ever, folded her arms and stared out the front window. "In my day, the bishop didn't allow buggy heaters or taillights. And that was in Wisconsin. You haven't seen anything until you've seen a Wisconsin winter. Isn't that right, Tim?"

"That's right, *heartzley*. That's the very reason we moved to Colorado. Our children won't freeze like icicles every time we take a ride in the buggy yet."

Linda smiled to herself. Mamm sounded a hundred years old when she talked about how things were "in her day," even though she was only forty-two. Mamm liked to reminisce about the good old days when they weren't allowed to have battery-operated lights or LP gas stoves, but she was as happy as anybody not having to live that way anymore. When Linda was nine, her parents had followed a bishop and a group of Amish people from their more conservative community in Wisconsin to settle in Colorado, where the bishop and the elders had made the *Ordnung* strict but not suffocating. They were still considered Old Order Amish, but heaters in buggies and LP gas refrigerators were allowed. Such things made life easier, while still keeping their community separate from the world.

"I'm not cold," Elmer Lee insisted, even though he clamped his arms around himself and leaned into Linda for warmth. At fourteen, Elmer Lee thought it was unmanly to be cold.

Linda put her arm around him anyway. Soon Elmer Lee would be a man and too old for a *schwester*'s affection. Elmer Lee grunted his disapproval but didn't pull away. Linda cocked her head to one side. "Did you hear that?"

Over the rhythmic thud of horse hooves against a snow-packed road and the sound of buggy wheels rolling over the ground, there was a strange creak and a faint swish-swish coming from behind them.

"Hear what?" Dat said with a grin. "Is Elmer's stomach rumbling?"

Linda frowned. "Something's behind us." She turned around and knelt on the bench so she could see out one of the tiny windows in the back. "*Ach, du lieva*," she muttered. An Amish boy was gliding over the deep snow on the side of the road behind their buggy, holding tightly to two ends of a rope. He had somehow attached his rope to their buggy, and they were pulling him along at a pretty good clip. "*Ach, du lieva*," Linda said again. "He's hitched a ride."

"What?"

"Someone is skiing behind our buggy."

Elmer Lee knelt on the bench and peeked out the other window. "I think it's Ben Kiem," he said. "He's not doing so *gute*."

Of course it was Ben Kiem, either him or one of the other troublemakers in the *gmayna* he hung out with. Ben was indeed wobbly on those skis, as if he'd never skied a day in his life, which he probably hadn't. Skiing wasn't a popular Amish sport, though Linda was always trying to convince *die youngie* to try it.

Mamm opened her window and stuck her head out of the buggy, letting in a blast of frigid air that obliterated any wisp of warmth from the battery-operated heater. "Stop, Tim. Stop the buggy!" she yelled. "He's going to die."

Before Dat could stop, Ben met a three-foot-deep drift of snow, went airborne, and crashed spectacularly into a snowbank. Right before the crash, there was a creak and a metallic pop from the buggy. It wasn't a heartening sound. Dat pulled on the reins and stopped Snapper in the middle of the road. Dat set the brake, and the family piled out of the buggy, except for Nora, who was more cold than she was curious.

Ignoring the body lying in the snow, Mamm bent over to look at the right-side taillight, which lay shattered on the road along with the bracket that held it to the buggy. It seemed Ben had looped his rope around the taillight and used that to hook himself to the buggy.

Linda and Elmer Lee went straight for the stupid boy lying in the snow, a twisted mess of arms and legs and skis. "You okay?" Elmer Lee said.

Ben lay on his back, gazing at the sky as if he'd been camped there for hours looking for cloud animals. His black church hat had stayed on his head the whole ride, but now it was caked with snow, and the brim had partially torn away from the cap. Breathing heavily, he tried to sit up, fell back, and grimaced.

"Are you hurt?" Linda said, holding out her hand to help him up.

"I'm fine," was his curt reply. He ignored her hand and managed to sit up by himself.

"You broke our turn light," Elmer said.

"A rock tripped me."

Linda smiled, glad that he wasn't seriously hurt and glad no one in her family was as *dumm* as Ben Kiem. "You're a terrible skier."

Ben raised his eyebrows in surprise and indignation. "Nobody asked you." He tried to stand, but it was going to be almost impossible the way his rope was tangled around his skis and his skis were tangled around his legs.

"Elmer, can you untwist the rope?" Linda bent over to see what she could do about removing the skis from his feet. And burst out laughing. She laughed until it hurt and still she couldn't stop.

The resentment grew like mold on Ben's face. "What's so funny?"

"These are water skis," Linda stuttered between giggles. "You're snow skiing with water skis. Oy, anyhow, you look silly."

"I do not. I was just having some fun, and they worked fine." Elmer pulled the ropes away, and Ben tried to stand, but the skis were just too cumbersome and slick for him to gain any traction.

Linda took hold of the tip of one water ski.

Ben jerked his foot back. "Go away."

Linda blew air from between her lips. "Let me help you get those things off, or your *hinnerdale* is going to freeze. You don't enjoy sitting in the snow, do you?"

He narrowed his eyes in her direction. "Don't make fun of me."

"I only make fun of people when they deserve it, like when they do something *deerich* and immature and suffer the consequences. You have to admit you look wonderful funny."

"Leave me alone," Ben hissed. He made a feeble attempt to reach out and pull off one of his skis, but he couldn't bend his leg close enough to get a good grip on the ski.

Linda sighed loudly. "*Ach*, don't be such a baby. Elmer Lee, come on this side." She wrapped both hands around the tip of Ben's left ski and tugged firmly. Elmer Lee did the same with the right ski.

Ben gasped as the left water ski came off his foot, along with his black boot. Fortunately, his stocking stayed put, though he did have a rather large hole where the big toe stuck out. Elmer Lee managed to get the other ski off without removing Ben's boot. Linda yanked the boot from the rubber toehold of the ski and handed it to Ben. He took it grudgingly and without looking at her, quickly put it back on his foot, and pushed himself from the ground. His church trousers were soaked, and his coat and mittens were caked with snow and ice. And his hat! Oh, dear. Linda couldn't keep a giggle from tripping from her lips.

He turned on her as if she had attacked him with a knife. "What is so funny?"

She couldn't speak without erupting with laughter, so she clapped her hand over her mouth and simply pointed to his head.

Elmer Lee still had the power of speech. "The brim of your hat is ripped." It was literally hanging on to the crown by a thread.

Ben reached up, grabbed his hat by the crown, and snatched it off his head. The force of Ben's tug was too much for the brim. It gave up its hold, ripped from the crown, and fell to the ground.

Elmer Lee and Linda burst into laughter. Ben's face grew even redder. Linda felt a tiny bit bad about laughing, but Ben Kiem had gotten his just desserts. Besides, the more she tried to suppress her laughter, the worse it got.

He tossed what was left of his hat into the snow. "That's not very Christian of you to laugh at me."

She was sorely tempted to scold him, but he'd probably had enough of her disapproval for one day. "Don't look so sour. A merry heart does *gute* like a medicine."

Mamm walked toward Ben carrying the shards of their

taillight in her outstretched hand. "You broke our buggy. And for sure and certain, you're going to pay for it."

Stiffly, Ben bent over and picked up his skis and his rope. "You should ask the man that made that buggy for you to pay. The taillight wasn't attached securely."

"Don't blame other people for what you've wrought yourself," Mamm said, shaking her finger at him as if he were a naughty toddler.

Ben took a step back and grunted. "Okay, okay. I'll pay to have it fixed. You don't have to get all worked up. I was only having some fun."

Mamm wasn't going to let him get away with that excuse. She never let anyone get away with anything if she could help it. "Fun at another person's expense is selfishness."

Ben shot a piercing look at Linda. "Or spite," he muttered.

Linda raised an eyebrow. She wasn't being spiteful when she'd laughed at him, was she? Mostly she was amused. And maybe a little bit smug that Ben Kiem hadn't gotten away with his mischief making like he usually did.

Mamm pinned Ben with a withering stare. "Not only did you break our buggy, but you were skiing on the Sabbath. Sabbath breaking is a serious sin, Ben Kiem. Are you going to tell your *dat* or should I?"

Ben's face seemed to lose all color. Ben's *dat* was the bishop, and if there was anybody who shouldn't break the Sabbath, it was the bishop's son. But like a cornered wild animal, he decided to attack. "I'm in *rumschpringe*. I can make my own choices."

Mamm shook her head. "*Rumschpringe* doesn't give you leave to break the commandments. Best to confess your sin to your *dat* and face the consequences like a man."

Ben paused and pressed his lips together, as if giving Mamm's advice serious thought. Or maybe he was contemplating how much trouble he'd be in when his *dat* found out about what he'd done.

Linda didn't feel quite so smug anymore. Maybe Ben really was sorry. And maybe she could try to make him feel better. "If you really want to ski, you need the right skis. Cross-country skis are best for . . ."

Ben scowled. "I don't care."

Okay then. She'd let him figure out his own skis.

Mamm frowned. "Skiing is folly, Linda. A waste of your money, if you ask me."

Linda grinned at her mother. They'd had some version of this conversation more times than Linda could count. Worrying and fussing was how Mamm showed her love. "Now, Mamm, I need sunshine and fresh air. You can't put a price on that."

Mamm harrumphed. "Need fresh air? Milk the cow or feed the chickens. Don't come crying to me if you get killed by a bear or drown in a river or fall off a cliff."

Linda giggled. "If any of those things happen, I promise not to bother you with it."

Mamm cracked a smile and waved her hand in Linda's direction. "*Ach*, stop teasing me."

Nora stuck her head out of the buggy. "It's really getting cold in here."

"Let's go home," Dat said. He put his arm around Elmer Lee and nudged him toward the buggy.

Mamm nodded as if everything had been settled to her satisfaction. "We will let you know how much it costs to fix the taillight. And you make certain you tell your *dat* what you've done today. Have a *gute* Sabbath."

Ben probably wouldn't have a *gute* Sabbath if he told his *dat* what he'd done, but Mamm probably hadn't thought that through. Mamm, Dat, and Elmer Lee climbed into the buggy.

Without acknowledging Mamm's *gute* wishes, Ben tucked his skis under one arm, turned away, and ambled down the road like a very old man.

"Wait," Linda said, running after him. "Let us give you a ride back."

"*Nae, denki*," Ben said. "I'll walk."

She hadn't expected him to say yes, but she'd done the right thing by asking. It was cold, he was soaking wet, and it was a long way back. He'd skied for at least a quarter mile.

She shrugged. "Okay. Let me know if you want to go cross-country skiing sometime. It's fun, and it's slower than downhill skiing so you're less likely to wipe out."

He shuffled down the road. "I'd rather go to the dentist," he said, without looking back.

He was obviously still mad at her, because who in their right mind would rather see the dentist than go skiing? At least she could say she'd done her best.

Chapter Two

Ben tried to walk without limping, at least until Linda Eicher's buggy was out of sight. He wasn't going to give that snobby girl the satisfaction of knowing that he'd hurt himself. He'd been laughed at enough for one day. And he wouldn't have gotten into that buggy even if a pack of angry wolves had been chasing him. The righteous indignation in there would have smothered him.

He glanced behind him. The buggy turned down the road. Now he could limp as badly as he wanted to. His leg burned something wonderful, and his shoulder would for sure and certain have a big bruise. He'd fallen on something hard and unforgiving under the snow, and now his whole body screamed in agony. After less than a hundred steps, he started wishing he'd taken Linda Eicher up on her offer of a ride home. His trousers were soaking wet, he didn't have a hat, and his shin hurt so badly, he seriously didn't know how much farther he could go.

If Linda Eicher hadn't laughed at him, he wouldn't have refused a ride in her buggy. His predicament was all her fault.

Needing to lighten his load, he tossed Wally's skis and

the rope off to the side of the road. He could come back for them later when the pain didn't make him feel like passing out. Something wet and sticky felt as if it was pooling at the bottom of his boot. A dizzying sight met him when he lifted his trouser leg. Oh, *sis yuscht*. An angry gash at least five inches long and who-knew-how deep ran down the length of his shin. The front of his trouser leg was soaked with blood, but Ben hadn't noticed before because his trousers were black and already wet. A long rip in the fabric showed where something sharp had torn through his trousers and cut his leg. He turned and squinted in the direction of where he'd fallen. Smears of dark red blood stained the snow. Neither he nor any of the Eichers had noticed. He'd also left a trail of tiny drops of blood on the snowy road. Oh, *sis yuscht*. Skiing behind a buggy was the stupidest idea he and Wally Bontrager had ever thought up.

But Wally had dared him to do it, and Ben was never one to back down from a dare.

Ben shivered violently, whether from the cold or his own stupidity, he wasn't exactly sure. He peered down the road toward the Troyers' house where they had held services today. It looked so far away. Like Linda had said, he'd gone a long way on those skis. One side of his mouth curled upward. It had felt like flying.

Where was Wally? Only two buggies were still parked in front of the Troyers' house. Most people had already gone home. Not wanting his parents to see what he was about to do with Wally's skis on the Sabbath, he had told his parents not to wait for him. He often walked home with Wally and Simeon. Ben heaved a great sigh. If he went to the Troyers' house, he'd have to confess to breaking the

Sabbath and breaking the Eichers' taillight. But could he make it all the way home before either freezing or bleeding to death?

He glanced down at his leg. He wasn't going to bleed to death, but it sure hurt something wonderful. He needed to get out of the wind and prop up his leg, maybe take a nice warm bath and then wash his clothes in the sink so Mamm would never know about his foolishness. It would be harder to hide the seven-inch tear in his trousers. Did he even know where Mamm kept her needles and thread? Could he figure out how to sew even if he found them?

To sew! His new sister-in-law, Esther, knew how to sew. According to his *bruder* Levi, Esther was one of the best quilters in the country. Surely she would repair his trousers without telling Mamm or Dat. Esther was nice like that and so was Levi. Neither of them would tell on Ben, and their house was closer. Easier than limping all the way home.

Ben glanced to the north. Would it be faster to cut across three pastures, wading through knee-deep snow, or to take the long route by way of the snow-packed road? He'd already made one stupid decision today. He wouldn't make another. The road it was, and he'd have to hurry. He sucked in a hard breath in anticipation of the pain. It was going to be a long fifteen minutes, but he'd brought this on himself. No doubt, Linda Eicher would say it was exactly what he deserved.

Every step was agony, but the bitter cold propelled him forward. How *deerich* he had been to hitch a ride behind Eicher's buggy without planning on a way to get back. Wally had probably been cornered by his *dat* and ordered to go home before he could help Ben. He was on his own.

After ten minutes of half limping, half dragging

himself down the road, Ben was almost breathless with relief at the sight of Levi and Esther's house. He had never seen a more beautiful sight than the tidy, red-brick house where his *bruder* and *schwester*-in-law lived with their adopted daughter, Winnie. Wisps of smoke curled from the chimney, and tiny icicles hung from the seams of the rain gutters. Those leaks would need to be caulked come spring. Ben would have to do it because Levi shouldn't be getting up on ladders now that he had a family to take care of.

The nearness of the house gave Ben new purpose. He limped double-time down the road and practically ran across the yard to their porch. He stopped himself right before he knocked. Even though he wanted to pound the door down and get into the warmth of the house, he didn't want to wake Winnie if she was taking a nap. He knocked softly, waited for a few seconds, then knocked again louder.

Levi opened the door, and his eyes nearly popped out of his head. "What has happened? You look froze to death." He ushered Ben into the house and closed the door behind him. "*Cum, cum,*" he said, leading Ben into the kitchen.

Winnie sat in her highchair with spaghetti sauce smeared all over her face. "Beh!" Winnie squealed, reaching for Ben with her tomatoey hands. *Beh* was how she said his name, and it was actually the only word she knew. Winnie loved Ben, even if everyone else thought he was a nuisance.

Esther stood at the stove stirring a pot of liquid that smelled wonderful *gute*, like Christmas morning in a warm house. Ben's sister-in-law always had something tucked behind her ear. Today it was a plastic spoon. She turned around to look at him, and her eyes flashed in alarm. No doubt, he was a shocking sight. "*Ach, du lieva,* Ben! *Ach, du lieva.* Sit down, sit down right now."

Levi pulled a chair out from under the table, and Ben sort of fell into it. His pants were so stiff, he couldn't bend his knees. Esther clucked her tongue, bent over him, and took his face in her hands. He hissed. The touch of her warm skin felt like a hot iron against his cheeks.

"Your face is like ice," she said. She curled her fingers around his ears. "And no hat. Your ears are bright red. They must ache something wonderful."

"Can I have a blanket?"

"No blanket for you." Esther glanced at Levi. "He needs a warm bath, but not too warm or it will burn his skin." She opened a drawer and pulled out a cooking thermometer. "Maybe a hundred degrees? Like we do for Winnie's bath."

Levi took the thermometer and marched down the hall to the bathroom.

Esther gasped. "There's blood." She turned her head in the direction Levi had just gone. "Levi, there's blood."

Levi shot out of the bathroom like a boomerang. "What?"

Esther pointed to three tiny drops on the floor. "Blood."

"Sorry to get your floor dirty," Ben said. "It should have stopped bleeding by now."

"Do you think I care about my floor at a time like this?" Esther knelt down next to him. "Let me see." She made a face and glanced up at him. "Left leg?"

He nodded then tensed when she reached out.

"Not to worry. I'll be careful. I just want to see what sort of mess you've gotten yourself into."

Ben gripped the armrests and shot a pleading look at Levi. "Don't tell Dat."

Levi didn't reply, just watched as Esther studied Ben's leg. She raised her hand and hovered it over his leg—thank Derr Herr she didn't touch it—then untied the sticky, blood-caked laces of his boot. She turned to Levi. "Can you help?"

Levi jumped as if he'd been shot from a rifle. He knelt down beside Esther, cupped his hands around the heel of Ben's boot and slowly pulled it off. The motion hurt a little, but mostly because his foot ached with cold.

"You've got a hole in your stocking," Esther said, the hint of a smile playing at her lips. "Why is it that boys never care about their stockings? It's an embarrassment to mothers everywhere." She gently pulled off his stocking and nudged his stiff pant leg up to his knee. It couldn't help but scrape against the gash in his leg.

He grunted in pain. Linda Eicher would say he deserved it.

A sound of distress came from the back of Esther's throat. "*Ach*, Ben. You got yourself but good." She looked at Levi. "We should take him to the hospital."

Ben's teeth started chattering. The sight of his leg caked with dried blood made him dizzy, not to mention that the cold had finally seeped into his bones. He could sure enough use a smoke right now. "I don't need a hospital. It's not that bad."

"Ha," Levi said, showing a lot less concern for his seriously wounded *bruder* than he should have. Something like a smile crept onto his face. "Your teeth are going to vibrate right out of your head. You need a bath, then we can talk about the hospital. I'll fill the tub."

Nothing in the world sounded better than a warm bath. Ben's joints were so stiff and cold, they felt as if they might snap if he tried to move them.

Esther turned off whatever was on the stove then removed his other boot, then his stocking. This one didn't have a hole, but she didn't mention it, even though he deserved a little credit for one good stocking. She helped him off with his coat and laid it on the table. "Do I need to walk you to the bathroom? Levi is going to need to help you off with your trousers and such."

For sure and certain, Levi was going to need to help. Ben's fingers were so stiff, he couldn't even make a fist. "I can walk, but I'll get blood on your floor."

Esther scrunched her lips to one side of her face. "Don't you just love how easy it is to clean linoleum?"

Ben cracked a smile. "I've never cleaned it, so I wouldn't know."

"Ben Kiem, it's high time you did more to help your *mamm* around the house." Esther offered both hands and pulled Ben to his feet. The kitchen spun in front of his eyes for a few seconds. It was a *gute* thing the bathroom wasn't far down the hall. Esther must have sensed how unstable he was, because she draped his arm around her shoulder and toddled with him to the bathroom.

The bath was pure torture and pure heaven at the same time. His skin stung something wonderful when the water touched it, but then the warmth seeped into his body and he melted like a bar of chocolate on a summer day. He washed his hair twice and gingerly washed his leg with strong soap and a washcloth. By the time he finished, the bathwater was pink.

Levi brought Ben some clean clothes and a fluffy white towel that smelled like a warm spring breeze. He didn't deserve a warm spring breeze, but he certainly wasn't going to refuse it. He put on Levi's blue shirt and a pair of Levi's underwear and wrapped the towel around his waist. It was embarrassing for his sister-in-law to see him without trousers, but they'd only get in the way when she fixed his leg. *If* she fixed his leg. She might refuse to help him and insist he go to the hospital.

His wound had started bleeding again when he'd gotten into the tub, and blood continued to seep from the cut as he got dressed. He really did feel bad about Esther's floor. The floor in the bathroom was laid with tile of all different shapes and colors. Esther had designed it herself, and now Ben's blood was ruining it.

Sheepishly, he limped down the hall and into the kitchen, clutching the towel around his waist like a shield. Esther stood right where she'd been when he'd first come into the house, stirring the same pot of something that smelled delicious. The spoon behind her ear had been replaced with a small pair of scissors.

She turned and pressed her finger to her lips. "Shh," she said. "Levi is putting Winnie down for her nap. He's always been better at it than I am."

Ben's trousers and stockings hung by the window on the round clothesline that Amish *fraaen* usually used for stockings and unmentionables. "Did you wash them?"

She nodded. "In the sink. I can't rightly hang them outside or neighbors will think I do laundry on Sunday. But the ox was in the mire, so I don't see as how Derr Herr will judge me harshly for that."

"*Denki*." He cleared his throat. "It wonders me if you could mend them."

Her lips twitched upward. "I can do that. In exchange for the story of what happened to your leg."

Ben groaned softly. Of course Esther and Levi would ask him to explain himself. There wasn't any way around it. "Okay. I didn't hope you wouldn't be curious."

She bent over and took a good look at his leg. "Oy, anyhow, it looks worse now that it's had a soak."

"I got blood on the towel."

She smiled. "You've bled all over my house. That means we're truly family now. We love you, Ben. I'm honored you came to our house when there was trouble."

A lump caught in Ben's throat. Maybe there was someone else besides Winnie who didn't think he was such a bother.

She turned back to the stove and gave the contents of her pot one more stir. "Sit down. You need some hot chocolate. Then we'll take a look at that leg." She poured some hot chocolate from the pot into a mug. "You like it with cinnamon, don't you?"

He nodded. How had she remembered that? Mamm never did.

Esther sprinkled cinnamon into his mug and handed it to him. "*Cum*. Let's go into the front room. You'll be more comfortable on the sofa, and I can look at your leg."

He followed her into the front room where a quilt on frames took up most of the space. Esther almost always had a quilt set up in the front room. She'd told him it was so she could put a few stitches in whenever she had a minute or two. This quilt was decorated with maroon fabric flowers and green vines, with intricate stitching in the white fabric underneath. Ben didn't much care about quilts and sewing, but he could appreciate that the quilt had taken hours to make.

Levi came out of Winnie's room and shut the door. He immediately placed himself on one side of the quilt and lifted the frames just as Esther lifted the frames on her side. They scooted it up against the front window so Ben would have room to sit on the sofa and they'd have room to tend to his leg. They'd obviously moved it before.

"Sit, Ben."

With his towel tucked securely around him, Ben sat on the sofa and stretched his legs on the cushions. Both Esther and Levi pulled folding chairs from under the quilt frames and set them facing the sofa, Levi at Ben's head, and Esther on the end where his legs were. Esther pulled a white box from under the sofa and smiled apologetically. "When Winnie came to live with me, I bought a first aid kit for every room of the house. You never know when you're going to need gauze." She opened the box, took out a roll of gauze, and pulled the scissors from behind her ear. "I'm *froh* to have these scissors handy." She cut a strip of gauze and folded it on itself. "I have to warn you, I'm not *gute* at this. I know how to do chicken pox and colic and how to make a bottle of formula, and that's it."

"But you have steady hands," Levi said. "And you're careful." He scooted his chair an inch closer to her and winked. "And so pretty."

Esther's blush made Ben grin. People in love were wonderful goofy.

"All you need to do is give me some antibiotic ointment

and slap a Band-Aid on it," Ben said. "Just so I don't bleed on my sheets at home. I don't want Mamm to know."

Esther dabbed lightly at his leg with the gauze. "*Ach*, Ben, you're going to need more than a Band-Aid."

"Okay, twenty Band-Aids. Or you can wrap the whole roll of gauze around it."

Esther ignored him and looked at Levi. "He's going to need stitches."

"Oh no, I'm not." Ben swung his legs off the sofa, being careful to secure his towel. "I'm not going to a hospital. Dat will find out for sure and certain."

"If you die of an infection, Dat will find out anyway," Levi said.

"Dat can't yell at me if I'm dead."

Levi cocked an eyebrow. "That will be a great comfort to all of us, I'm sure."

Ben growled and slumped his shoulders. Susie Eicher was bound to tell Dat all about it, but stitches and a doctor bill would make it so much worse. Dat would chastise him for breaking the Sabbath, but the lectures would never end if Dat found out about the blood and the hospital. Ben had already tasted the dull ache of Dat's disapproval many times. He'd rather not be reminded what a disappointment he was to the whole family. He wished he didn't care what Dat and Mamm thought about him. It would make life so much easier. And happier. Why couldn't Dat just let well enough alone?

"What is so bad that you don't want your *dat* to find out?" Esther said, gazing at him in concern.

He knew what she was going to think of him. It was what all adults thought of him. Dat told him all the time—he was irresponsible, immature, and an embarrassment to the whole *gmayna*. Linda Eicher had called him stupid and silly. Then she'd laughed right in his face. Shame and irritation flared to life inside his chest, and he felt his face get warm. "I didn't do anything wrong. I was just having a little fun. It's Linda Eicher who needs to repent. She mocks people. And she doesn't care if she hurts their feelings."

Esther tilted her head to one side. "Linda Eicher hurt your feelings?"

"*Nae*, not mine. I'm just saying that she doesn't care about other people. She's un-Christian, and she needs to repent right quick."

Esther tilted her head to the other side, but her expression was unreadable. "Are you and Linda Eicher . . . you know. Are you a couple?"

Ben grimaced with his whole face and made Esther giggle. "I just told you. She mocks people, and she thinks she's better than everybody. I wouldn't couple up with her if she was the only girl in Colorado."

Levi leaned back in his chair and folded his arms. "Maybe you better tell us what happened before we take you to the hospital."

Ben looked at Esther as if she could save him. "I'm not going to die. Just give me some gauze, and I'll do it myself."

Esther laid a hand on his foot. Her hand was warm, and his feet were like icicles again. "You need stitches, Ben."

A wonderful, painful idea struck him right between the eyes. "You're the best stitcher I know, Esther. You've got plenty of sharp needles and lots of thread. Why can't you sew up my leg?"

Esther laughed as if his request had taken her by

surprise. For sure and certain it had. "Your *dat* would never speak to me again."

"*Nae*, he wouldn't. You know what a liberal bishop he is. He lets you and Mammi play pickleball. He's given permission for Mammi to lift weights and do yoga."

"In her dress," Levi added, as if that made a difference.

Esther leaned away from him and held up her hands as if stopping traffic. "Pickleball is a far cry from pretending to be a doctor."

"Levi is always telling me what a *gute* quilter you are. It wonders me if your stitches aren't better than any doctor could make."

Levi shook his head. "Don't drag me to your side of the argument, Ben. Esther is a *gute* quilter, but she's not a doctor."

"That's right," Esther said. "I'd feel terrible if I left you with an ugly scar."

"Girls like scars. They get giddy when they see one," Ben said. He lifted his sleeve to show Esther his bullet scar. Dat had yelled at him for three days about that one.

Esther laughed, but her mirth came out more like a grunt, as if she was trying not to laugh but couldn't help it. "I'm sure someday your *fraa* will be very impressed with that scar, but it only reminds me of the time you almost accidentally killed yourself."

Ben scrunched his lips together. "*Ach vell*, Wally almost accidentally killed me, but my friends are impressed at how close I came to death. It makes me more interesting. Just think how interesting I'll be with a six-inch scar on my leg."

"The girls will come running," Levi said drily.

"And I deserve some thanks for helping you put up that

barn last fall. Esther didn't have a horse or a place to put it when you married her."

Levi made a face. "You and thirty other men from the *gmayna*. I'm not *that* grateful."

Ben snatched Esther's hand and squeezed it. "Please, dear *schwester*. Please sew it up for me."

Esther expelled a long breath. "It's going to hurt something wonderful."

"I can take the pain. I'm tough."

Esther grinned. "You are as charming as your big *bruder*." She glanced at Levi. "And almost as handsome."

Levi laughed. "Don't try to butter me up. I don't think you should do it."

Esther wasn't one of those *fraaen* who thought she had to obey her husband in everything he said. And Levi wasn't one of those men who insisted his word was law. To Ben's way of thinking, Levi and Esther's way seemed like a better path for a marriage. When the husband was the only one who was allowed to be right, he was also the one who had the responsibility on his shoulders when he made the wrong decision. Ben couldn't see but that it was nicer to share the blame and the credit, the good and the bad, with your *fraa*, instead of holding so tightly to your own authority that you squeezed everybody else out of your life.

Esther was already on her feet, rummaging through the box of thread that sat on the floor next to the quilt. "I'll do it on one condition."

Ben would have done almost anything to keep this last little mishap from his *dat*, but he stiffened anyway. What would Esther want him to do? "If you want me to babysit, I can do that. I don't mind babysitting Winnie. She adores me."

"You already babysit for us plenty. And that's too easy."

"You want to ask me something hard?"

Esther picked a spool of thread and a needle from a little box. "I'm going to have to sterilize this." She sat back down and rummaged through the first aid kit. "There should be some alcohol wipes in here." She looked up and smiled one of her sweetest, most devious smiles at Ben. "In exchange for me using my excellent sewing skills on your leg and possibly giving you the most brag-worthy scar in the history of scars, you're going to drive Linda Eicher home from the next gathering."

Ben groaned. Was it too late to choose the hospital option?

Chapter Three

Linda donned her bonnet, her rubber boots, and her coat and tromped outside to feed the chickens. There was still a lot of snow in their yard, but it was a warm enough day that the icicles were melting off the house. The water droplets made a pleasant drip-drip sound on the ground as Linda made her way to the chicken coop. Dat had built a clever little door in the small coop so the chickens could get in, but big dogs and coyotes couldn't squeeze through. Not that there were any big dogs in the neighborhood, but Linda did occasionally see a coyote prowling around.

She stopped in the barn for a pan and feed, called her chickens, and scattered feed around the coop. One by one, the four Rhode Island Reds poked their heads out of the coop and came waddling down the ramp for their breakfast. Once they were distracted, Linda lifted the roof and collected their eggs in her basket. She closed the coop and took the feed pan back to the barn. As she did every morning but Sunday, Linda walked around to the front of the house to get the mail.

Linda gasped. Splashes of red, blue, and purple color covered the snow in her front yard as if someone had spilled pitchers of colorful juice during the night. What in the world?

It was . . . it looked like some sort of a picture. Linda walked down the gravel driveway and stood next to the mailbox to get a better look. Her heart skipped a beat. It was a big purple head, probably eight feet in diameter, with red circles for eyes, a green triangle nose, and a blue gaping mouth with pointy purple teeth. Beneath the head in big block letters was her name: LINDA.

The painter had managed to spray the whole picture on her front yard without marring it with footprints, except for two prints right in the middle of the triangle nose.

Oh, *sis yuscht*. How annoying.

There was only one person she knew who could be so spiteful and childish. For goodness sake, she'd laughed at him and called him silly. Was he really that thin-skinned? When Mamm saw it, she'd give the bishop a report for sure and certain.

If Mamm saw it.

The fewer people who knew, the fewer people to get worked up about it. Nobody but Linda had to know about this. *Ach vell*, Linda and *dumm* Ben Kiem. What was he, an eleven-year-old? Linda huffed out a breath, set her basket on the ground next to the mailbox, and stomped on the *L* with her boot. Then she stamped down her whole name until there was nothing left but a mash of slushy color. She ran around the circle, stomping the purple paint into slush, then the beady eyes and that horrible mouth. Ben Kiem obviously thought she was ugly, but he was a terrible artist and had no imagination. *Ach*, had she ever known anyone more idiotic?

Linda's annoyance gave way to amusement, and she

giggled as she ran around and around the yard, kicking up snow and stomping the paint into the grass beneath. Her rubber boots made that funny squishing sound in the slush under her feet. It meant spring was just around the corner, and she could spend more time outdoors in the glorious warmth. March had come in like a lion but was definitely going out like a lamb.

Linda saved the nose for last because green was her favorite color. With the rest of the face destroyed, the nose was just a pretty green triangle sitting in the middle of her front yard. Linda stood in the center of the triangle in the very footprints of the painter—Ben Kiem, without a doubt. She had to admire his ingenuity and his determination. Many Christmases ago, Mammi Edna had filled spray bottles with water and food coloring and let Linda and Yost go outside and spray colors onto the snow. The color hadn't lasted long and hadn't been very bright. Ben had used real spray paint on Linda's snow. It was ten times brighter than food coloring and didn't sink into the snow over time. Obviously, he wanted to make sure it lasted long enough for Linda to see it. Painting that face in the snow couldn't have been a five-minute job, especially with spray paint. It probably took an hour at least. That was dedication.

If that boy put his efforts into something useful, he might actually make something of himself someday.

Should she tell him that? She had half a mind to march over to Ben Kiem's house and scold him for wasting his life on petty pranks and idle activities. But there was probably nothing Linda could say that Ben's *dat* hadn't already said. It was too bad. Ben seemed determined to throw away his youth. He hung around with Wally and Simeon at the park, smoking cigarettes and listening to Wally's boom box.

Why did he still act like a rebellious teenager? He seemed healthy and capable enough. His broad shoulders and muscular arms proved he knew how to work.

One thing was for sure and certain. If he didn't change his ways, he was going to ruin his life. It made Linda sort of sad. She didn't like to be sad, so she shook her head and thought about spring and camping and stargazing and hiking to the top of Mount Lamborn. Ben Kiem's life was none of her business, even if she did hate to see him throw it away. She couldn't help everybody, and a boy who painted ugly pictures of her in the snow certainly didn't want her to meddle.

Still, Ben Kiem's squandered life was all she could think about as she picked up her egg basket and checked the mail. She glanced at the front yard, which looked like a herd of cattle had trampled all the snow, but Mamm would never guess what had gone on here this morning. Linda smiled. Ben was safe.

Ben frowned as he watched Linda climb out of the buggy with Freeman and Suvie Sensenig. Nothing but the deepest respect and gratitude for his sister-in-law could make him go through with this. But Esther had sewed up his leg liked he'd begged her to, and Dat hadn't found out about his little skiing mishap, at least not yet. Linda's *mamm*, it seemed, hadn't told Dat yet. Maybe she felt sorry for him. Maybe she had completely forgotten about it. Old ladies forgot lots of things.

While keeping his gaze on Linda, Ben took one last

drag on his cigarette, threw the butt to the ground, and stamped it out. He'd agreed to ask Linda if he could drive her home from the gathering, but he didn't actually have to do it. She wouldn't consent to let him drive her home in a million years. Linda Eicher was far too good for him, and she knew it. But last night he'd started to worry that maybe Linda would say yes out of pity or just so she could make fun of him behind his back. So he'd hiked over to her house in the middle of the night and painted that ridiculous face in her front yard. It was childish and immature and mean, but he had to make sure she hated him so badly that she would never even consider getting into a buggy with him.

He'd told Esther he would ask, so he would, and then he could honestly report that Linda had refused him, and Esther would be satisfied. Or if not satisfied, at least convinced that he'd done his best to fulfill his part of the agreement. Linda was going to laugh at him and turn up her nose and glare at him like he was a fresh pile of manure. He wasn't looking forward to it at all.

With arms linked, Linda and Suvie practically skipped up the sidewalk of the Sensenigs' house where the gathering was being held. Ben wanted to catch her before she went into the house. Might as well get this over with or the dread would hang over him all night. Ben could be brave when he wanted to be. With purposeful steps, he came up behind the two girls and tapped Linda on the shoulder. Linda turned around and peered at him with a slightly amused, slightly surprised expression on her face, as if he were wearing a shoe on his head. "Linda, can I talk to you privately?"

Suvie giggled. Linda gave her friend a knowing look

and smiled like she was the smartest girl in Colorado. "Okay."

With a lump the size of a horse in his throat, he turned and led her to the edge of the grass, far enough so no one would hear them talking, close enough so no one would think he wanted to be alone with Linda Eicher.

She didn't lose her smile, but Ben wasn't fooled. She was mocking him. "So, Ben Kiem, you ski, you paint, you smoke. Is there anything you can't do?"

He swiped his hand across his mouth. "Look, let's get this over with, okay? I'm wondering if . . . can I drive you home from the gathering tonight?"

Her mouth fell open and there was a breathless pause before she started laughing. She doubled over and laughed and laughed until she couldn't breathe. What was it with Linda and laughing? It seemed like whenever she wasn't in church, she was either laughing or getting ready to laugh. Was her life really that funny?

Ben had known he was going to embarrass himself just by asking the question, but he didn't expect his face to get warm and his gut to ache. "I'll take that as a no," he snapped. "You can quit laughing now."

She grabbed his arm before he could walk away. "I'm sorry," she said, though the remains of her laughter tripped from her mouth. "I didn't mean to embarrass you or hurt your feelings or whatever."

"You didn't hurt my feelings. But you shouldn't make fun of people."

Linda took a deep breath and sighed, the wide smile still in place on her lips. "*Ach*, Ben. I'm not making fun. Truly I'm not. But you have to admit you're acting strange, and it struck me as funny. I know you don't want to drive me home from the gathering tonight, so why did you ask?"

"So your answer is no? That's all I needed to hear." He could tell Esther he'd tried.

She stepped in front of him and propped her hands on her hips to block his escape. "Is it another one of your tricks? Because they don't upset me, if that's what you're trying to do. Your pranks and little paintings say more about your character than mine."

She was so smug. "What do you know about my character?"

Her blue eyes danced in amusement. "I know that you're not a very *gute* artist or skier."

"Very funny."

"But I know you're determined and persistent when you put your mind to something. I mean, who else would spend that much effort painting my face in the snow? And then you were so careful with your footprints."

He folded his arms, turned his face away, and stifled a smile. He *had* gone to quite a bit of trouble to paint that picture. Linda had actually noticed. "Do you think I know what you're talking about? A face in the snow?"

"I felt kind of bad stomping on it, but if my *mamm* had seen it, she would have told your *dat* for sure and certain. You should have thought that one through better."

"I take risks."

"You're reckless. It's not the same thing as taking risks. You should never dive into a lake until you've checked how deep the water is. It's foolhardy to put yourself in danger like that."

Ben shrugged and did what he always did when someone disapproved of his choices. He simply told himself he didn't care. It made life easier when you didn't worry about what other people thought of you.

"But I also know you're tough," she said.

Ben looked at her in surprise. She didn't seem to be teasing him.

"You're coordinated because you stayed on those water skis as long as you did, even though you don't know how to ski. And then you wouldn't get in my buggy, even after you were hurt, because you wanted to prove a point. I'm not sure what point you wanted to prove—maybe how manly you are—but stubborn or not, you're definitely tough."

Ben narrowed his eyes. "What are you talking about?"

Amusement gave way to some other emotion on her face. Sympathy maybe? "I saw the blood."

"You did?"

"That's why I offered you a ride. But I didn't want to make a big fuss about it. You were embarrassed enough already."

"I wasn't embarrassed," he said, just to be contrary.

"Okay, okay. You weren't embarrassed." She rolled her eyes and laughed, then stopped and studied his face. "I'm not making fun of you. Oy, anyhow, you need to learn to laugh at yourself, Ben."

"I don't like it when people laugh at me."

She sighed and tempered her smile. "I'm not laughing *at* you. I'm laughing *with* you. It looked like you were having a *gute* time on those skis until you crashed. You got some good air, then fell out of the sky like a duck full of buckshot."

He couldn't keep his lips from curling upward. "I got pretty high. And I was going really fast."

"How bad did you hurt yourself? You're here, so you didn't bleed to death."

Would Linda be impressed with his wound or just find it another reason to laugh at him? He decided to trust her. He motioned for her to follow and led her to the bench swing in Millers' front yard. After brushing off the snow and seeing that the metal was reasonably dry, he sat down and lifted his trouser leg up to his knee. Esther had wrapped the entire bottom half of his leg with gauze and made him promise to change it every twelve hours, as if she knew the magic number for gauze changing.

Linda's lips formed into an O. "I can't see a thing, but it looks serious."

Ben found the edge and slowly, carefully unwound it from his leg. Square gauze pads underneath covered the cut. The rolled gauze was just to keep the square gauze pads in place, and they also had to be changed every twelve hours—because of Esther's random magic number.

Linda bent over his leg, her eyes full of excitement. Her eyes were an interesting color of blue, like an icy lake in the moonlight. "This is looking interestinger and interestinger."

"Are you bothered by the sight of blood?"

"*Nae*. I help my *dat* butcher a pig every year."

Ben found himself smiling, though he didn't know why. He handed her the roll of gauze, then pulled the gauze pads from the gash in his leg.

"*Ach, du lieva*," Linda said, her voice thick with awe. "Does it hurt?"

"Something wonderful."

"If I'd known it was as bad as all this, I would have

thrown you over my shoulder and forced you into my buggy."

The resolve in her voice made him chuckle. "You and your whole family couldn't lift me off the ground."

She looked him up and down as if trying to guess his weight. "You might be right. Muscle is denser and heavier than fat. I read that in a magazine. And you've got plenty of muscle to go around. Of course, before too long you're going to waste away from the cigarettes. Mark my words."

Ben ignored her little lecture on smoking. He'd heard it all and more from his parents.

She hunched over to get a better look at his leg. "You got stitches."

"*Jah*. Esther gave them to me."

Linda caught her breath. "Esther? Your sister-in-law?"

"She's a *gute* quilter, and I didn't want to go to the hospital."

"*Ach*. Did it hurt?"

He couldn't help but smile at her intense interest in his leg. He knew his wound would impress the girls. "Something wonderful. But I didn't want to go to a doctor."

"How many stitches?"

"I don't know."

"You don't know?" she said in disbelief. "You're supposed to know so you can tell people, 'I got three stitches.' Or 'Remember that time I got seven hundred stitches?' It's a number you can brag about." She pointed to her elbow, which was covered by her coat. "I got two stitches here when I fell on my scooter."

"I think it's between three and seven hundred," he said. She cuffed him on the shoulder. Fortunately, it wasn't the sore one. "Ask Esther. Or maybe I could count them right now."

She leaned over again and squinted at his leg. Her hair smelled like roses and vanilla. *Ach*, the heady scent attacked his senses and made his pulse race. He drew back slightly. It was just a smell. What was wrong with him? "The stitches are small. I'd guess maybe forty."

"Okay. Forty is a *gute* number."

"Like I said, Ben. You're tough. I would have bawled like a baby."

He hadn't bawled, but he might have yelled pretty loud when Esther first poked that needle into his skin. But Linda didn't need to know that. She thought he was tough. That was something.

She stood up straight, taking her enticing smell with her. "You should get a tetanus shot."

"I got one last year when I snagged my ankle on a barbed wire fence."

She raised an eyebrow. "How did that happen?"

He wasn't about to tell her. He'd said enough already. Linda didn't need to know that he, Wally, and Simeon were tipping an old, abandoned outhouse on Rierson's farm, and Rierson's two big dogs had chased them off the property. Ben hadn't quite cleared the fence when he was running away. "It was nothing. Simeon and me were out having some fun, and I ran into some barbed wire, that's all."

Linda shook her head. "Sounds like you're kinda slow to learn your lessons."

Why did everybody think they were smarter than he was? "There isn't anything wrong with enjoying life. It was on a dare from Simeon. That makes me tough *and* brave."

"*Nae*. It just makes you reckless."

He wasn't going to argue about that. He didn't care what Linda Eicher thought. He gingerly placed the gauze pads back on his gash.

"Here," she said. "I'll wrap." Bending over again, she took the gauze and gently wound it around his leg.

Ben held his breath while she worked. He didn't want to be attracted to her smell or her eyes or the strand of yellow hair that escaped her *kapp* and brushed against her cheek like a kiss. He refused to like anything about Linda Eicher.

When she finished, he pulled down his trouser leg and stood up. "Okay then. I'll see you later."

She inclined her head toward the front door. "Aren't you coming in?"

"*Nae*. I think I'll go home."

Her eyes twinkled. She was silently laughing at him again. "You came all this way to ask if you could drive me home?"

"*Nae* . . . well, *jah*. But I knew you'd say *nae*."

"Of course you knew I'd say *nae*. Why did you ask?"

"It's not because I like you," Ben said. The very thought was beyond belief.

She folded her arms and scrunched her lips together. "I already got that idea from the picture you painted in my front yard."

He wasn't going to let her make him feel guilty about that. It was a means to an end, that's all. "Esther wouldn't sew up my leg unless I agreed to ask to drive you home from the gathering."

Linda drew her brows together. "Why would Esther want you to ask me?"

"She wanted to punish me for the skiing. She knew it would be pure torture for me to drive you home."

That didn't seem to offend Linda. Instead she fell silent, as if thinking hard about something. She squinted at him, and he could see she was trying not to smile. "I accept your offer."

"What?" That was not in the plan at all. His gut clenched. Never in a million years would he have expected her to say yes. His work of art on her lawn was supposed to have made sure she didn't.

"But instead of driving me home from a gathering, you have to come skiing with me and my friends. Cross-country skiing, if you can keep up."

Ben didn't even try to hide his horror at such a thought. Cross-country skiing with Linda? He didn't know how to ski, his leg ached, and he hated the thought of spending one more minute with Linda Eicher. He groaned loudly.

That should be enough torture to satisfy even Esther.

Chapter Four

Ashley honked her horn before Linda could stop her. "Don't honk," Linda said. "I'll go get him."

"What?" Ashley said, rolling her eyes. "Amish guys don't know what a car horn sounds like?"

Linda smiled wryly. "Like as not, he'll pretend he didn't hear. I'll be right back." She jumped out of the car and hiked across the snow to Esther's front door. Instead of her usual plain dress, she wore her black snow pants and warm boots that were really the only proper thing to wear for snow sports. She sported a dark blue beanie on her head, but underneath, her hair was tucked up in a bandana, something many Amish girls and women wore when doing chores.

Would Esther be shocked at her attire? Maybe. But everybody knew how much Linda liked to ski and snow-shoe. And she was still in *rumschpringe*, her running around time, as was Ben. Most people in the community just wrung their hands or clucked their tongues at what *die youngie* did during *rumschpringe* and didn't do much to discourage them. Of course, everybody wanted to keep their children as close to the straight and narrow path as they could, even during *rumschpringe*, but Mamm told

Linda that if skiing was the worst Linda ever did, Mamm would be satisfied. And Linda might even be able to ski after she got baptized. Nobody had asked the bishop yet if skiing was against the *Ordnung*.

Meeting at Esther and Levi's house had been Linda's idea. That way Ben could prove to his sister-in-law that he'd fulfilled his part of the agreement, and he wasn't likely to back out with his sister-in-law watching him get into the car with Linda. Linda was kind of surprised that Ben cared so much about pleasing Esther. He seemed like the type who didn't care about much of anything, especially not anyone else's feelings.

Linda wasn't exactly sure what had induced her to invite Ben Kiem to go skiing. She certainly didn't like him much. He'd broken their buggy, painted that very unflattering picture of her in the snow, and made himself generally unpleasant to be around. It was crazy to have anything to do with him.

She felt bad that she hadn't been more sympathetic when he'd injured himself. That was one nasty gash, but Ben hadn't cried one tear over it or made any sort of fuss. Then again, why should she feel sorry for someone who made his own trouble and then suffered the consequences?

Mamm always said that Linda was her practical child, which was Mamm's way of saying Linda didn't have a nurturing bone in her whole body. Linda had no patience for those who didn't pull their own weight or whined about things that couldn't be changed. What was the use of complaining? Complainers wore Linda's tolerance down to a nub. Of course, people who didn't know her well thought Linda was insensitive with her pull-yourself-up-by-your-own-bootstraps attitude. Her siblings certainly didn't like it. Nora liked to be coddled when she was sick, and Linda refused to baby her.

But her invitation to go skiing wasn't just about trying to be more sympathetic to Ben. Maybe it was his brown, puppy-dog eyes that always seemed to be so sad or the tense and guarded way he approached people, as if someone might bite off his hand if he let them get too close. Maybe it was to prove to herself that she had forgiven him for being such a *dumkoff*, and maybe she was secretly impressed that he'd gone to all that trouble to ask her, even though he hadn't really wanted to.

Whatever the reason, she only had to take him this one time, and then she never had to talk to Ben Kiem ever again in her whole life, unless he decided to draw more artwork in her yard.

Linda knocked on the door, and Esther opened it as if she'd been waiting just inside. A stubby piece of white chalk sat behind Esther's ear, four fabric clips were fastened to her apron, and a spatula stuck out of her apron pocket. "Linda, how *gute* to see you. Ben says you're taking him skiing."

"*Ach*, *vell*, we've decided to go snowshoeing. It's easier, and the snow isn't so *gute* this time of year for skiing."

Esther nodded thoughtfully. "Snowshoeing is *gute* enough." She ushered Linda into the front hall. "*Cum reu.* It's wonderful cold out there."

Esther's front room was just off the entryway, where a stunning blue quilt sat on a set of frames. Little white fabric flowers traveled around the edges of the quilt, accented with tiny leaves in every shade of green. "*Ach*, Esther. That is so pretty."

"I always have a quilt up so I can take a stitch or two

when Winnie isn't paying attention. If she thinks I'm more interested in my quilt, she hangs on my skirt and uses it as a swing. If that doesn't work, she starts chewing on my quilt frames." Esther laughed. "I hope she has some teeth left when she gets older."

"Do you need help?"

"Of course. I'm always looking for friends to help me finish my latest quilt."

Linda stepped to the quilt and ran her hand over the fabric. "I don't mind quilting, as long as you're not fussy about stitches. I'm not very patient."

Worry lines appeared around Esther's eyes. "*Ach*. I heard you were a *gute* quilter."

"That's just my *mamm*'s wishful thinking. She thinks if she says it out loud, I'll feel guilty enough to try to be better at it."

Esther fingered the chalk behind her ear. "Don't take this the wrong way, but if you're not a *gute* quilter, you're not allowed to work on my quilt. I hope that doesn't offend you. And I hope you'll still take Ben snowshoeing."

The troubled expression on Esther's face made Linda laugh. "I don't get offended easily." Somebody had spray painted an ugly picture of her in the snow, and she had invited him to go skiing—which, come to think of it, was a little bit crazy and a whole lot unnecessary. "Take everything my *mamm* says about me with a grain of salt. I'm afraid I'm a huge disappointment to her."

"Of course not." Esther blew air from between her lips. "Every Amish girl or *fraa* thinks they can quilt. Most get offended when you question their skill, but I hate unpicking bad work. It leaves holes in my fabric. And then I get so angry, I have to go outside and throw something or yank up my flowers or tear tufts of grass from the lawn."

Linda didn't know Esther well, but she liked her better and better all the time. How many Amish women would admit to having a bad temper? "For the sake of your lawn, I won't quilt a stitch."

"*Denki*. My grass and my husband are very grateful."

A loud thump-thumping noise echoed down the hall. Ben came galloping around the corner with Esther's daughter, Winnie, riding on his back, her chubby little arms wrapped as far as they would go around Ben's neck, her delighted, ear-piercing squeals filling the house. Ben's grin lit up the whole room as he pranced and whinnied enthusiastically, but when he caught sight of Linda, he stopped short as if Winnie had pulled back hard on the reins. "*Ach*," he said, losing his buoyant energy, "you're here."

Linda wasn't happy about the fact that she seemed to have completely ruined Ben's day, but there was nothing she could do about it. Or maybe there was. She glanced at Esther. Would Esther object if Linda called the whole thing off? Just why had Esther wanted Ben to drive Linda home?

"Come on, sweetie," Esther said, peeling Winnie off Ben's back.

Winnie protested by squeaking loudly and wrapping her little fingers around Ben's collar. "Beh!" she said.

Esther grinned at Linda as she wrestled Winnie into her arms. "That's how she says 'Ben.' It's the only word she knows. Ben is Winnie's favorite person in the whole world."

It was nice that someone—anyone—liked Ben, even if that person was a sixteen-month-old. He seemed pretty harmless, but he wasn't all that likable. Linda tilted her head and studied his face. Children weren't fooled by insincere adults. Winnie was probably a better judge of character than Linda was. And Linda shouldn't judge at all. That was what it said in the Bible.

Winnie still reached for Ben. Ben took her from Esther's arms and planted a quick kiss on Winnie's cheek. Something warm and sweet tingled down Linda's spine. There was something very appealing about a young man who liked children. She hadn't expected it from Ben.

Esther smoothed her hand down Winnie's hair. "Ben usually crawls around on all fours with Winnie on his back, but he can't crawl at the moment. He hurt his leg. It's a *hesslich* wound. Very deep." Her eyes twinkled as if she was thinking of something funny. "Show Linda your leg, Ben. For sure and certain, she'll be impressed."

"*Ach*, I've seen it," Linda said. "It was nice of you to sew it up."

Esther's eyes grew round. "He told you?"

"*Jah*. It was my buggy he hitched a ride on. I saw the blood."

For whatever reason, Esther seemed disproportionately pleased that Linda had already seen Ben's cut. "Do you like it?"

Ben growled. "Like it? Of course she doesn't like it." He gave Esther a pointed glare. "I don't care if she likes it."

Linda laughed. "Okay, okay. Nobody cares about your leg." Ben nodded in agreement, but Esther frowned. Linda cleared her throat. She should be a little less blunt and at least pretend to be sympathetic. "I mean we all care that Ben got hurt, but what's done is done. No use dwelling on it or making a fuss."

"That's what I think," Ben snapped. He glanced at his sister-in-law and the lines around his mouth softened. "I'm wonderful grateful to you for giving me stitches."

Esther heaved a sigh. "I know you are, and I know you wish you'd been wiser, but you don't have to get touchy about it. You asked quite a bit of me, insisting I sew your leg. It is very upsetting to cause someone that much pain. After you left, I had to go outside and have a snowball fight with Levi."

Linda laughed. Ben cracked a smile. "I'm sure he's glad to let you throw anything at him you want," he said.

Esther's grin took over her entire face. "He's very sweet that way."

A long, loud, impatient honk came from the car outside. Linda was startled, mostly at how she had been enjoying the conversation so much she'd almost forgotten why she'd come. Ben really shouldn't be forced to go snowshoeing with her. And she didn't really want him to come. "You know," she said, looking at Esther doubtfully, "Ben doesn't have to come. He doesn't want to, and maybe it's better if we just all forgive and forget."

For the first time ever in Linda's life, Ben smiled at her. It was a nice smile like berry pie fresh from the oven or sun sparkling on newly fallen snow. "I . . . that . . . that's wonderful kind of you. I'd rather not go."

A twinge of disappointment caught Linda off guard. There was no reason to feel that way. She hadn't expected anything different from Ben, and snowshoeing would be much more fun without him.

Esther practically snatched Winnie from Ben's arms. "*Ach*, no excuses. I spent over an hour giving you stitches.

I got lightheaded and almost threw up twice, and you twitched and groaned until I thought you'd faint."

Ben blew a disgusted puff of air from between his lips. "I don't faint."

Esther acted as if she didn't hear him. "We had an agreement, and you're going."

"The agreement was that I'd ask to drive Linda home. Going skiing wasn't the agreement."

"We're not skiing," Linda said. "We had to change it to snowshoeing."

"*Ach*, that makes it so much better," Ben said, the sarcasm dripping from his lips.

Esther glared at Ben, pulled the chalk from behind her ear, and pointed it at him like a knife. "One full hour and forty-five stitches. My hands shook until bedtime, and Levi accidentally hit me in the cheek with a snowball. You're going snowshoeing if it kills me. I'll have none of this talk about forgiving and forgetting. There will be no forgiving and forgetting in this house. You're going."

"But why do you want me to go so bad?"

"I won't debate this a second longer," Esther said, obviously unwilling to talk about her reasons. "You're going."

Ben pinched his lips together and turned back into the petulant boy Linda had found in the snow by the side of the road after skiing behind her buggy. After that brilliant smile he'd given her, his current expression was quite a contrast.

Winnie reached for Ben again, but Esther bounced the baby on her hip and kissed her three times on her forehead. "Hush now, *heartzley*. Onkel Ben has to go. He'll be back soon to play with you." She pointed to a duffle bag sitting on the sofa next to the quilt. "I've packed your coat and Levi's snow pants, boots, and gloves. Take them with you. I'd rather not have your frozen self show up on my doorstep again. Your ears were so cold, I could have snapped them off your head like pea pods."

Ben shook his head and turned his face away from Esther, stifling an affectionate smile that stole Linda's breath. Ben Kiem truly was a puzzle. One minute he was pleasant and funny, affectionate with his family, the next he was pouty and irritated, guarding his emotions behind a wall of resentment. What kind of person was hiding behind all those layers of flesh and stone? And why did she suddenly feel sorry for him?

Linda squared her shoulders and stopped staring. She didn't really want to know.

Ben moved reluctantly to the sofa and hooked his fingers around the handle of the duffle bag. Then he kissed Winnie again and took a step toward the front door. Sighing, Esther grabbed his sleeve, pulled him back, and planted a swift kiss on his cheek. Linda pretended not to notice. The Amish in her community in Wisconsin and even here in Colorado tended to be more reserved with their affection.

Ben made a face and swiped his hand down his cheek as if trying to wipe off any hint of Esther's kiss, like a schoolboy might do after being kissed by a girl at recess. Esther laughed, and he grinned in spite of himself, his eyes dancing with amusement. For some reason, Ben, in all his prickliness, seemed to blossom with even a small measure of Esther's approval. Even though Linda was known to be insensitive and unsympathetic, she could see that Ben needed Esther's acceptance, needed her kindness, no matter how much he pushed her away. How nice that Esther saw it too. Linda liked Esther more and more all the time.

Ben Kiem was the most annoying, childish boy in Colorado, or at least the most annoying boy on the trail. "Haven't we gone far enough? This is *dumm*," he said, huffing and puffing as if gasping his final, dying breaths.

Was there anyone in the world besides Esther and Winnie Kiem who even liked Ben? Who cared if he had a nice smile? Nobody ever saw it.

Ashley glanced back at Linda who in turn glanced back at Ben. Ben was so slow, Dylan, Sissy, and Ashley had passed him, and he was lagging a good twenty feet behind Linda. They weren't even really going uphill. And it had nothing to do with the fact that this was his first time snowshoeing. Snowshoeing was easy enough for anyone with even an average amount of balance and fitness. Ben was dragging his feet, literally, and being completely lazy about where he put his snowshoes and how fast he moved. Linda didn't know whether to be annoyed at Ben or embarrassed for him.

Ashley paused to glance at Ben and curled one side of her mouth. "Why did you want to bring him?"

Linda laughed, not even caring if Ben heard her. He was being deliberately difficult and didn't deserve her consideration.

Linda had met her *Englisch* friend Ashley one day last summer when she and Elmer Lee had been canoeing at Home Lake. Ashley had given them some pointers on paddling, and they'd become friends because of their shared love of outdoor activities. Ashley invited Linda whenever she went skiing, snowshoeing, hiking, or canoeing. Linda owned her own pair of cross-country skis, but she never went downhill skiing. It was too expensive and time consuming, and Linda didn't want anyone paying her way, even though Ashley had offered several times.

It was nice to have a friend who owned a car and could drive them all over the valley or out to the sand dunes. Ashley's brother Dylan usually joined them in their adventures. Dylan's girlfriend, Sissy, was a new addition to the group. Even though she was a beginner, Sissy seemed to be doing just fine on her snowshoes. Ben simply had an attitude problem.

The sharp, cold air did nothing to mar the beautiful sunny day. There wouldn't be many more days like this for months. In another three weeks or so, the snow would start to melt, and ski season would be over. Linda had hiked or snowshoed the Rock Creek Trail many times over the last year, and the view of the valley at the end of the trail was spectacular. If Ben could just hold on for another mile or so, he'd get the view of a lifetime. Or maybe he wouldn't. He didn't seem like someone who would appreciate the aspens and lodgepole pines and the breathtaking scenery as much as he would a spray-painted wall or a free pack of cigarettes. There was no accounting for taste.

"Linda," Ben called, now thirty feet behind the rest of them. "I'm going to head back. I'll meet you by the car."

Linda made a full stop and turned around. "Don't go back. It's the first rule of the wilderness. Never hike alone. You'll get lost."

"I won't get lost. I just have to follow the trail."

"Don't, Ben."

He stabbed one of his poles into the ground as if to protest all the injustice he'd ever suffered in his entire life. With his pole firmly in the snow, he tried to turn around. Because he was favoring his injured left leg, he didn't lift it quite as high as he should have, and he ended up stepping on the back of his right snowshoe with his left foot. When he tried to disentangle his snowshoes, he tripped over one of his poles, teetered off the trail, and disappeared into a bank of powdery snow.

"Ben!" Linda called, more annoyed than alarmed. The snow wasn't extremely deep, and his landing would have been sufficiently soft. One pole and one snowshoe stuck out from the snow, the only sign that Ben was there. He was going to panic, and panic would only make it harder to get out of the deep snow. She glanced at Ashley. "We'll catch up."

Ashley smirked. "I guess it wouldn't be very nice to leave him there."

"Probably not." As fast as was physically possible, Linda shuffled to the spot where Ben had fallen off the trail.

Ben's head popped out of the snow, followed by his arms. He coughed and flailed about as if he were drowning. Standing up was hard with a pair of snowshoes on your feet, especially in deep, powdery snow. It was much like being an upside-down turtle. You just couldn't gain enough traction to help yourself out.

The thought of turtles, flailing arms and legs, and Ben's wounded pride struck Linda's funny bone, and she couldn't stop herself from bursting into laughter. He looked ridiculous, and he'd brought it on himself.

His scowl could have melted all the snow on the trail.

"Don't laugh at me," he said, trying to push himself up with his poles.

"Don't," Linda said, swallowing her laughter. "You'll break your poles and hurt your back."

"Like you care."

Ach, dumm boy. He was so pigheaded. "Stop fighting the snow. You'll just sink deeper." Linda stepped to the very edge of the trail where the snow was soft and powdery. She reached out to him. "Give me your hand."

"Nae, denki."

Linda propped her hand on her hip. How did he think he was going to get out of there without her help?

He clutched both his poles in one hand, rolled onto his stomach, and pushed himself to a kneeling position. On his hands and knees with the tips of his snowshoes dragging on the ground, he crawled out of the deep depression in the snow and onto the snow-packed trail where he scooted his feet under him and stood up.

Linda's smile grew as she watched his progress. "That was smart."

His dark eyes flashed with anger. "I'm not as much of an idiot as you think I am."

"I don't think you're an idiot. You got out of that hole."

He narrowed his eyes. "No thanks to you."

"I offered my hand."

"You couldn't have pulled me up. I weigh at least forty pounds more than you do."

That was probably true. Ben looked like he was made entirely of muscle. She slapped the snow off Ben's coat sleeve. He pulled away from her. "We need to get the snow off so you don't get wet," she said. "The cold is worse when you're wet." He must have given her credit for knowing something because he bent over and brushed off his snow pants while Linda worked on his sleeves and the back of his coat. "You wouldn't have fallen if you hadn't gone off the trail. The snow on the sides can be deep and soft. Sometimes you can't even walk on it with snowshoes."

"If you'd told me that instead of making fun of me, I wouldn't have fallen. But maybe you'd rather help me off a cliff than help me up the mountain."

"*Ach*, for goodness sake, all you've done is whine since we got here."

"And all you and Ashley have done is laugh at me. I knew you'd make fun of me. That's why I didn't want to come."

Guilt niggled at her, like a mosquito buzzing on the ceiling of her conscience. "I'm not making fun of you." It wasn't a lie, but it wasn't exactly the truth either. She definitely thought he'd gotten his just desserts. "I'm laughing with you, not at you."

"I'm not laughing," he said, his gaze accusing her with its intensity.

"You don't have to be so . . ."

"So what? Embarrassed? Irritated? You brought me here just so you could humiliate me in front of your friends. Is this punishment for the broken taillight or that picture I painted in the snow? Or maybe just because you hate me?"

"What a *dumm* thing to say. I laughed because it was funny the way you sort of teetered on your tippy toes before you fell, like a three-year-old dancing."

"This is my first time snowshoeing. How am I supposed to know what I'm doing?"

"Sissy's doing fine."

"Because her boyfriend cares enough to help her." He pointed up the trail. Dylan was stuck like glue behind Sissy, calling encouraging things to her and pointing out places where the trail might be tricky.

Linda's stomach sank past her knees. Okay, maybe Ben had a point.

And maybe he didn't. She cleared her throat and clenched her jaw. Linda wasn't trying to humiliate him. She simply refused to coddle someone who didn't need any special treatment. "Dylan is nicer than I am."

"That's for sure and certain. All you've shown me is contempt, like you think you're so much better than me. Well, I have news for you. You're not better than anybody. So quit laughing, and let me alone."

Linda found Ben's stupidity kind of funny, but she clamped her lips together to keep from laughing. Laughing only irritated him. And maybe he wasn't exceptionally stupid. He used words like "contempt." "It seems you don't want to think on your own sins, so you accuse me of something that isn't even true. Believe me. I don't think I'm better than anybody."

"You think you're better than me. You brought me up here to put me in my place."

Ben Kiem was determined to see it his way. "Oh, *sis yuscht*! I didn't bring you up here to humiliate you. You've humiliated yourself by acting like a baby. You're perfectly able to pull your own weight, but all you've done is complain."

He crossed his arms. "Why did you bring me up here?"

"Why did you say yes?"

"I said yes because I promised Esther. But you could have said no and that would have been the end of it."

"I wish I'd said no."

"Me too," he said. "But you didn't answer my question."

"What question?"

"I agreed to come up here with you because of Esther. But why did you invite me?"

"*Ach.* I'm not sure."

"That's a *dumm* answer."

He was the most difficult boy. "It's a *dumm* question."

"You only say that because you don't want to answer, because you really did bring me out here to embarrass me in front of your friends."

"That's not true, and I've already told you it's not true. *Ach*, Ben, you're so thick sometimes." She cocked an eyebrow. "Well, not just sometimes."

"Not too thick to know there's a reason you invited me today."

Linda sighed as if it took great effort to explain everything to him. Mostly it took great effort to understand her own reasons. "Well, I wanted you to know what it really feels like to ski, but then Ashley thought snowshoeing would be easier for a beginner."

His gaze was a little too piercing for her comfort. "You wanted me to learn how to ski?"

"I suppose. And actually, I was kind of impressed that you had the courage to ask if you could drive me home."

He smirked. "It wasn't courage. I'm afraid of Esther."

Nae. Linda didn't believe it was fear. It was affection for his sister-in-law. "I invited you because a boy should get out and do other things besides smoke behind the barn and listen to that ridiculous boom box and paint useless pictures on people's property."

"So you don't approve of my life?"

"It doesn't matter if I approve."

"I enjoy my life," he said.

"Do you?" She didn't believe him for a second. Ben Kiem was a lot of things, but happy wasn't one of them. He walked around with his shoulders slumped as if he carried the weight of the world. He couldn't muster a smile to save his life, and he kept his head down at *gmay* and never sang the hymns. He sneaked around with his friends playing pranks on his neighbors, maybe finding fleeting pleasure, but little happiness and no meaning. "There is no happiness in bad choices."

"So you brought me up here to make me change my ways?"

"I don't believe I could make you do anything," Linda said.

"I don't want to change, and you can't change me."

"*Gute*, because it's an impossible project." She flashed him an I-couldn't-care-less look and peered up the trail. Her friends were far ahead. "*Cum*. Let's catch up."

"You go on. I'm going back."

"I was telling the truth, Ben. You can't go back by yourself. It's the first rule of the outdoors."

He frowned. "I've been humiliated enough for one day."

Linda bit the inside of her cheek. She'd brought this on herself, first by inviting Ben to come and second by laughing at, er . . . *with* him when he fell. Of course someone as self-conscious and touchy as Ben would take her laughter the wrong way. Maybe she should swallow her exasperation and try coaxing him, even though coaxing was right next door to coddling, and coddling was a step away from babying. "I'm sorry I laughed. I truly wasn't laughing at you."

"You could have fooled me."

She pressed her lips together and remembered to be patient. "Elmer Lee says I laugh too much, and Mamm says I think everything is a joke, but I'd rather laugh than cry. Crying gives me a headache."

He studied her face as if he might be thinking about believing her. Either that or deciding whether he should shove her head in the snow. "I've never seen you without a smile," he muttered.

He probably didn't know she considered that a compliment. "And I've only seen you smile like twice in my whole life."

"What have I got to smile about? Nobody likes me."

"Well, of course nobody likes you. You never smile."

He swiped his glove across his mouth, rubbing away the hint of a pleasant expression. "Now we're talking in circles."

She took a couple of steps up the trail in hopes he'd follow. "I'm sorry I haven't been more help. I'll stick by you to the end of the trail. It's wide enough for us to walk side by side so you don't feel left behind."

He slowly shuffled up the trail. "I'll look like a child if you walk next to me."

Was he purposefully being difficult? Of course he was. Did he want her help or not? "*Nae*, you won't. We'll look like two friends who'd rather visit with each other than get to the top first."

"*Ach, vell.* At least we'll look like that, even if we're not friends."

Linda shrugged. "Maybe we're not friends, but I don't consider you my enemy, even if you did paint that *hesslich* picture of me in the snow."

A deep shade of red traveled up his face. He expelled a deep breath and avoided her gaze. "That was mean."

"It sure was."

"I had to be sure you'd say no when I asked to drive you home. That didn't work out so well, and I wasted all that paint."

She gave him a sideways grin. At least he regretted the paint. "Well, I didn't cry for three days or anything like that. I stomped on it with my boots and forgot about it."

"Okay. I guess I'm glad."

She pointed up the trail with her pole. "So will you come? The view from the meadow is *wunderbarr.*"

She sensed the moment he chose to move ahead instead of turn back. Maybe he'd decided to trust her. Maybe he didn't want to look stupid in front of her friends. Maybe he wanted to finish what he'd started. "Okay, but don't laugh at me again, or I'll go sit in the car." He took off his straw hat and tapped it against his thigh to knock off the snow.

Linda clapped her hand over her mouth before a giggle could escape.

He narrowed his eyes. "What?"

"Your hat," she squeaked.

He examined his hat. At the back, the brim had come away from the cap, just like his black church hat after skiing. His features darkened momentarily, as if he was going to scold her for laughing, then his face relaxed and his lips twitched as if wanting to smile but not knowing how. "*Ach*," he grunted. "Two hats in one month. Mamm will think I did it on purpose."

Linda let the laughter spill from her mouth. "Maybe you should wear a plastic hat. It wouldn't rip."

"That would be worse. Plastic snaps when it gets cold."

They started up the trail, but Linda held no hope of catching her friends until they stopped at the meadow. As they walked and Ben got more out of breath, Linda did most of the talking. She told him about cross-country skiing at the golf course and on Old Monarch Pass Road where the snowmobiles zoomed past like birds of prey. She told him about the time Elmer Lee lost his shoe in the river and about when they had gone to the sand dunes and tried sand skiing.

A few hundred feet from the meadow, Ben was breathing hard, and Linda feared he might faint. "Are you okay?" she said, stopping and jabbing her poles into the snow so he could catch his breath.

He eyed her suspiciously, as if expecting her to laugh at him. When she didn't laugh, he said, "I'm okay. I'm just out of shape, I guess."

"Ben, you're six feet of solid muscle. You're not out of shape. Your lungs are clogged with cigarette smoke. It's a wonder you can breathe at all."

His eyes flared with anger, but the emotion soon disappeared. He was probably too concerned with sucking air into his lungs to be irritated with her. "I breathe fine."

"I'm a girl, I'm three years younger than you and several inches shorter, and I could still beat you up this mountain with one hand tied behind my back."

"You could not." The deeply offended look on his face

was kind of cute. He had thick, dark eyebrows that drew close to the bridge of his nose when he frowned.

"It wonders me why you smoke."

Ben coughed as if to prove her point. "I like to smoke. It helps me relax, and it's fun."

Linda snorted. "Fun? Fun like lung cancer is fun?"

"I won't get lung cancer."

"That's what they all say."

He bent over and adjusted the strap on one of his snow-shoes. "Wally and Simeon started smoking, and I wanted to fit in. They're my only friends."

She tapped her gloved finger to her lips and looked at the sky. "Isn't there a saying about if your friends jumped off a cliff?"

He surprised her by curling his lips into what might have passed for a smile. "The best part is, smoking makes my *dat* mad."

"You like annoying your *dat*?" Linda couldn't imagine wanting to deliberately hurt her parents.

"He doesn't expect anything better. I'm already a huge disappointment to him."

Maybe if you tried harder. Linda pressed her lips together. It wasn't her place to lecture Ben or judge him. She had no idea how hard Ben did or didn't try at anything.

As soon as Ben was breathing somewhat normally, they pushed on for the last hundred yards where the trail dropped down through the pines into the meadow on the hillside. Ben stopped at the edge of the meadow full of snow, looked to the east, and whistled long and low. "What . . . is that the valley?"

Linda nodded. "You can see almost the whole valley from here. And look out there. See the sand dunes?"

"I see them," Ben said before falling silent and staring dumbly at the view before him.

Ashley, Dylan, and Sissy had walked farther into the meadow. Ashley shielded her eyes from the sun as she looked down at the valley. "Isn't it pretty, Ben?" she called. "Worth the climb."

Ben gave Linda a dazzling smile, but she only felt extra breathless because of the hike. "It was worth the climb. Why didn't you tell me?"

Linda rolled her eyes at him. He didn't seem to take offense to it. "I tried. Believe me, I tried."

She and Ben hiked closer to the others, and the five of them stood in the meadow, savoring the stillness, taking in the beauty of the valley below. Then Linda pulled five ham and cheese sandwiches from her backpack. Dylan took bottles of water from his, and Ashley produced trail mix and chips from hers. Linda handed everyone a sandwich.

"You made these?" Ben said.

Ashley passed out the chips. "Linda makes the sandwiches, I provide the transportation." It wasn't an even trade, so sometimes Linda gave Ashley gas money from her earnings at the grocery store where she worked two days a week.

Ben eased himself to the ground and sat with his legs and snowshoes spread out in front of him. Linda sat next to him. He took a bite. "It's good," he said. "You put horseradish on it, didn't you? I love horseradish."

It was probably the first nice thing he'd said to her all

day. Of course it would be something about food. Boys weren't so annoying when they were fed properly.

He finished off the first half of his sandwich in four bites. "I guess I should have carried your backpack."

"Don't be silly. You barely got yourself up here."

"I'll carry it next time."

Next time? Did Ben think there was going to be a next time? Did Linda want there to be a next time? She had no idea.

"Is that blood?" Sissy's eyes widened as she pointed to Ben's leg.

There was indeed a circle of dark red blood at the top of Ben's white stocking in the gap between his boot and the leg of his snow pants.

Ben glanced at his leg as if he didn't especially care he was bleeding. "Probably."

That unwelcome feeling of guilt returned with full force. Linda tried to push it away. How could she have known Ben had reinjured his leg? The pain in his leg had probably slowed him down from the very beginning, but it was hard to tell if someone was limping when they walked around in snowshoes. It certainly wasn't Linda's fault she hadn't noticed. If Ben was in that much pain, he should have told her.

But maybe she would have accused him of whining.

Ach. Sometimes she was a little too sure of herself.

Sissy's breathing quickened. She hurriedly loosened her straps, stepped out of her snowshoes, and ran to Ben's side as if he were choking. "Oh, my heck. Oh, my heck. Are you okay? Let me see. Do you need me to put some pressure on it?"

Linda never would have guessed that Ben could smile

so sweetly. He'd certainly never smiled at her like that. "That's nice of you, but I'll be okay. I hurt my leg last week, and I must have popped a couple of stitches when I fell back there. I'll go home and put a Band-Aid on it."

"A Band-Aid?" Sissy protested. "You need more than a Band-Aid. You need a field dressing."

"And some essential oils," Linda said, because nobody should forget the essential oils.

Ashley popped a chip into her mouth. "I guess it's okay that you whined. That's a serious amount of blood."

It was obvious Ben was in some pain. All one had to do was note the lines of discomfort that creased his forehead or watch how gingerly he moved his leg, but he maintained that soft, easygoing smile while Sissy nudged his stocking down to get a better look at his cut. Ben liked that Sissy was making a fuss over him. But why should she make a fuss? Ben had only brought his pain upon himself. Still, a lump of self-reproach lodged in Linda's throat.

Was she sensibly unsentimental or simply uncaring?

Ach. No use trying to figure that out now. No use trying to figure it out ever. She liked how she was, and if Ben took offense, that was his problem, not hers.

Linda tried not to stare at Ben's interesting face while Sissy talked on and on about how her mom was a nurse and Ben needed to see a doctor. His eyes were the color of *kaffee*, black, no sugar, no cream, no nonsense. His eyebrows were dark, much darker than the light chestnut hair that hung over his ears in straight tufts. Not one bit of curl like his *bruder* Levi had. There was a one-inch long scar at his chin. Linda's lips curled upward. Her *bruder* Yost had a scar like that. It came from running around wildly and leading with your chin when you fell.

Ben also had a scar that cut across his right eyebrow and another small round scar on his forehead, most likely from the chicken pox. The scars did nothing to mar his face. If anything, they made him more handsome.

Not that she thought Ben was handsome or not handsome or anything. Ben was just Ben, rebellious, irresponsible, and a real pain in the neck.

After Sissy lectured Ben about antibiotics and he assured her he'd watch for infection, everyone finished their lunches, stuffed their garbage into their packs, and headed back down the trail. Ashley insisted that Ben take the lead, because on a hike, the slowest person always went first. Sissy walked directly behind Ben, probably to make sure he didn't faint or something, and Linda went last. Ashley and Sissy made such a fuss about Ben that Linda felt no obligation to worry about him at all. Ben didn't like to be embarrassed. Was Sissy's fussing any better than Linda's laughter?

Who knew? Nobody but Ben.

Linda smiled to herself. Ben had certainly gotten more than he bargained for today. If he had known what was going to happen, a team of Percheron horses couldn't have dragged him out of Esther's house. She giggled softly at the thought of Ben on a pair of skis being dragged up the hill by a team of eight—with his hat brim dangling around his neck like a necklace. Wouldn't that be a sight?

Dylan moved aside a low-hanging branch in his way. When he let it go, it snapped back and smacked Linda in the face. The pointy end of a stick scratched her cheek. "Ouch," she said, pressing her glove to her skin to lessen the sting.

Dylan halted abruptly and turned around. "Linda, I'm

sorry. That branch had more spring to it than I thought. Are you okay? Let me see."

"I'm okay," Linda said, though her face hurt something wonderful. She pulled her hand away. "Did it leave a mark?"

Dylan hissed. "Oh, shoot. You're bleeding. I'm sorry. I'm such an idiot."

"No. It's okay. Just a little scratch. I'll be fine." She gave him a teasing smile, even though it made her cheek hurt. "Maybe you should be in the back."

He chuckled. "Maybe I should, but just my luck I'd slip and fall forward and take you out with me."

"You're fine, Dylan. It barely hurts."

"Everybody knows you never let go of a branch without warning the person behind you."

Linda glanced ahead at Ben. "Well, not everybody."

Dylan took off his beanie and wiped the sweat from his brow. "It was a rookie mistake."

"You're forgiven," she said. "But I'll let you take up the rear just in case." She giggled at the expression on his face.

"Okay, but watch for falling bodies."

Ben led the trip back at a faster pace than he'd taken the trip up, but that was probably because it was easier going downhill and he didn't want to go embarrassingly slow. He was definitely limping now, and the limp got more pronounced the farther they went. Linda caught her lip between her teeth. Thank Derr Herr, they'd be back to the car in less than an hour, and she could quit feeling guilty and responsible and just a little bit like a goat. She liked goats, but they made a lot of noise, butted in where they weren't wanted, and certainly weren't very sympathetic creatures.

With about a mile left to go, Ben glanced back, way back, at Linda, and frowned. Fine. She certainly didn't care that he was still mad at her. She hadn't meant to embarrass him, and she wasn't going to stop laughing just so Ben wouldn't get offended. There was nothing wrong with her.

He said something to Sissy, and she trudged on ahead while Ben stepped off to one side of the trail and waited. Was he waiting for Linda? Was he going to tell her to quit smiling? Maybe he thought she was being smug instead of cheerful. Perhaps he didn't care about Linda at all. Maybe he wanted to strike up a friendly conversation with Dylan. Or maybe he wanted to be in the back so he could step on Linda's snowshoe and trip her while no one was looking.

"You're bleeding," he said, when Linda got closer. That was nice of him to notice, but that didn't mean he wasn't going to try to trip her later on.

Dylan stopped. "My fault. The old tree branch trick."

"Dylan," Sissy called. "What are you guys doing?"

"Coming." Dylan stepped around Linda. "Mind if I go ahead? My lady misses me."

Linda nodded and smiled, which only served to remind her of her aching face. "Sure. But beware. I might take this opportunity to get my revenge."

"You're bleeding," Ben said again when Dylan walked away.

"I'm okay."

"There's a big scratch on your face and a smear of red

and a big glob of blood on this end that looks like a red booger."

Linda exploded with laughter. "It does not."

Ben pulled off one glove, stuffed his hand into his coat pocket, and fished out a handkerchief. "At least let me get the booger. People will look at you funny."

"I'm fine," Linda said, giggling and dodging his attempts to wipe her face. "Leave my booger alone."

He laughed then gazed at her with mock contrition. "I'm laughing at you, not with you."

It was the first time she'd ever heard Ben laugh. "*Ach*," she said. "That isn't one bit funny."

"But you're laughing."

"So are you." Linda hadn't ever seen this side of Ben, the side that thought things were funny. The side that wasn't so uptight about looking stupid.

He cocked his thick eyebrows. "Will you just let me wipe your face?"

She huffed out a breath and came to rest. "Okay. But only because I don't want Sissy to have a fit and tell me I need to get my face amputated."

She riveted her gaze to his face as Ben dabbed carefully at her cut with his handkerchief. This close, his eyes were two dark, stained-glass windows with specks of gold that seemed to let in the light of his soul. She saw pain there and kindness and confusion. "The blood is mostly dry now." He bent over, picked up a small handful of snow, and closed his fist around it. When the snow melted, he dipped his handkerchief in it and wiped her face again.

Linda held perfectly still as his gentle fingers caressed the side of her face, sending a strand of something warm and thick threading into her veins. This was not at all anything she'd expected from Ben Kiem. Or from herself. But that didn't mean it wasn't entirely pleasant or that she wanted it to stop.

He bent over for more snow and continued wiping her scratch until she thought maybe all the blood was off and he was lingering close to her for a different reason entirely. She swallowed hard. "Is . . . is the booger gone?"

He stepped back, balling the handkerchief in his hand. "The blood is gone, but that scratch looks angry."

"I'll put some essential oils on it when I get home."

"But it's got to hurt." He sounded so sympathetic, so sorry, with much more concern than Linda had ever shown him.

It shocked her how much she liked that he cared. "Not near as bad as your leg must be hurting. I'm sorry I laughed."

"*Ach, vell,* you were laughing with me, not at me."

"I was!" she protested. "But I guess I didn't think it would upset you."

"I don't like to look stupid. I don't like people making fun of me."

"I wasn't making—"

He held up his hand to stop her. "No sense talking about it again. You talk too much."

His bluntness made her laugh. "Well, that's about the silliest thing I've heard ever. Just because you don't like what I say doesn't mean I shouldn't say it."

"You can behave how you want to behave, and I can think what I want to think."

"I suppose that's true," she said, but she'd rather win

the argument than come to some sort of truce. Where was the fun in agreeing to disagree?

He glanced down the trail. The others had slowed down, but they were still far ahead. "We should go."

"Now that I don't have any embarrassing smudges on my face . . ."

"Or boogers."

A giggle tripped from her mouth. "Or boogers, it's safe to get closer."

They headed down the trail side by side. "How much longer do you think there will be snow up here?"

Linda shook her head. "I don't know. Three weeks. But it doesn't matter. When the snow melts, we start hiking."

"Do you think you'll go snowshoeing again this winter?"

She studied him out of the corner of her eye. "Probably. When the snow is good like this but it's not too cold, we like to go every Saturday."

"So." He suddenly seemed uncertain. "So."

"So what?"

"Can I come next time?"

Linda thought maybe her eyes were going to pop out of her head. "I thought you were having a miserable time."

"I am having a miserable time, but I can't let your challenge go unanswered."

"What challenge?"

Determination flashed in his eyes. "You said you could beat me up this mountain with one hand tied behind your back. I'm going to prove you wrong. And I'll even let you use both hands."

"You can't beat me, Ben." It wasn't even a boast. She'd already seen him on the mountain.

He squared his shoulders. "You scared?"

"Of course I'm not scared. I'm managing your expectations. I don't want you to be crushed when I rub your face in the dirt."

He thought about that for a minute. "Sounds like a *gute* reward. The winner gets to rub the loser's face in the dirt."

Linda couldn't hold back her smile. "I'll look forward to it."

Chapter Five

Wally clicked his lighter, held the flame to his cigarette, and puffed a couple of times to get the burn going. He glanced at Ben who'd left his lighter in the buggy and his cigarettes at home. "You out of smokes? I've got an extra. You can pay me back later." Wally never offered a cigarette for free. Smokes were expensive, and Wally didn't have a job. He earned money doing the occasional chore for his *Englisch* neighbor, and that barely paid for his cigarette habit.

Smoking was expensive—for sure and certain a good reason to quit. Ben had tried to quit twice before when his savings had run low and Dat had threatened to fire him from the family's remodeling business. But quitting was a whole lot harder than starting, and Ben just hadn't had the willpower. Even now, after giving cigarettes up for twelve hours, his hands shook, and a headache was building right between his eyes.

Ben shook his head. "*Nae. Denki.*"

Rolling his eyes, Simeon pulled out his Camels, tapped out a cigarette, and offered it to Ben. "Here. And you don't need to pay me back."

Ben licked his lips, looked longingly at Simeon's cigarette, and backed up against the fence. "I'm okay. I'm thinking of quitting."

Wally looked at him as if he'd jumped on top of the fence and started dancing. "Quit smoking? Why? The judgey girls leave us alone, and it makes our parents crazy. Both *gute* reasons to never stop."

"I'm thinking maybe I should start exercising or something. My *onkel* Perry had a heart attack last year."

Wally glared at Ben, his cigarette hanging from his lips. "He's an old man. Smoking doesn't do nobody no harm."

Simeon lit the cigarette he'd offered to Ben and took a long drag. "You won't be any fun if you don't smoke."

Was that all it took to be considered fun with these two? Maybe he needed different friends.

Who was he kidding? Nobody but Wally and Simeon wanted to be his friend. They always stuck by him. He didn't need different friends. He was better off without those self-righteous types anyway.

"I'm not going to quit for very long," Ben said, modifying his plan just a bit. "But I need to quit for a couple of weeks to get in shape."

Simeon grunted in disgust. "Just so you can go snowshoeing with Linda Eicher? Who cares about her? Tell her you changed your mind."

Ben hesitated. Did he want to change his mind? He obviously hadn't been thinking straight when he'd scheduled another snowshoe outing with Linda. It had been miserable enough the first time—well, not completely miserable. The view had been nice and the sandwich was good and he'd discovered that Linda's eyes were the color of cornflowers. Still it was crazy of him to volunteer to do that again. He still felt the sharp pain in his lungs and the burning ache in his leg.

But Linda had challenged his manhood, more or less, and he wasn't about to lose to a girl. She wasn't going to poke fun or laugh at him ever again. But if he had any chance of beating Linda up the mountain, he had to be able to breathe. And that meant no smoking. He could pick up smoking again in a week or two.

He pulled out yet another piece of gum and chewed it until his jaw ached. Why had he let Linda get under his skin? She was snobby and hard-hearted and obnoxious. And she said exactly what she thought right out loud.

She also seemed very comfortable in her own skin, as if nothing bothered her or made her sad. As if she liked herself and was happy just being alive. Ben didn't know if he was envious or skeptical. Her life seemed too good to be true. How could anybody walk around being that happy? Was she pretending? Didn't she have any problems? Of course, Ben had more problems than anybody, so everyone was happier than he was, but still, Linda should at least show some sensitivity to people less fortunate than she was.

Like Ben.

She had no sympathy because she'd never had a bad thing happen to her ever. And she had no sympathy for Ben because she hated the very ground he walked on.

Or . . . at least . . . maybe that was true.

She'd smiled at him, and not just when she was making fun of him either. She smiled when he ate her sandwich. She smiled when he wiped the blood from her face. She smiled when he helped her take off her snowshoes. His heart beat a little faster thinking about her soft skin and the delight in her face when she looked out over the valley.

Maybe she didn't hate him.

But she didn't like him either. He'd warned her not to try to change him, and then she'd come right out and said that changing him would be impossible, like she'd already decided he was a lost cause. Well, she could get in line. Everyone thought Ben was a lost cause, even Esther and Levi. Even Mamm and Dat. Even Wally. It probably didn't count with Wally because Ben thought Wally was a lost cause too. At least they understood each other.

Wally, Simeon, and Ben stood just inside the pasture gate behind Mr. Bateman's barn. It was the halfway point between Wally's house and Ben's, and Mr. Bateman's field was lying fallow this year so there weren't any crops to trample. Last year, the three of them cut across Mrs. Leavey's hay field, and Mrs. Leavey accused them of trampling her crop when they'd only stepped on a few measly stalks that were so dry they were bound to die anyway.

The year before that, they'd gotten in trouble for riding a farmer's water-wheel sprinklers. All three of them had ridden the sprinklers. Ben was the only one who had gotten in trouble. Ray Sarle owned one of those giant center-pivot irrigation systems on wheels that went around in a huge circle, automatically watering the field with sprinklers mounted on the top. The contraption even had footholds for climbing. If people weren't supposed to ride them, there shouldn't have been a way to climb them. The three of them had straddled the sprinklers like cowboys on horses, which had been awkward at best. They had whooped and hollered and waved their hats in the air while getting soaking wet. They had pretended riding a sprinkler was more fun than it really was. That thing went so slow, it was just about as exciting as riding home from church in Dawdi David's buggy.

Ben pressed his lips together. What was the fun of standing out in a field smoking a pack of cigarettes or riding a sprinkler traveling three miles an hour?

Levi asked Ben that question every time Ben got in trouble with Dat. But the fun wasn't in riding sprinklers or cutting through someone's field. The fun was in doing something you weren't allowed to do. The fun was the feeling that you might get caught at any moment. The fun was seeing if you could get away with something you weren't supposed to be doing, pulling the wool over Dat's eyes and making him so frustrated he didn't know what to do with you. That was power. That was the fun.

Except the sprinkler ride hadn't been so fun. It had been painful and humiliating, like most of Ben's recent adventures. Riding that sprinkler, Ben had gotten over-confident and slipped off the pole, falling nine feet to the ground and separating his shoulder. Wally and Simeon climbed down to help him just as Mr. Sarle had come at them with his four-wheeler and a shovel. Ben had been forced to run, even with the wind knocked out of him and his shoulder on fire. Wally and Simeon got away, but Ray Sarle had hauled Ben into his house and called Dat on his business phone. Dat wouldn't let Ben sleep in the house until Ben had made it right with Mr. Sarle, which meant he worked his farm for a whole week after his shoulder healed. That was a lot of nights sleeping in the barn for a *dumm* sprinkler ride. Linda was right. How stupid could one boy be?

Still, Wally and Simeon were his only friends, and he wanted to make them happy. He wanted to fit in. And not sharing a smoke with his two best friends wasn't going to help the relationship.

Ben hated to admit his failure at snowshoeing, but Simeon might understand why he needed to quit smoking. "Linda laughed at me. She practically dared me to race her up that hill. What else can I do? I can't let her beat me again, and I can't beat her if I can't breathe." And maybe he wanted to impress her just a little. Maybe she wouldn't think he was so *dumm* if he sped up that hill like a race-horse. "It's just for a week. We're going snowshoeing on Saturday while the snow it still good."

Simeon shrugged, threw his spent cigarette on the ground, and stamped it out with his boot. "I guess. But don't go healthy on us. Healthy people always look down on the smokers, as if we're dirt or something. As if this wasn't a free country."

They never talked about what they would do about smoking if they got baptized. The *Ordnung* didn't exactly prohibit smoking, but most of the rules were understood behavior even though they weren't written down. Ben drew his brows together. Did he want to get baptized? Would that make Mamm and Dat love him? Or would they be happier if he left home and never came back?

Wally turned on his boom box and cranked it up loud. It was his way of making sure everyone knew he didn't care what anyone thought. He didn't care if the Batemans were bothered by the noise. He didn't care if they complained. Wally's boom box was a dare he waved in front of *Englisch* and Amish alike. *Kick up a fuss if you dare.*

Threaten me if you dare. I will make you mad at how much I don't care.

Wally puffed his cigarette and leaned closer to Ben. "If I were you, I'd forget about Linda Eicher," he said, yelling to make himself heard over the music coming from his boom box. "Who cares if she wants to race again? She's just trying to get under your skin. Besides, I met this *Englisch* girl at Dairy Queen who said she'd take us to the drive-in on Saturday."

Simeon squinted in Wally's direction. "Who's paying?"

"We can all pitch in some."

"Might be fun," Simeon said. He looked at Ben. "More fun than snowshoeing."

"I guess," Ben said. He didn't really want to go snowshoeing with Linda anyway, did he? "But for sure and certain it will be cold. Is the drive-in even open yet? Maybe I could go snowshoeing and then come to the movie."

Wally grunted in derision. "I guess. But why would you want to? I don't get you."

Ben didn't get it either, but snowshoeing with pretty Linda Eicher sounded much better than being crammed in the back of some *Englisch* girl's car at a boring drive-in movie. But Wally would be irritated if Ben disagreed with him. "Okay," Ben said. Wally could take that answer any way he wanted, and Ben wouldn't have to commit to anything yet. Maybe he'd go to the movie. Maybe he wouldn't. But for sure and certain, he was going to go snowshoeing with Linda Eicher.

Suddenly a sharp knife of frigid water hit him on the back of the head. He raised his hands in front of his face and turned around. Mr. Bateman, the farmer whose field they were standing in, was holding a hose with a brass nozzle on the end of it, and a hard, powerful stream of water shot through the nozzle. The water hitting Ben in the face and chest felt as if Mr. Bateman was hurling baseballs at him. Ben bent over and cradled his head between his arms. He'd rather not lose an eye.

Mr. Bateman turned the hose on Wally next and sprayed the cigarette right out of his fingers. Wally turned his head to keep from getting shot in the face. "Run!" he yelled.

Ben grabbed Wally's boom box, and the three of them took off across Batemans' field.

"That'll teach you to smoke on my property," Mr. Bateman yelled when they were out of reach of the stream of water.

While still on the run, Wally grabbed his boom box from Ben. Water dripped off of it, and one of the speakers was crooked. It had stopped playing. Wally turned back and scowled at Mr. Bateman. "I hate you," he yelled. "You'll be sorry."

"Stay off my property," Mr. Bateman yelled back. "Or you'll be the one who's sorry."

Wally stopped in his tracks, glaring in Mr. Bateman's direction. "We'll see about that."

Chapter Six

Cathy Larsen nearly missed Ben's road, slammed on her brakes, and turned her steering wheel hard to the right. Linda held tightly to the convenient handle just above the window, but Elmer Lee slid all the way across the seat in back.

Cathy glanced back at Elmer Lee, who at that moment decided to put on his seat belt. "You're a victim of centrifugal force, Elmer Lee," she said. "Always take it seriously."

Linda giggled, even though she had no idea what Cathy was talking about. Cathy had a way of saying things that made them sound like she was scolding you, even when she was talking about the weather.

Cathy weaved down the road as if looking for Ben's house, but Linda knew for a fact that Cathy had been to Ben's house several times and knew exactly where it was. "The doctor says I need cataract surgery, but he really just wants to take my money. My eyes are good for at least another year. That doctor is so young, he doesn't even have to shave yet. What does he know?"

The need for cataract surgery explained the erratic driving. Linda tried not to think about it. If she was supposed to die in a car accident, there was nothing Cathy or anybody else could do to prevent it. Lord willing, she would live many more years, but Gotte was in charge, and she wasn't going to worry about it.

The car jerked to a stop in front of Ben's house. "*Denki* for driving today," Linda said, opening the door. "I'll fetch Ben."

"Don't lollygag or dilly-dally," Cathy said. "I don't have all day to wait."

Would Ben's *dat* think it was strange that an Amish girl dressed in *Englisch* winter clothing was coming to pick Ben up for a snowshoeing adventure? Linda smiled to herself. It did sound strange, but Ben's *dat* was unlikely to object when Linda was probably the most well-behaved person Ben hung out with. And by "hung out with" she meant Ben had broken her buggy taillight and gone snowshoeing with her once. Was it proper for the girl to be the one picking up the boy? *Ach, vell*, it couldn't be helped. Linda had invited Ben snowshoeing, and if she actually wanted him to show up, she'd have to go to him. It was highly likely he'd back out on her anyway.

Ben answered the door, looking like he was ready for snowshoeing. He wore his coat and snow pants and carried a pair of gloves in his hand. He had a tentative, almost regretful smile on his face. She liked that smile. He was so much better looking when he wore it. "*Ach*, Linda. I'm sorry. I can't come."

Having expected an excuse, she wasn't quite sure why disappointment knotted her stomach. She shot him a teasing grin to cover any irritation he might see in her face. "*Ach*, don't tell me you've chickened out. I brought Elmer

Lee along to help lift you out of all the holes you're going to fall in."

He smiled. That kind of talk usually annoyed him. Okay. This was progress. "I wasn't planning on falling in any holes. In fact, I was planning on passing you so fast on the trail that my wake would blow the bonnet off your head."

She snorted. "As if that would ever happen."

Nanna Kiem, Ben's *mammi*, came to the door and stood beside Ben. Nanna always smiled like she meant it, like there was no use smiling partway when a smile that showed all your teeth was better. Nanna had chin-length, salt-and-pepper hair that looked strange down like that under a *kapp*. Nanna had lost all her hair to cancer last year, and it hadn't grown back enough to pin up into a bun. "Linda Eicher. *Vie gehts*? Esther said something about you the other day."

"Esther?"

Her eyes twinkling merrily, Nanna waved her hand as if swatting a fly. "*Ach*, never mind. Did you come to talk to Ben? We were just going out."

"Mammi asked me to drive her into town," Ben said. The look of affection in his eyes was unmistakable. Apparently there was someone else in addition to Esther whom he cared about very much. Linda found his fondness very sweet.

Nanna hooked her hand around Ben's elbow and pulled Ben toward her. "Ben is so good to me. I don't like to drive the buggy or run errands by myself. If I didn't have such a *gute* grandson, I don't know what I'd do."

Linda certainly wasn't going to get in the way of Ben

doing something nice for his *mammi*. And it was nice, even if he was just using it as an excuse to get out of snowshoeing.

Nanna's gaze traveled from Ben to Linda and back again. "Well then, I will go get my bonnet and my coat while you two have a nice long visit."

Linda didn't know how long of a visit they could have in the time it took for Nanna to get her coat, but it was just as well. There wasn't really that much to say.

"I'm sorry," Ben said. "I really was looking forward to running circles around you today. I stopped smoking and everything."

Linda stared at him. "You stopped smoking?" For her? Well, not specifically for her but definitely because of her. A little warm spot grew right in the middle of her chest.

"Just for a week."

"That won't do any good. A week hardly gives your lungs a chance to clear out. You've got to stick with it for at least a month." Linda didn't even know if that was true, but if she said six months, he might just give up.

The combination of alarm and irritation in his expression made Linda want to laugh. "A month?" he said. "It's been seven days, and I can't stop shaking." He held out his hand so she could take a look.

"I don't see any shaking. Maybe you're getting better."

"That's easy for you to say. You weren't throwing up all week. Nothing but the thought of beating you to the top kept me going."

That was sweet in an awkward sort of way. "Well, what did you expect? You've been abusing your lungs for years."

He leaned against the doorjamb. "*Denki* for the sympathy."

She smiled and rolled her eyes. "I'm not good at sympathy."

"I hadn't noticed."

He had gotten himself into this mess, but she'd already mentioned that a few times. For sure and certain he didn't want to hear it again. "I'm sure there's an essential oil for tobacco addiction. I'll ask my *mamm*."

"Sounds like a bunch of nonsense to me."

She didn't take it personally that he was unconvinced. "Doubt is not a destination. You should try some essential oils and find out for yourself. They work if you believe in them. Kind of like faith."

It was his turn to roll his eyes. "And now you're going to give me a sermon."

She giggled and backed away, holding her hands palms up. "No sermons. It's no skin off my teeth if you choose not to believe."

"*Denki*. I'd be grateful if you didn't try to convince me." He smiled slightly, as if he didn't really think she was a huge bother. "Your cheek looks better. I can't even tell where you got scratched."

Linda felt her face get warm. She wasn't exactly sure why, except Ben's gaze seemed to pierce right through her skull, as if he was looking at something deeper than her face. "It's myrrh."

"What was that?"

"Myrrh and tea tree essential oils. They're wonderful *gute* for wounds."

He threw back his head and laughed. Linda smiled in

spite of herself. There was a certain amount of satisfaction in making someone as gloomy as Ben Kiem laugh.

Nanna Kiem reappeared at the door with her black bonnet and the bag of fabric scraps she always carried. "I hate to cut your conversation short. Why don't you come with us, Linda? I'm going to the fabric store."

Linda pointed her thumb in the direction of Cathy's car. "*Denki*, but we're going snowshoeing while there's still some snow left."

Nanna stuck her head out the door and frowned. "I didn't even notice the car there. Is Cathy driving you?"

"*Jah*."

Nanna folded her arms and pinned Ben with a stern look. "Were you supposed to be going snowshoeing with Linda?"

"*Jah*."

Nanna seemed extremely annoyed. "Why didn't you tell me?"

Ben shook his head. "You need me to drive worse than I need to go snowshoeing."

"Stuff and nonsense," Nanna said. "I'm not an invalid. I'm not even that old. Who am I to keep you from a fun outing with a pretty girl?"

"It's not really an outing . . ."

Nanna did not pause her indignation. "You should have told me. I feel so selfish, not to mention that Linda has made all these plans."

Linda jumped in. "You didn't know. And I think it's sweet that Ben is such a devoted grandson." Ben grinned at her. She felt the warmth of it clear to her toes.

Nanna shed every ounce of irritation in an instant and reached up and put her arm around his shoulder. "He is a wonderful *gute* grandson. He drives me wherever I want to go and doesn't complain about eating my chicken pot pie."

"I love your chicken pot pie, Mammi."

"*Ach*, *vell*, nobody else does. But I'm over it."

"I can just go snowshoeing with Elmer Lee," Linda said. "He's funny-looking and smelly, but we'll have a *gute* time." She looked at Ben out of the corner of her eye. It might have been fun, but it didn't matter anymore.

Nanna shook her head. "No sirree, Bob. This old lady isn't going to get in the way of your snowshoeing trip."

"I don't mind taking you to town, Mammi."

Nanna patted Ben on the cheek. "I know you don't. But I'm not going to ruin your fun. My errands can wait. I'm coming with you."

Linda was struck speechless. By the look on Ben's face, he was thinking the same thing. "You're . . . you're coming with us?" Ben stuttered.

"I don't want to miss out on the fun. I've never been snowshoeing."

"But, Mammi, it's kind of hard for someone . . ."

"For someone my age?" Nanna seemed only slightly offended. "Stuff and nonsense. It's snowshoeing. How hard can it be?"

"That's just what Linda said," Ben murmured, looking at Linda as if this was all her fault.

Linda didn't know what to say except to go along with it. "Do you have snow pants?"

Nanna pursed her lips. "I'll wear my long underwear."

"Mammi!" Ben said, as if the thought of his *mammi*'s underwear shocked him to the core.

Linda giggled. Nanna was blunt and unembarrassed.

It was exactly how a cancer survivor in her sixties with improperly short hair should behave. "I don't know if you can snowshoe in a dress."

Nanna nodded decisively. "I can. I play pickleball in a dress. I can certainly snowshoe."

Linda didn't even hide her surprise. "You play pickleball?"

"*Jah*. Esther, Hannah, me, and some *Englisch* friends. Cathy plays with us."

"Cathy? But she's almost eighty years old."

Nanna's eyes danced with amusement. "Eighty-three."

"I don't think we have enough snowshoes," Ben said. He actually seemed disappointed instead of just pretending to be disappointed.

Linda's heart sank. If Nanna didn't go, it was unlikely she could convince Ben to go. "I only have three pair."

Nanna tapped her finger to her lips. "I think Ben's *dat* has a pair of snowshoes, the old-fashioned kind made out of wicker or some other such thing. They're hanging in the barn."

Ben jumped into action. "I'll go get them and meet you at the car."

Nanna winked at Linda when Ben walked down the hall. "I'll get into my long underwear. Cathy has been waiting a long time, and she's not a patient person. You'd better get out there and make sure she isn't having some sort of attack."

They crammed into the car, Cathy driving and Nanna in the front passenger seat. Linda sat between Ben and Elmer Lee in the back. Ben was a nice solid presence, and

Linda found herself leaning toward his side of the car to take in his nice scent. "You smell like wintergreen gum and fresh cut wood."

He gave her a half-confused, half-amused look. "*Denki*. The gum is to keep my mind off smoking. And the wood is because I helped my *dat* cut floor joists this morning."

"Much better than stinking like an ashtray."

He cocked an eyebrow. "I'm glad I meet with your approval."

She gave him a teasing smile. "I wouldn't go that far." Cathy pulled onto the road, and Linda leaned even closer to Ben. The confusion on his face deepened. "I don't think we should go to Rock Creek," she whispered. "You're *mammi* doesn't think she's old, but I think the trail will be too hard for her."

Ben seemed to be holding his breath and purposefully avoiding her gaze. "It is a hard trail, but what can we do? She wants to go snowshoeing."

How to change plans without Nanna getting suspicious? "Cathy," Linda said, "since we got a late start, I think we should snowshoe at the golf course instead of up the canyon. The snow is still pretty good down here."

"Wherever you want to go. I've never been to the golf course. Golfing is the most boring sport in the entire world, except for maybe football. I mean, what's the point?" Cathy turned north instead of south, and Nanna didn't seem to notice the plans had changed because of her. *Gute*. She could still enjoy snowshoeing without having a heart attack or breaking a hip, Lord willing. And on the flatland, Ben might think he had more of a chance to beat Linda to the end of the trail. He wouldn't, but she didn't want to crush his hopes right at the beginning.

There were a few other cars parked at the golf course. Not many, because the good snow was mostly gone. But it would be good enough for Linda, Ben, Elmer Lee, and an elderly woman who insisted on being included. They climbed out of the car, and Cathy popped her trunk. Nanna's ancient snowshoes came out first, then the three pair Linda had borrowed from Ashley. Ashley and Dylan had gone skiing this weekend, but Ashley had been happy to lend Linda her snowshoes. Cathy reached under a blanket in her trunk and pulled out another pair of snowshoes and some walking poles. "Alrighty then. Which trail do we take?"

Linda couldn't keep the sheer panic from her voice. "Um. What do you mean?"

Cathy set the snowshoes on the ground and pulled out a hot pink, sparkly parka from under the same blanket. "You don't think I'm going to sit in the car and wait for you."

Actually, Linda had thought Cathy was going to drop them off and come back later. Apparently not.

Ben glanced at Linda, the alarm on his face probably matching the alarm on hers. Nanna Kiem joining them was one thing. Eighty-three-year-old Cathy Larsen was quite another.

Eighty-three-year-old Cathy in a hot pink parka with fake fur on the hood and rhinestone buttons down the front.

Cathy reached under the blanket and pulled out a bright yellow beanie that could have blinded someone in full sunlight. "I found this on Amazon. It's good for if you're out on the road in the middle of the night."

Ben's lips twitched upward. Linda turned away from him

so she wouldn't burst into laughter. Okay. The snowshoe adventure had just become a lot more interesting. She hoped Ben could hold his own this time, because Linda was going to have to give her complete attention to the two senior citizens.

"Mammi," Ben said. "Let me wear the old snowshoes. You wear these new ones. They'll be easier."

Nanna looked at both pair. "Are you sure? I invited myself. I don't mind wearing the old ones."

Ben nodded vigorously. "I'm sure."

Linda peered at the old snowshoes. The frames were made of some kind of pliable wood, stained a pretty reddish brown and tapering to a point at the back. Leather weaving crisscrossed the wood, and a piece of rope hung where the bindings should be. The wood frames were cracked in three or four places, and the leather was old and dry. Lord willing they would be just fine, and if they disintegrated into a thousand pieces, this was the golf course, not a wilderness trail. Ben could hike back to the car in his boots without encountering snow much past his ankles.

Golf course or not, Ben was going to have a hard time in those snowshoes. Linda picked them up and pulled Ben aside. "I'll wear them. They don't look very easy to walk in."

Ben gave her a dazzling smile. What was it about him today? He'd smiled more in the last hour than she'd seen him smile in the last ten years. "That's wonderful nice of you, but I don't mind. I quit smoking for just such a time as this."

Linda giggled. "I don't wonder but this is your Queen Esther moment."

He nodded in mock seriousness. "I don't wonder either."

Ben and Elmer Lee helped Nanna on with her snow-shoes while Linda directed Cathy to sit in her car with her feet on the ground. It was better to put on snowshoes while you were actually in the snow so you didn't bend the metal crampons on the pavement, but it was definitely safer for Cathy to sit while Linda helped her. Linda strapped Cathy's snowshoes to her boots and adjusted the bindings. "These are nice snowshoes, Cathy."

Cathy studied her feet as if she was reconsidering all her life choices. "I bought them yesterday. They were the most expensive ones in the store. I could have bought a pony for what I paid for these."

With both hands, Linda pulled Cathy to her feet. Cathy wobbled slightly as if her feet were stuck to the ground. "Move your feet. Walk just like normal."

Cathy scrunched her lips together. "I've never walked normal. I've had shin splints for fifty years." Linda moved back, and Cathy took a step forward. Her hand shot out and clamped onto Linda's shoulder.

"Are you okay?"

"As long as my vertigo doesn't get too bad, I'll be fine."

Ach. The way things were going, they'd end up at the hospital by noon. They'd have to call an ambulance be-cause Cathy was the only one who knew how to drive. Linda glanced at Ben who was holding tightly to his *mammi*'s arm. Did he know how to drive? It seemed like that would be something a boy like Ben would have learned how to do. Maybe some wild *Englisch* friend had taught him. It would come in handy if they needed to take Nanna or Cathy to the emergency room.

Gripping her poles, Cathy made a wide arc around the snow at the edge of the parking lot. It was all Linda could do not to run to her, grab her around the waist, and pull her back to the car for her own safekeeping.

Cathy glanced up at Linda before looking back down at her feet. "I look ridiculous, but I can do it, even with my lumbago." Linda offered her arm to Cathy to lead her to the trail, but Cathy wouldn't take it. "Don't bother with me. I'll be just fine. I didn't pay three hundred dollars for these snowshoes for nothing."

Three hundred dollars? She really *could* have bought a pony for that much.

Linda wasn't a worrier, and she certainly wasn't going to fuss over Cathy if Cathy didn't want to be fussed over. Cathy played pickleball. She drove too fast. She complained about a lot of health maladies, but she moved well on those snowshoes. Linda shouldn't underestimate her just because she was eighty-three. Linda certainly didn't want to be underestimated simply because she was nineteen.

Linda hadn't coddled Ben on his first snowshoe outing. She didn't need to baby Cathy either. Probably.

Ben held tightly to his *mammi* as she made her way to the trail, but as soon as she got onto the snow, she nudged him away from her. "*Denki*. You are so *gute* to me. Now go get your own snowshoes on."

Ben set the old snowshoes on the ground and peered at them as if he didn't even know what they were. He swiped his hand down the side of his face and glanced at Linda. "Don't laugh, but I have no idea how to put these on."

Linda let her jaw drop in mock indignation. "What makes you think I would ever laugh?"

"Just a guess," he said dryly.

She sat on the ground next to Ben's snowshoes. "I'm not sure either. Give me your foot."

Ben chuckled. "Will you give it back?" He stepped into the left snowshoe, and Linda tried to figure out how to secure his foot with the rope. She looped the rope around the center pole of the snowshoe, secured it around his toe then his ankle, and tied her best knot to secure the whole thing into place.

"This should hold it," she said. "Give me your other foot."

Ben stepped into the other snowshoe. "How did you do that so fast?"

"Years of milking cows," Linda said.

"Cows don't wear snowshoes."

Linda laughed as she secured Ben's other foot. "Very funny. I have strong fingers from milking cows."

"How many cows do you have?"

"Two. I've milked one every day since I was six. My older *bruder*, Yost, used to milk the other. Now Elmer Lee helps me." Linda finished the last knot and stood up. "Okay. I don't know how well it will work, but I guess we'll see."

"I guess we will. I plan on beating you to the top."

Linda smiled at the determined look on his face. "There is no top. It's pretty flat clear to the end of the trail."

"It's just an expression. It means I'm going to win the race and be king of the hill."

"It's not a race."

Ben flashed a playful grin. "Don't chicken out on me."

Linda rolled her eyes. "We both know I can run circles around you."

"I don't think so. I haven't had a cigarette for a week, and my legs are longer. You're scared."

Linda laughed at the teasing expression on his face. "We can't race." She leaned closer and lowered her voice. "If you haven't noticed, the other three have never been snowshoeing before, Cathy is eighty-three, and your snowshoes will fall apart if you step on them too hard. When I win, I don't want you blaming it on your antique snowshoes."

"*When* you win? It wonders me if you're a little over-confident."

"*Nae*. Just realistic."

He grunted. "I can't let that boast go unanswered. I challenge you to a race next Saturday, up Rock Creek without my *mammi*."

Linda got breathless all of a sudden. He wanted to do this again? "Okay, but don't get your hopes up. I'm still going to beat you."

"I don't think so."

Cathy started walking in the wrong direction. "Cathy," Linda called. "That way is a dead end. Let's go this way."

Linda grabbed her snowshoes, took them to the trail, and quickly put them on. She'd given Elmer Lee her poles because she only had one set, and he didn't know what he was doing, but nobody really needed poles snowshoeing on the golf course. It was hard to fall.

Ben shuffled awkwardly to the trail, but he seemed to grow accustomed to his snowshoes the more steps he took. Nanna and Cathy took off with Ben between them, and Linda walked behind with Elmer Lee.

"He's not bad," Elmer Lee said, motioning at Ben, who was making sure Nanna's gloves were secure.

Linda watched as Ben helped Cathy loop her poles around her wrists, his broad shoulders easily visible from behind. "He can be contrary and he likes to argue, but he's very *gute* to his *mammi*. And he's got a pretty tough skin. You should have seen that cut he got from skiing behind our buggy."

"Was it deep?"

"Esther gave him forty-five stitches. He wouldn't go to the hospital so she just used a quilting needle, and he sat there and watched while she poked him."

Elmer Lee's eyes widened with surprise. "They didn't even numb it first?"

"*Nae.*"

His expression turned to one of awe. "I'd like to see that scar."

"It's pretty bad. But I wouldn't admire him too much. That scar came from doing something he shouldn't have been doing. There's no honor in that."

"LaWayne Nelson says Ben got shot trying to stop a robbery."

Linda drew her brows together. "Don't make a hero out of him. He and Wally were being stupid, and Wally accidentally shot him." That had been almost five years ago. Everybody knew about it, and everybody said Ben had gotten what he deserved for playing with his *dat*'s rifle. Linda had agreed with the general opinion, but now she wasn't so sure. Ben was reckless and *dumm*, but he wasn't a bad person. He could have been killed, and maybe the world would have been worse off without him. Maybe he would have missed out on the chance to make his life right with Gotte. Her heart beat a little bit faster. How glad she was Ben hadn't died.

Nanna stumbled over her own feet, and Ben grabbed her arm before she could fall. "You're doing *gute*, Mammi. Walk as normal as you can but lift your feet higher. That will help you get a more secure step."

Nanna glanced behind her. "Elmer Lee, come up here and tell us what you're learning in school. This is your last year, isn't it?" She inclined her head in Ben's direction. "I'll be fine. You go walk by Linda so we can talk to Elmer Lee."

Elmer Lee caught up with Nanna and Cathy, which wasn't too hard. Elmer Lee's legs were longer than Nanna's, Nanna was wearing a dress, and she and Cathy were taking it nice and slow. They were doing well, but they weren't going to win any races, even against other old people.

Ben turned around and waited for Linda. The grin on his face made her heart smile. "Did you hear me giving Mammi instructions? I bet you never thought I'd be one of the experienced ones on the trail."

"Today, you're the best I've got."

"Well, nobody has died yet or fallen into a snowbank."

"Not even you," she said, in mock surprise.

He poked her with his elbow. She squeaked in protest. "Considering I'm wearing these ancient snowshoes, you should be impressed."

"You're doing well for a beginner." He growled and shoved her harder this time. Laughing, she veered off the trail but got right back on it without missing a step. "I see you got a new hat."

He reached up and ran his finger along the brim of his straw hat. "Thirty dollars."

"Considering your history with hats, this one should last you another half hour."

"It isn't me. You've been there both times my hats got ruined. You're bad luck."

"Amish don't believe in luck."

His smile faded, not for any reason Linda could see. "Maybe I don't want to be Amish."

Linda didn't know what to say to that.

Ben fell silent for a full minute, and the only sounds between them were the swish-swish of their snowshoes and Ben's labored breathing. He may have quit smoking, but he had quit very recently, and he was a long way from being in good physical condition. "Do you want to be baptized?" he finally said.

She glanced at him in surprise. It was a deep question she never would have expected from Ben Kiem. "*Jah*. Of course. When I find a boy I want to marry, someone who is good enough for me." She nudged him playfully, but he didn't act as if he'd heard her.

He stared down at the ground. "I don't know if I want to be baptized."

Of course he didn't know. Linda had never met anyone who liked to kick against the pricks more than Ben. "It's a big decision."

"I would have thought you wouldn't want to join with the *gmayna*. You'd have to give up skiing and snowshoeing, plus swimming and hiking."

Linda scrunched her lips to one side of her face. "Not really. Your *mammi* has been baptized. She plays pickle-ball."

Ben shook his head. "That's only because her son is the

bishop, and he gives her permission. Dat won't go so easy on you. Or me. The *Ordnung* is about tradition and behavior. It's about what the community thinks is proper and righteous. That's why I'd have to give up smoking even though it's not specifically forbidden in the *Ordnung*."

"I thought you'd already given up smoking."

He ignored her attempt to make a joke. "You won't get to swim. You won't be allowed to do anything you can't do in a dress."

Linda gave Ben a half smile and pointed at his *mammi*. "As we have seen, there's a lot more you can do in a dress than you might guess." She stopped walking and pulled him back. "Don't think I haven't pondered on the consequences of my decision. There are some things I know I'll give up. I'll trade in my swimsuit for one of those special swim dresses. I might not feel it's proper to go skiing, but I can't see how hiking in the mountains and enjoying Gotte's beautiful creations can be bad. My *aendi* Edna and *onkel* Luke paddle all over the lake together in their canoe. My work will be to serve and praise Gotte. What better way to praise Him than to take joy in His world? Gotte wants us to be happy."

Ben grunted his disagreement. "*Nae*, He doesn't. If He wanted us to be happy, why won't He let us have any fun? Why all the rules?"

Linda pinned Ben with a stern eye. "Is it really that much fun to tip over outhouses and play music so loud you lose your hearing? Is it fun to stand outside in the freezing cold because your *mamm* won't let you smoke in the house?"

"It's more fun than sitting in *gmay* listening to the minister."

She shook her head. "I don't think sitting in *gmay* is fun, but I find it nourishing."

"I don't even know what that means."

"Faith is my anchor, Ben. Obedience keeps me safe. I yield myself to Gotte's will, and I am happy."

He moved away from her, as if an extra foot between them would make him feel better. "Maybe that makes you happy, but don't judge me for not feeling the same way."

Ach. He was so touchy. She started walking again because Nanna, Cathy, and Elmer Lee had slowed down so Ben and Linda could catch up, which now meant the three ahead of them were barely moving. "I'm telling you how I feel, Ben. And you're right. I was judging you when I said that about outhouses and smoking. If that is how you find happiness, I'm not going to try to talk you out of it."

"Well, that stuff does make me happy," he said, though he sounded more like he was trying to convince himself than anyone else.

She stifled a smile. Ben was twenty-one? Twenty-two? But still so childish. "Don't think I'm judging you, but you don't seem happy."

He lifted his chin. "I'm wonderful happy."

"I'm glad to hear it." Linda had nothing else to say about such an obvious lie, so she picked up her pace just to remind him how much better off she was for not smoking. What did she care if Ben Kiem was too stubborn to admit to his own stupidity?

Ben matched her pace even though he sounded like a rattly, raspy diesel engine. "My friends and I like to hang out together. We have fun. We go to movies or have a smoke. Maybe we drive around with some *Englisch* girls. Wally plays rap music on his boom box. It's like the rhythm goes right to your bones. We like it when people complain that the music is too loud. It means we're getting their attention. We talk and laugh, and we don't pretend to be righteous. Everybody else just pretends to be righteous. They're so fake."

Linda couldn't help but laugh. Who was being fake? "Are you trying to convince me how happy you are? Because it's not working."

He pressed his lips into a hard line, and she could see the muscles of his jaw tighten. "Don't laugh at me."

She tilted her head so he could see her smile. "I'm sorry. That time I was laughing at you and not with you." She didn't get the response she hoped for. His hardened expression didn't melt one bit. "I'm sorry, Ben. You're trying to be honest with me, and I'm being insensitive."

"*Jah*. You are."

Ach. She was too plainspoken for her own good. She should never say exactly what she thought. "You're right. Who am I to judge what is fun and what's not. Most people think sliding all over the country on a pair of skis is stupid and unnecessary."

Ben's lips softened into something that might have passed for a smile. "Snowshoeing is even dumber. It's cold, and all you do is walk to nowhere in particular."

"I'll try not to judge your choices if you don't judge mine."

He nodded, lowered his head, and concentrated on his snowshoes. "I'm happy the way I am. Nobody likes me, so I'm not going to waste my time trying to get the *gmayna*'s approval. They're all hypocrites anyway. Everybody thinks

I'm a good-for-nothing, so nobody expects anything of me, even my parents."

There was so much pain in the casual way he talked that even Linda, as insensitive and practical as she was, felt like crying. But what could she say? She'd told him she wouldn't judge, but his heart was clearly hurting. How would it be to feel completely friendless, even with two "best" friends? She tried to smile. "I expect something of you."

He glanced at her, puzzled and defensive.

She stretched her lips wider across her face. "I expect you to lose our race next week."

He rolled his eyes. "Don't count on it. I'm going to win."

Happy to be back on more comfortable ground, Linda relaxed and her smile felt more genuine. "I shouldn't give you any advantage, but I'll bring over some essential oils to help you quit smoking. Then at least it will be a more competitive race."

He groaned as if he were in pain. "What is it with you and essential oils?"

Ben teased her about essential oils while the five of them walked the rest of the loop around the golf course and ended up back at Cathy's car. "Is everybody ready for a snack?" Linda said, pulling the backpack off her shoulders.

"*Ach, du lieva,*" Ben said. "I didn't even notice you were carrying it. I would have carried it. You should have asked me."

"*Nae.* You were huffing and puffing enough as it was."

"I was not."

Linda laughed. He seemed offended but was good-natured about it. "Oh, yes, you were. Besides, you had to wear the ancient snowshoes. It was the least I could do."

Ben started to say something, but a sudden bout of

coughing caught hold of him, and he was useless for a full minute.

"What have you got?" Cathy said, taking out her keys and popping her trunk. "I've recently gone gluten free. And dairy free. And sugar free. I'm learning very quickly that freedom isn't free. It's expensive."

Nanna peeled off her gloves. "What do you eat, Cathy?"

"Cabbage and avocadoes. And I can have some nuts but only half a cup a day."

"Sounds miserable," Nanna said.

Cathy didn't look too happy about it either. "It is. Last night for dinner, I fixed cabbage steak with a side of Brussels sprouts. Lon took one look at his plate and went to Dairy Queen."

Ben held Linda's backpack while she pulled out the sandwiches she'd made this morning. "I've got tuna fish with pickles and without. And potato chips."

Cathy squinted at Linda's sandwiches. "What kind of chips?"

"Salt and vinegar."

Cathy's face brightened a little. She never really smiled. "Gluten free, dairy free, and sugar free. I'll take three bags."

Linda only had four bags of chips, but she didn't want Cathy to starve. The rest of them would have to settle for tuna fish. And a little bag of peanuts at the bottom of her backpack.

A big, noisy pickup truck rumbled down the road as if it was racing itself. The truck pulled into the parking lot, and the driver honked the horn. Loud. Did they think Linda's group hadn't already noticed them?

Ben's friends Simeon and Wally and some *Englisch* girl

sat in the truck bed grinning like cats and smoking like chimneys. That must have been an unpleasantly cold ride. There were three more *Englischers* in the cab of the truck. Two girls and a boy. The girl driving looked like a raccoon, with black and white striped hair, thick black eyeliner, and deep purple lipstick smeared across her lips. The windows were closed, but Linda could still hear the pounding bass notes from the music they were playing. They were going to go deaf.

Wally stood up when the truck came to a stop and lifted a case of beer above his head. "Ben, let's go. Zoe says we can use her hot tub after the movie."

Ben was just about to take a bite of tuna fish with pickles. He slid the sandwich back into the bag and stuffed it into Linda's backpack as if he'd been caught stealing. "Okay. I'm coming." He glanced at Linda, a bright flush of red overspreading his face. At least he knew enough to be embarrassed.

Nanna frowned. "We were having such a nice time."

"We're just going to a movie," Ben said, without lifting his eyes to his *mammi*'s face.

Linda's heart sank to her toes. Hot tub and movies and beer. How fun. And Ben liked to have fun.

She shouldn't judge, but no matter how happy he protested to be, Ben needed better friends. And maybe a swift kick in the *hinnerdale*. She looked the other way and took a bite of her sandwich. Why she even cared was a mystery.

Ben handed Linda the backpack, quickly loosened the ropes around his boots, and stepped out of his snowshoes. He opened Cathy's trunk and set them inside. He couldn't look Nanna in the eye, but he motioned toward her feet. "Here, Mammi, let me help you take those off before I go."

"No need," Nanna said. "You go along. Have a nice time."

"It's just a movie, Mammi."

"Of course." Nanna gave him an uncertain, reassuring smile.

Ben wasn't comfortable, but Linda didn't see as that was anyone's fault but his own. He paused and half-smiled at Linda. "*Denki* for taking me snowshoeing."

The look he gave her sort of melted her heart. Ben was an idiot, but he was nice about being an idiot. "You're welcome. I expect you to be ready for our race next week."

The *Englisch* girl honked the horn. Was she trying to break everybody's eardrums?

Ben glanced behind him. "Maybe we should just forget about the race." He jogged to the truck and climbed in the back.

Cathy opened her first bag of chips. "That boy could use fewer good looks and more brains. Why are the good-looking ones often the most stupid?"

Why indeed.

Before Ben could secure himself in the truck bed, the raccoon driver gunned the engine and made a loop around the parking lot to get herself going in the right direction. Ben's hat caught the sudden rush of wind, flew off his head, and fell to the ground. The truck's front wheel ran over it on the way out.

Laughter exploded from Linda's mouth. *Ach*, *du lieva*. There went another hat, flattened like a pancake.

Ben was always good for a laugh.

Chapter Seven

Ben paced back and forth in Esther's kitchen, unable to sit, unable to concentrate on anything but the overpowering need for a cigarette and the overpowering urge to dump a pile of snow over Linda Eicher's head. Why had he ever let her talk him into giving up smoking?

Esther sat at the table feeding Winnie spoonfuls of soup while Winnie fed herself bits of peanut butter and jelly sandwich. Seven or eight quilting clips were clamped to the bodice of Esther's apron, and she wore a drink packet behind her ear, one of those long, narrow, single-serve packets that people used to flavor their water. Ben was never sure what Esther was going to wear behind her ear, but he always noticed. "Would you like something to eat?" Esther said. "There's plenty of soup."

Ben halted temporarily as a fit of coughing overtook him. Why was he coughing more now that he wasn't smoking than he did when he was smoking? "I'm bothering you. I'm sorry."

"You're no bother. And if you wear a furrow in my floor, Levi knows how to fix it." She smiled at him. "You could fix it yourself, I guess."

That was one thing he liked about Esther. She noticed things. Levi and Ben both helped Dat with the remodeling business, but Levi was the older one, the more responsible and capable one, and people usually ignored Ben in favor of Levi. Ben knew how to do everything Levi did, but Dat and everybody else had more confidence in Levi. He couldn't blame them. Levi was just better at everything than Ben would ever be. Still, it was nice of Esther to acknowledge that maybe he had some floor-laying skills. "I didn't know where else to go. Dat and I finished at the shop, but if I go home, Mamm makes me do jobs. I don't want to do anything but eat and smoke."

"My *mamm* used to do that too. If I had any time to myself, she thought I must be bored. She didn't want me to sit idle, so she always found a job for me to do. I wiped a lot of walls as a child."

"Exactly," Ben said. "Mamm makes me wash windows. And it's cold out there." He paced another line in the kitchen. "Have you got something besides soup? Something sweet?"

Esther frowned, stood up, and rummaged through her cupboards. "*Ach.* Tomorrow is shopping day. I don't have hardly anything. I've got some old candy corns." She pulled a bag from the shelf. "They're hard as rocks, but if you suck on them, they'll soften up."

"I'll take them." Beggars could not be choosers, especially beggars who were trying to quit smoking with white-knuckled determination.

With her eyes full of sympathy, Esther handed him the half-eaten bag of candy corns. "The first couple of weeks are the hardest. My sister Ivy got the shakes and these terrible headaches. Of course, Ivy is a complainer, so I don't know how bad it really got with her and how much was just her making sure I knew how bad it was."

"*Ach*, for sure and certain, it was bad." Ben stuck three candy corns in his mouth and pressed his teeth into them as far as they would go. It wasn't far.

Esther grabbed a glass from the dish rack and filled it with water. "Here. Stay hydrated. I'm very proud of you for quitting cigarettes."

"You don't have to say that." Ben took a gulp of water. There was nothing to be proud of. He was doing this so he could beat Linda in a snowshoe race, and also maybe to prove to her that he wasn't as stupid as she thought he was. She wasn't going to have a reason to laugh at him ever again.

Besides, this smoking thing was nothing for Esther or his parents to get their hopes up about. He'd probably go back to smoking as soon as the race was over. He never succeeded in anything, and his parents certainly didn't expect much of him. They'd be astonished if he was able to quit altogether, but not surprised if he started smoking again tomorrow. That was just how they saw him. They were already disappointed in him, and he'd stopped trying to gain their approval years ago. There was nothing he could do to change their minds about him.

Esther was sweet, and she acted like she loved him no matter what, but she was only saying she was proud of him because there was nothing else she could say. In the end, he'd only disappoint her too.

Esther sat back down, picked up the spoon, and immediately set it down again. "*Ach.* I could make you some lemonade." She stood up and pulled the flavor packet from behind her ear. "I've got mix."

"*Nae, nae.* Sit down. I'm okay."

"But it's right here," she said, showing him the yellow packet.

He shook his head. He didn't want her to go to any trouble, and it would hurt her feelings to know it wasn't especially appetizing to think of drinking something that came out of a packet that had been sitting behind her ear for who knew how long.

They heard the front door open and footsteps down the hall. Linda Eicher and that old Cathy lady walked into the kitchen. Linda's gaze immediately fell on Ben, which he knew because his gaze immediately fell on her. It was annoying that he found her so interesting, annoying that he cared what she thought about him. Well . . . he didn't really care what she thought about him, but she sure knew how to make him madder than a wet hen. And was she aware that lavender was a wonderful-*gute* color on her?

She smiled as if she wasn't mad at him for running out on her snowshoe outing, as if she didn't care that he'd gotten into a truck with some *Englisch* kids. She smiled as if she was his friend. But he wouldn't be fooled.

Cathy wore a bright yellow pantsuit and a necklace of round orange beads. She definitely wouldn't be missed in a crowd. "We let ourselves in," she said. "It's cold out there, and the cold isn't good for my asthma." She pulled out a chair from the table and sat down. "Besides, what is that quote about friends who come in without knocking? Something about they're the best kind of friends in the world?"

Ben didn't know about that. Like as not, friends who walked into houses without knocking would stop getting invited over.

"How nice to see you both," Esther said, even though Ben couldn't see any reason why that might be true. All Cathy did was complain about her health, and all Linda did was laugh at people and make boys feel uncomfortable when she smiled at them.

Linda's eyes danced with a light all their own. He couldn't decide if it was because she was happy to see him or she just found him amusing. But she was like that with everybody. She smiled and laughed more than her fair share. "I hope you don't mind that we came over, Esther," she said. She set a canvas bag on the table. "I went to Ben's house, and they told me he was here."

Cathy sighed. "It was a wild goose chase, but I promised Linda I'd get her here, no matter the inconvenience. I'm not one to refuse when someone has a health emergency."

Esther paused with the spoon halfway to Winnie's lips. "A health emergency? Is someone sick?"

Cathy pointed to Ben. "Linda's been concerned."

Linda was concerned about him? Why? He cleared his throat. He didn't need to get worked up. Linda was concerned for his soul, like Mamm and Dat and everyone in the *gmayna*. She certainly wasn't concerned for him as a person or for him in particular.

Linda pulled some small glass bottles from her bag. "Ben has been having headaches and nausea since he quit smoking. I feel bad for him, so Mamm gave me some essential oils to try."

"How nice of you," Esther said.

Ben eyed her skeptically. "They won't work."

Linda, of course, wasn't offended. "They'll work. My *aendi* Luann got pregnant using essential oils. My cousin Vernon was cured of asthma."

Ben crossed his arms and shook his head. "Don't believe it."

Linda laughed. "*Ach*, if I didn't have to drag you kicking and screaming, this would be much easier, but I don't mind dragging." She pulled a package of chocolate chips from her bag. "If the essential oils don't work, we can always try chocolate."

Ben tried to snatch the package from her hand, but she held it out of reach and pressed her palm against his chest to keep him from lunging forward. A warm sensation radiated from the spot where she touched him, as if her hand was a heater and he was a piece of ice. Then his heart started acting funny, like a skittish horse trying to escape its pen only to run full speed into a wall. If she noticed how wildly his pulse was racing, she didn't say anything. Since when did chocolate make him that tense?

Linda set the chocolate chips on the table. "Chocolate later. If you like, we can make cookies. Right now I'm going to brew you some tea and see if we can't help that cough."

"I drink a tablespoon of apple cider vinegar every morning," Cathy said. "It's sour, and it makes my bladder hurt, but it's supposed to be good for you."

Linda gave Ben a sideways grin. Cathy had no problem talking about her bladder anytime she wanted to. Her bladder, her arthritis, her varicose veins, and her hysterectomy. What was it they said about friends who could tell you anything, no matter how private? They stopped getting invited over.

"First," Linda said, pulling a small glass tube from her bag. She took the cap off and came at Ben as if she was going to paint his face. He backed away. "Ben, stop it. I'm going to give you some aromatherapy."

"I don't know what that is, but it sounds dangerous and completely unnecessary."

"It's not dangerous," Linda said, slapping his hands away and backing him into the wall. Her aggravated smile gave way to laughter, and Ben couldn't help but laugh with her. *With* her this time. They must have looked ridiculous, Ben trying to avoid getting killed by her essential oils and Linda trying to force him to be still. "Ben," she scolded between giggles, "stop moving." She expelled all the air from her lungs in a deep, deafening sigh and handed him the tube. "Smell it. It won't hurt you."

"You might be trying to poison me."

"I am not trying to poison you, though sometimes I'm sorely tempted." She folded her arms and shook her head. "You and your *Englisch* friends," she muttered.

So she *was* mad that he'd left her on the golf course that day. He studied her face. Maybe *mad* was too strong a word. She seemed more aggravated, as if he hadn't hurt her feelings as much as he'd done something stupid she had already forgiven him for, as if there wasn't anything he could do that would make her hate him. As if she was a friend who would stick by him, no matter what he did to offend her.

There it was again, the warm sensation right in the center of his chest, the heart palpitations, the clenching of his gut. What was going on?

"Well, try it," Linda said.

What was it she had asked him to do? He couldn't for the life of him remember. It was just too easy to jump into those blue eyes and go swimming. He cleared his throat, gathered his wits, and reminded himself how judgmental Linda was. It didn't matter the color of her eyes. He raised the tube to his nose and took a short whiff. "It smells like oranges."

She nodded as if he'd just paid her a compliment. "*Jah*. It's orange and cedarwood oil. If you apply it behind your ears and on your throat, that will help the headaches."

"I don't believe it."

"Try," she said, the annoyance building in her voice. She took the tube from him. "*Ach, vell*. You don't have to believe they'll work for them to work. Let me do it."

With Cathy and Esther looking on, he couldn't very well run away without looking stupid. But putting some smelly oils behind his ears would *also* look pretty stupid. Which would make him look less stupid? Which would keep Linda from laughing at him? "Okay. You can do it, but just this once."

Her smile could have lit up every house in Byler. "I'm giving you this whole bottle. You can go home and put it on in secret as many times as you need. No one has to know." She sidled closer, put a hand on his shoulder, and nudged his chin to the left. Her skin was warm and soft against his face. He sucked in a breath. "Don't worry. It's not going to hurt," she said. "It has a little roller ball, so you can roll the oils right onto your skin."

Linda's hand crept farther up his shoulder as she took the bottle, tipped it on its side, and slid the roller up and down behind his ear. Her warm breath tickled his cheek and played at the short hairs on his neck. At the intimacy of this simple movement, his stomach tightened and his pulse raced out of control. Ben gritted his teeth and focused on Cathy, with her yellow pantsuit and bladder problems. It was a helpful distraction.

Linda scooted around to his other side and applied the oil behind his other ear. The second ear wasn't as bad as the first because Ben's attention was firmly focused on Yellow Cathy and those chocolate chips sitting on the table. He liked chocolate chip cookies. He liked chocolate. The beads on Cathy's necklace looked like pieces of candy. Where had Cathy purchased that pantsuit?

Linda moved so she was face-to-face with Ben, which prevented him from staring at Cathy. "How does that feel?"

He wanted to resist, but it felt *gute*, oh so *gute*. "Um . . . *ach* . . . I don't know. It smells *gute*, I guess."

Without even checking to see if it was okay, she curled her fingers around the back of his neck and rolled the bottle back and forth across his throat. He swallowed hard and resisted the urge to clamp his eyes shut. Was she purposefully trying to make him lose all sense of reason?

Finally, mercifully, regrettably, she pulled away and smiled at him. "Now, just give that a few minutes. Lord willing, it will help. I'm going to make you some tea. It will clear out your lungs."

Esther gazed at Ben with a funny, twitchy smile on her face. "How do you feel?"

He didn't know how he felt, and that was the honest truth. "It's not going to help."

Linda rolled her eyes. "Whatever you say, Mr. Know-It-All."

He did feel like sitting down. He sat between Cathy and Esther where he had a full view of Linda at the stove warming the teakettle. "What kind of tea are you making?"

"Peppermint and lemon with honey. I'll make it nice and strong."

Esther stared at him as if she was trying to read his mind. He needed to divert her attention from him and whatever she was looking for in his face. "It wonders me if Cathy could use some tea for her asthma."

He didn't need to say more. Cathy launched into a speech about her asthma and the drugs she was currently taking for it and how the doctors just wanted your money. Unfortunately, Esther didn't stop her scrutiny. Her wide gaze never left his face, and her lips never stopped twitching. Had she been able to hear his heart pounding? Had she noticed his labored breathing? He should have asked Esther about Winnie or her apricot tree. It was too easy to sit in silence and think deep thoughts when Cathy talked about her problems.

As soon as the water boiled, Linda poured it into a cup with a few drops of peppermint oil, a few of lemon, and a spoonful of honey. She stirred her concoction and set it on the table for Ben. He lifted the cup to his lips, and the peppermint made his eyes water before he even tasted it. He took a sip, being careful not to burn his tongue, and the hot liquid traveled down his throat. He immediately started coughing, as if his body had rejected the tea and everything Linda had given him.

"That's *gute*," Linda said. "The tea will loosen that cough and help clear the cigarette smoke from your lungs."

Ben cracked a smile. "You think you're so smart."

Linda took it as a compliment. "*Denki*. I am."

It wasn't the Amish way to appreciate a compliment. Ben found her confidence refreshing.

After Ben finished his tea, he didn't feel quite so antsy,

but he wasn't ready to say it was because of the essential oils. It might have been because Cathy had so many health problems, his didn't seem so bad. Cathy made him feel better just by wearing that pantsuit. Yellow was a cheery, healing color.

Esther wiped up Winnie and the highchair and left to put Winnie down for a nap. Winnie insisted on giving Ben a goodbye kiss. Ben kissed her cheek and caressed the top of her head. He'd never get over how soft her hair was.

Linda washed the few dishes while Cathy gave Ben a rundown of her mole surgery and showed him her scar. Linda finished wiping the counter. "Do you want to make cookies?"

For some reason, making cookies with Linda sounded more fun than listening to Wally's boom box or tipping over outhouses or even hearing about Cathy's moles. "*Jah*, okay."

"I'll help," Cathy said. "Even though I can't eat them because of the gluten and sugar."

Ben's enthusiasm crashed like a bee against a picture window.

Linda's smile faltered. "Okay. The three of us." She set a mixing bowl on the table. "Ben, you have the muscles, so you can stir." Her eyes sparkled. "But I warn you, it's a hard job."

He pretended to take offense. "Do you think that's all I'm good for is the heavy lifting?"

"*Nae*. I don't doubt but you're good for a far sight more." The way she said it made his heart skitter around in his chest. Oy, anyhow, what was in that tea she'd given him?

"Too bad you Amish don't use electricity," Cathy said. "This would be easier with my KitchenAid."

Linda pulled four sticks of butter from her bag, unwrapped them, and plopped them into the bowl. Then she measured the sugar, two cups of white sugar and two of brown.

Ben chuckled. "These are going to be wonderful *gute* cookies."

Her fingers brushed against his when she handed him a tool he'd never seen before. "You need to blend the butter and sugar together. This is a pastry cutter. Do you know how to use it?"

He examined it for a couple of seconds. It had a handle with six hard steel prongs attached to it on either side of the handle. "I think I can figure it out." He pressed the prongs into the butter, which separated into sections. "Like this?"

She looked up, and it was a little disconcerting how close her face was to his. "I knew you were smart."

Did she have any idea how those five words affected his breathing? Or how the smell of her hair made his heart race?

"He's smart enough," Cathy said, "even if he doesn't always act like it." Cathy peered into the bowl. "You really should cut down on your sugar, Linda. This much sugar will give you diabetes before you're thirty. And all that butter will clog your arteries."

Linda finished measuring out the sugar. "People crave sugar when they go off cigarettes. These cookies are for Ben."

"She's trying to kill me slowly," Ben said. He grinned at Linda so she knew he was teasing, but he didn't have to do that. She thought everything was a joke. But it was nice of her to think of him. Linda was usually more the practical type than the thoughtful type.

Ben mixed the butter and sugar together, and Linda handed him a giant spoon. "Start stirring," she said. "And don't stop until I tell you."

"How long will that take?"

She laughed. "Hours and hours."

"Hmm," he said, pretending to think about it. "Can I take time out to go to the bathroom?"

A giggle burst from Linda's lips. "We'll see how hard you work. Slackers don't get bathroom breaks."

Cathy cracked an egg into Ben's bowl. "I have to take bathroom breaks or I'll get a bladder infection."

Neither Ben nor Linda could stifle their amusement. Ben had to step away from the table as his laughter turned into a fit of coughing. Linda pounded on his back as if to keep him from choking, but it was mostly to cover her own laughter. Cathy probably wouldn't appreciate their mirth at her expense.

Four eggs went into the bowl, and Ben mixed them with the sugar and butter. "I hope you notice what a wonderful-*gute* job I'm doing."

Linda watched him stir. "You might get that bathroom break after all, but don't get too confident. We haven't got to the hard part yet."

"Now I'm scared," he said.

"You should be."

Esther came into the kitchen. "Thank Derr Herr, she's finally asleep." She propped her hands on her hips. "Are you finding everything you need, Linda?"

"*Jah.* I hope you don't mind."

"Of course not."

Cathy sprinkled a teaspoon of baking soda into the bowl. "I'm glad my arthritis isn't as bad today so I can help with the cookies. I'm good at making treats. My gluten-free cake is to die for."

Esther shifted her gaze from Ben to Linda to Cathy. Her lips started doing that twitching thing again. "Cathy, it wonders me if you could help me with my quilt in the front room."

"I saw it on the frames," Cathy said. "I'm not fond of your color combination, but it's your quilt so I guess you can choose. Did you use the cut-away method?"

"Yes I did. Will you take a few stitches?"

Cathy glanced at Ben's bowl. "I'd love to quilt, Esther, but these two will ruin the cookies without my help."

"We'll be fine," Linda said.

Esther put her arm around Cathy's shoulder. "You're a very good cook, Cathy, but you're an even better quilter. Come, and I'll show you how I did the appliqué."

Cathy hesitated, obviously torn between being desperately needed in two places. "Okay, Esther. I'll help you. I suppose I can monitor for burning cookies from the front room."

"I suppose you can," Esther said. She led Cathy out of the kitchen and into the living room.

Linda's face was just barely wide enough for her smile. "We're on our own. Are you up for the challenge?"

Ben laughed. So far his biggest challenge had been trying not to sniff at Linda's hair. "I'm ready."

Linda measured out four cups of flour and poured them into Ben's bowl. Her eyes flashed with delight. "Now for the hard part." She poured in five cups of oatmeal, one by one, making the dough very hard to stir. She opened the bag of chocolate chips. "Open wide," she said. She moved one step away from him and threw a chocolate chip at his open mouth. She missed and caught him in the forehead. The chocolate chip bounced to the floor.

"You're a terrible shot," he said. "Let me." He grabbed a handful of chocolate chips out of the bag, popped three in his mouth, and tossed one in Linda's direction. It sailed past her head and plinked against the fridge.

"Now who's the terrible shot?" She retrieved another chocolate chip and launched it at his open mouth.

It hit him hard on the cheek. "Ouch. Stop that." She wound up as if to throw another one, and he grabbed both her hands and pressed them against his chest, laughing so hard his gut ached. "Stop, stop. You're going to take out my eye."

Unfortunately or fortunately, depending on how he wanted to look at it, Linda's hair was mere inches away from his nose, and he couldn't resist the urge to smell her. And then there was the feel of her hands, like smooth silk, tucked into his, as if they belonged there, and the brilliant color of her eyes, which he wanted to gaze into all day long without even taking time out for meals. It was a very unfamiliar sensation.

Instead of struggling to break free, her whole body stilled, as if she could read his mind and was trying to decide if she approved or not. "I think," she said slowly. "I think it's more about who's catching than who's throwing."

"Huh?" was all he could say. He had been concentrating so hard on her lips, he hadn't been paying attention to what she'd said.

She cleared her throat and nudged herself away from him. He didn't want her to move, but for sure and certain it made it easier to understand what she was saying. "The person . . ." She took a deep breath. "The person catching the chocolate chip has to try to catch it."

"Okay?" Ben said, elongating the syllables so it took him like ten minutes to say the word.

Linda's smile was more normal now. "Throw one at me. But toss it in the air so there's a nice arc. Then I can get under it and catch it."

Ben should have thought of that. He and Levi used to play this game with M&Ms when they were little. M&Ms, or pebbles if they didn't have anything else. "I swallowed a rock once when I was a kid."

"A rock?"

Ben held out his hand. "Get ready."

Linda held her arms perpendicular from her body, as if she needed extra balance to catch a chocolate chip in her mouth. Ben gently tossed a chocolate chip about three feet into the air. Linda kept her gaze glued to the chocolate chip, bent her knees slightly, and caught the chip in her mouth. It pinged against her teeth and nearly bounced out, but she clamped her lips around it.

"Yes!" Ben yelled, as if he'd just run some world championship race.

"Woohoo," Linda squealed. "That was amazing."

Cathy stuck her head around the corner from the living room. "Is everything okay in here? Do you need my help?"

Ben couldn't help but laugh. Cathy was just so nosy and so pushy. And so yellow.

"We're fine," Linda said. "We haven't even put the cookies in the oven yet."

The wrinkles deepened around Cathy's eyes. "Okay then. I'm just three steps away if you have an emergency."

She pulled back but reappeared a second later. "Don't eat the raw cookie dough. You'll get Ebola."

Linda pressed her lips together as if even the thought of eating raw cookie dough would never cross her mind. When Cathy went back into the living room, she glanced at Ben. "I suppose we should try to perfect our chocolate chip trick later. These cookies are much better with chocolate chips in them."

He nodded. "There's plenty of rocks outside we can use."

She scrunched her lips together. "Not unless you want to break a tooth. Sounds like you had an interesting childhood. I'd like to hear about it sometime."

"I'm sure you would."

She poured the rest of the chocolate chips into the bowl. "What does it feel like to swallow a rock?"

He shrugged. "Nothing. I guess it passed right through me."

She held up her hand. "I don't want to hear it, unless there's a possibility that rock is still rolling around in your stomach. That would make you a much more interesting person."

"I'm not a very interesting person, even with an assortment of rocks in my gut."

She looked at him as if he'd just said something outrageous. "Of course you're an interesting person."

His lips curled involuntarily. "I am not."

"You're interesting, just not obvious like other boys."

"Obvious? I don't know what you mean."

"It takes time to get to know you. To understand you."

"There's nothing to understand. I'm just another Amish boy with a boring life." He most certainly didn't want Linda to truly understand him. She'd turn and run the other way as fast as she could, and try as he might, he couldn't talk himself into wanting her out of his life, disagreeable and troublesome as she was.

Smiling, she took his spoon and stirred the chocolate chips into the dough. "That's what you want people to think, but you're not just any other Amish boy. You're deep, like a treasure buried in a field."

He snatched his spoon back. That dough was stiff. His arms were much stronger for stirring. "Sometimes you make no sense."

"*Ach, vell*, there's the side you show to the *gmayna*. The boy who doesn't care about anything or anyone, the boy who gets into mischief with his friends. I don't think that's who you really are."

Ben stabbed at the dough with his spoon, the panic rising inside him. "Why do you care?" He tried to sound flippant and disinterested, but he only managed to sound defensive.

She either didn't notice his prickly tone or she ignored it. Laughing, she pried the spoon from his fingers. "Ben, Ben. The dough is already dead. You don't have to kill it again."

He cracked a smile. This was safer ground, and that was where he wanted to stay. "I was just trying to be a *gute* stirrer so you'd let me have a bathroom break."

Linda rummaged through Esther's drawers. "Here we go," she said, holding up a tiny ice cream scoop.

Ben widened his eyes. "There's ice cream?"

Linda giggled. "*Nae.* This is a cookie dough scoop so our cookies are uniform."

"I've never cared about my cookies being the same size."

She pretended to be shocked. "It's *gute* one of us cares or these cookies would be a disaster."

"I'm just as happy to eat the uncooked dough."

Cathy's voice carried all the way from the living room. "Don't eat raw dough. You'll get salmonella."

Ben choked on his laughter when he tried to swallow it. Linda clapped a hand over her mouth. "Cathy has a lot of health problems," she whispered, "but there's nothing wrong with her hearing." She pulled a cookie sheet from above the fridge and started making perfectly round balls of dough with the cookie scooper.

Ben watched her work, mesmerized by her long, thin fingers and her fluid movements as she turned lumps of dough into cookie balls. "You're wonderful *gute* at that."

"Years of baking." She nudged him with her elbow. "I didn't mean to make you uncomfortable when I talked about buried treasure."

"You didn't," he lied.

She smiled like she didn't believe him. Of course she didn't. She knew him too well already. "I understand you better than I did, and I'm surprised that I like you so much."

Ben didn't know whether to be offended at her surprise or overjoyed that she admitted to liking him. Or wary. Did she really like him, or was she just trying to be nice to a poor, misguided youth? He hadn't known her long, but Linda didn't seem like someone who was nice just to be nice. She was more plainspoken and hardheaded than that. So . . . she liked him? That was big news.

"There's a whole treasure buried under there some-where," Linda said. "I'm curious."

He shrugged, trying not to let her concern get to him. "It's just a bunch of rocks."

Amusement danced across her face. "Are you talking about your stomach now or your person?"

"Both."

She glanced toward the living room, took a spoon from the drawer, and scooped a small glob of dough from the bowl. "Here," she whispered. "Before Cathy sees you." She raised the spoon to his lips. Never pulling his gaze from her face, he opened obediently and let her feed him. His senses reeled as if he'd been hit over the head with a two-by-four. How could something as simple as a spoonful of cookie dough be so unsettling? Esther fed Winnie all the time. Neither of them seemed to have a problem with it.

"What do you think?" Linda watched him expectantly.

What did he think? He thought he should probably get out of here before he pulled her into his arms and kissed her. "*Ach, vell.* I . . . I don't know."

Linda drew her brows together. "Isn't it good?"

Ach. The cookie dough. What did he think about the cookie dough. He cleared his throat. "It's wonderful *gute.* Do you think I'll get Ebola?"

"Probably. But it will only make you more interesting."

He chuckled to hide the fact that he felt so off-kilter. "Sick people are not interesting."

Linda slid the cookie sheet into the oven and set the timer. "Only a few minutes now."

She scooped more cookie dough onto another cookie sheet with her handy-dandy tool while Ben washed dishes and wiped the table. He even wiped the legs of Winnie's highchair because they never got cleaned, and he ran a damp paper towel on the floor around the table. He wasn't usually so tidy, but maybe today he felt like being helpful. And maybe he was hoping Linda would feed him some more cookie dough.

He glanced at her and swallowed hard. Or maybe he didn't care if she did or not. Linda wasn't his friend or anything. Wally and Simeon were the only true friends he had.

"I'm going to make you more tea while we're waiting," she said.

When the timer rang, Linda pulled the cookies out of the oven and set them on top of the stove. They smelled *appeditlich*, almost as good as her hair.

Linda handed him a cup of tea and two cookies. "The tea will probably overpower the taste of the cookies. Maybe you should drink it first."

Ben did as he was told, sipping his tea quickly so he could get to those cookies. The first bite melted in his mouth. "Soft," he said. "I like them soft."

"It was your *gute* stirring," Linda said, pouring them both a glass of milk.

Ben laughed. "I like to think I was important to making these cookies, but you could have done it yourself."

"I could not. They really are hard to stir, and you were very kind to stick with it."

She was teasing, but Ben didn't mind. Maybe he had helped her just a little.

Linda finished her third cookie and set down her empty glass. "I have something else for you."

He cocked an eyebrow. "If it's more essential oils, I'll pass. I already smell like a candle store."

"Maybe, but who doesn't like a candle store? How's the headache?"

"It's gone, but I think it was the cookies." Or maybe it was Linda. The minute she'd walked into the house, he'd forgotten all about the need to smoke.

Linda shook her head, always so sure of herself. "It was the oils." She reached down into her canvas bag, pulled out a straw hat, and set it between them on the table.

Ben's face got warm remembering what had happened to his last one. "You . . . you didn't have to get me a new hat."

She laughed and pulled his ruined hat out of her bag. The cap was flat like a pancake, and a black tire mark cut a diagonal path across the brim. "I felt so sorry about how this one died. Being run over by a truck is a horrible way to go."

Ben rolled his eyes. He slid the new hat closer and pressed his fingers along the brim.

Linda tilted her head to one side so she could look him in the eye. "I know you don't like to be laughed at, but it was funny how your hat blew off your head."

"I guess it was. But you laughed at me in front of my friends."

"Didn't your friends think it was funny?"

Ben shrugged. "They made fun of me for snowshoeing."

"*Ach*, *vell*, that's just silly. They've obviously never tried it." She pressed her lips together and giggled with her mouth closed. "And then Raccoon Girl ran over it."

"Raccoon Girl?"

Linda's lips formed into an O, as if she hadn't meant to say that out loud. "That was mean and judgmental. I'm sorry."

"Who is Raccoon Girl?"

She turned her head, but looking away did nothing to hide her smile. "That girl driving the truck. Her eye makeup was so dark, she looked like a raccoon or someone with severe hay fever. I do have an essential oil blend for allergies."

Ben cracked a smile. Zoe liked to layer on the makeup. "She does sort of look like a raccoon."

"Or someone who is sick with the plague." Linda grimaced. "I'm sorry. Raccoons are cute animals. She probably thinks she looks really *gute*."

"She wants to shock people. She likes it when people look at her funny. I think she likes annoying her mom too."

Linda's smile faded, and she dipped her head and looked at her hands. "Now it sounds like we're talking about someone besides Raccoon Girl."

Ben pretended not to know what she meant. He just stared at his new hat, unable to thank her because of the thick wall of disapproval between them.

She gritted her teeth. "*Ach*. I'm being judgmental again. I blurt out what I'm thinking and usually end up offending somebody. I'm sorry."

"You say 'I'm sorry' too much."

Her eyes narrowed in confusion. "It's important to admit to your mistakes. I'm not too proud to apologize."

Ben straightened. "That's not what I mean. If you tried to be considerate and hold your tongue more often, you wouldn't have to apologize so much." Her piercing, thoughtful look made him want to squirm, but he held his ground and stared right back at her.

"You're right."

He leaned closer to make sure he'd heard her correctly. "I'm right?"

She couldn't stay somber for long. A grin played at her lips. "Well, partly right. I like to laugh, and people usually laugh with me. But with you, I rarely know what's going to offend you until I say it. Sometimes I think things are funny that you won't even smile at. So in a way, it's your fault that I have to say 'I'm sorry' so often."

He couldn't stay mad at her, not when she had that playfully sweet glint in her eyes. He raised his hands as if stopping traffic. "My fault? Don't put this on me."

She propped her elbow on the table, rested her chin in her hand, and glued her gaze to his face. "Okay then. I'm going to ask you something, and I don't want you to be offended because I'm not trying to offend you, and seeing as you don't like me to say 'I'm sorry,' I'm not going to apologize."

"Okay," he said. What was it about Linda that made him uneasy and eager at the same time?

"Did you have fun with those *Englisch* kids on Saturday?"

He tensed. "You're judging me again."

"I'm not judging, just asking."

"Of course it was fun," he said, because what else did he want Linda to think?

"I'm *froh* it was fun. You just . . . you just . . ."

"What?"

"You seem so angry."

Ben shifted in his chair. "I have fun with my friends. I'm mad at everybody else."

He saw real concern in her eyes. "Why?"

Vell, if Linda couldn't take the truth, she shouldn't ask *dumm* questions. "Why do you ask so many questions?"

She curled her lips. "I'm curious."

"My parents hate me."

"And you're mad at them for hating you?"

He leaned back and folded his arms. "At least you didn't try to convince me that my parents *don't* hate me."

"*Ach*, I *do* disagree with you. I'm sure they don't hate you, but if that's what you believe, I would be foolish to try to talk you out of it, even though I think it's silly."

"You think a lot of things are silly. That doesn't make you right."

She shrugged. "I guess not. So you're mad at your parents for hating you, and you want to make them feel as bad as you're feeling. Is that right?"

She was too smart by half. "I guess so."

"But when they feel bad, they make you feel worse, and then you want to make them feel even worse, and then they make you feel worse. It sounds like you're going around in circles."

He shook his head. "I have no idea what you just said."

"I'm hoping you'll just give up and agree with me."

He smiled grudgingly. "I'll agree with you if you promise to stop talking. My headache is coming back."

Cathy sidled around the corner as if she'd been standing outside of the kitchen for ever so long. "Are you doing drugs? Because that's sure to give you a headache."

Linda had her back to Cathy. She drew her brows together and mouthed, "I'm sorry."

Now she was apologizing for other people. Ben stifled the urge to laugh at the expression on Linda's face. Cathy was a busybody, but it wasn't anything he hadn't heard before. He purposefully hadn't given anybody a reason to think better of him. Of course Cathy thought he was doing drugs. His parents probably assumed that too, but he didn't care what they thought of him. Their opinion of him was already so low, an ant couldn't get all the way under it. He certainly wasn't going to break his back trying to make them love him. It was wasted effort. They'd never see him as anything but a rebellious son who broke their hearts every day.

Ben's gaze shifted to Linda. Did she assume he was doing drugs? What exactly did she think of him? Did she care about him or was he a project to her, like sweeping the floor or cleaning the toilet? He didn't want to be on anyone's to-do list, even at the top. *Things to do today: Feed the chickens, milk the cow, convince Ben Kiem to change his ways.*

"Of course Ben isn't doing drugs," Linda said, so confidently that Ben wanted to give her a hug. Maybe she truly thought better of him, even though she'd already told him she thought he was stupid for smoking.

Cathy placed a hand on the table and stared into Ben's eyes. "I guess you're right. He doesn't have that glassy stare, and he's not drooling."

Linda gave Ben a secret smile. "I didn't know using drugs made you drool."

Cathy nodded. "Oh, yes. I know all about it. I watch *Dateline* every week. I know as much as any doctor does."

"For sure and certain you do," Linda said, her smile curling higher onto her face. "I always know to ask you all my medical questions."

"You should. I don't charge money for my advice." Cathy picked up a cookie and examined it. "These look good, but you've underbaked them. Nobody likes a soft cookie."

Linda laced her fingers together, not the least bit upset that Cathy had criticized her baking. "I'll remember that."

Cathy glanced at Esther's clock. It had quilt blocks where the numbers were supposed to be, and it said TIME TO QUILT. "Well, we've been here longer than either of us planned. We'd better go before we get roped into another project."

Linda's smile faded, as if she was slightly disappointed to be leaving. Ben was slightly disappointed to see her go, but not *very* disappointed. He didn't need her hassling him about his friends or throwing chocolate chips in his face or painting his neck with essential oils. But she had really nice eyes, and she made him laugh, and she cared enough about him to try to cure his headaches. Linda wasn't too bad. As long as she didn't try to change him or save his soul, they might be friends.

Linda handed him the little bottle with the orangey oil. "Rub this behind your ears and on your throat whenever you feel a headache coming on. And take the peppermint and lemon oils. Make yourself some tea to help that cough."

"*Denki*," he said. Even though he didn't believe in essential oils, it was nice that she cared.

Cathy picked up Linda's canvas bag from the floor. "Peppermint makes my bladder hurt. If your bladder starts hurting, stop using it."

Ben winked at Linda when Cathy wasn't looking. "Words to live by."

Linda stood up, pointed at Ben, and gave him the stink

eye. "I don't care if you don't believe. Use those essential oils."

"Okay," he said, as if she was asking him to pluck the hairs off his chin one by one. But even though he acted reluctant, he secretly determined to use Linda's essential oils every day. Linda had gone to a lot of trouble for him. The least he could do was follow instructions. The worst that could happen was that he'd start smelling like an orange or a stick of peppermint. There were worse things he could smell of, like cigarettes.

She grabbed another cookie from the plate and took a bite. "*Appeditlich*," she said.

Cathy made a face. "Might as well eat poison."

Linda gave Ben one last amused look before slinging her bag over her shoulder and following Cathy out the door. Ben stood still for a minute, breathing in the lingering scent that Linda carried with her. He flinched when he heard the front door close. There was something he still needed to do. He snatched his new hat from the table.

Passing Esther and her quilt in the front room, he hurried to the front door, opened it, and called to Linda, who was halfway across the yard. "Wait," he said.

She turned, and her smile almost blinded him. She couldn't be that happy to see him. They'd just said goodbye.

Cathy didn't turn around, didn't stop walking until she reached the car. "Come on, Linda. If he'd wanted to do more chitchatting, he should have thought of that while we were still in the house."

"I'll be right there," Linda said, never taking her eyes from Ben.

Cathy turned and leaned on the hood of her car. "Don't take too long. My arthritis acts up when I get cold."

In three long strides Ben was at Linda's side. She looked up at him as if she couldn't wait to hear what he had to say. Why? Ben had never been anyone special. His collar suddenly seemed too tight. "Uh, Linda, *denki* for the hat. It was wonderful nice of you. And you don't have to apologize for laughing when my hat got run over. I deserved it."

She reached out and wrapped one hand around his upper arm. He felt a zing down to his toes. "I was laughing with you, Ben, not at you."

He could feel a smile sprouting on his face. "I don't believe you for a second."

She threw back her head and laughed. "What else is new?" She seemed to realize she had a hold of his arm and quickly dropped her hand to her side. "Will I see you on Saturday for our race?"

He inclined his head as a yes. "I've got clear lungs and essential oils. I'm going to win."

"Don't count your chickens just yet."

"Sounds like fun," Cathy called from her perch by the car. "What time should we go?"

With her back turned to Cathy, Linda widened her eyes as if pleading with Ben to do something. He shrugged. What could he do? He wasn't about to tell Cathy she couldn't go snowshoeing with them.

Ben cocked an eyebrow at Linda. "Can you pick us up at eleven?"

"Sounds good," Cathy said. "I bought some new snow pants."

Linda pinned him with the stink eye, but there was

nothing Ben could do. He certainly didn't want to hurt Cathy's feelings. "Okay then," Linda said through gritted teeth. "We'll see you on Saturday. And don't count on Cathy slowing me down. I plan on soundly beating you up the trail."

"Only in your dreams," Ben said.

She tilted her head to one side, and her gaze explored his face. "See you then." She turned and ran to the car before Cathy could make one more peep about her bladder or her moles or her arthritis.

What did Linda see when she looked at him? Was it something more than his parents saw? Or any of the other girls in the *gmayna*? The thought made his heart race with anticipation and his throat constrict in terror. Linda didn't know him. He didn't want her to know him. Sooner or later she'd understand what everyone else already knew.

Ben was no good.

Chapter Eight

"You people don't know anything about keeping a fire going," Cathy said, throwing another log on their already tall campfire.

Linda glanced at Ben. He was looking at her. It was dusk, but by the light of the fire she had no trouble seeing the smile he flashed at her. Her heart did two somersaults and a back flip. Ben's smile was almost a common occurrence these days. Not that any smile of Ben's was commonplace, but he certainly smiled more often than he used to.

"Cathy," Levi said, standing up and poking a stick into the fire. "If you put too much wood on it, it will take longer to burn down to the coals. We don't want a raging fire. We want hot coals so we can roast marshmallows." Levi was usually patient and good-natured, but it seemed Cathy Larsen was wearing on his nerves just a bit.

Cathy pinned Levi with a no-nonsense frown. "Do you know how much sugar a marshmallow has in it?"

Esther laughed. "We're willing to take the risk, Cathy. You can't have a campfire without marshmallows."

Linda pulled the blanket around her neck and leaned closer to the fire to borrow more of its warmth. It was only the third week in May, and it got wonderful cold when the sun went down, especially in the canyon.

Ben sat in a camping chair next to her with his arms and his blanket tucked tightly around Winnie, who was sitting on his lap. It was a sweet sight, Winnie watching the fire, her eyes wide with delight, Ben with his arms securely around her, lending Winnie warmth and keeping her safe. At first, Winnie hadn't liked being restrained. She'd wanted to jump in the fire pit and test the fire for herself. Ben had scooped her into his arms and held her tightly on his lap until she had quit fussing and squirming and settled in to enjoy the dancing flames from the safety of Ben's lap.

It had been Esther's suggestion to have a pre-Memorial Day hot dog roast, before the crowds got too big at the campground. As usual, Cathy had invited herself to join them, and since they needed a driver, she was a convenient choice.

Linda slanted her gaze in Cathy's direction. Did Cathy enjoy spending time with a bunch of Amish people?

Cathy had invited herself on their outing with Ashley, Dylan, and Sissy three weeks ago, where Ben and Linda had finally planned to run, or rather snowshoe, against each other. Cathy seemed determined to tag along, as if she was suspicious of Ben and wasn't going to let him out of her sight. Or maybe she thought she was in charge of Linda and wanted to keep her safe from Ben and gluten.

They had planned on snowshoeing, but it had turned warm enough to rain, and there was more mud than snow. They had hiked instead, and Cathy had insisted on walking between Ben and Linda the whole time, holding onto each of their arms to keep her balance. Ben and Linda canceled the race because neither of them felt good about leaving an eighty-three-year-old woman to fend for herself, even if she hadn't really been invited. Hiking wasn't as physically taxing as snowshoeing, but Ben had still done a lot of heavy breathing, even as slow as they were with Cathy in tow. Linda had expected as much. Ben had smoked for three or four years. His lungs weren't going to clear out that quickly. But the longer he went without a cigarette, the better he would do.

The Saturday after that, Ashley and Dylan had taken them canoeing. Unfortunately, Cathy had again invited herself, and Linda hadn't figured out a polite way to say no. Besides, surprisingly enough, Mamm felt better about Linda going off with her *Englisch* friends when Cathy tagged along. Mamm probably saw Cathy as a good chaperone or a voice of reason in case Ben or Linda's friends wanted to do anything *deerich*, which wasn't likely. Ashley was a true outdoorswoman. She followed the rules and didn't do anything that would put herself or anyone else at risk.

Ben was less cautious, but he was still unsure of himself in the wild, so he usually did what Ashley told him, even though he didn't like being bossed around.

The canoe trip had been glorious. Ashley and Dylan had shared a canoe, and Cathy, Ben, and Linda had climbed into the other one. Linda and Ben sat in the back of the canoe and rowed while Cathy sat up front and told them what they were doing wrong. At one point, she had nodded off sitting straight up, and Linda had been terrified that she would fall into the water. But she had seemed very comfortable like that, so they hadn't awakened her.

Linda smiled to herself. Ben was better at canoeing

because his upper body was stronger than hers, with those broad shoulders and all those muscles rippling down his back and arms. When she had admitted he was a better rower than she was, he had flexed his biceps and let her feel for herself how hard they were. She'd been so giddy, she'd almost fainted.

The more time she spent with Ben Kiem, the more ashamed she felt for how little she'd thought or cared about him in the past. Ben Kiem had done some *deerich* things—everyone knew about the embarrassing incident in primary school—but no one should be forever judged by the worst thing they've ever done. Of course, Ben hadn't exactly changed his ways since then. He and Wally and Simeon always seemed to be making trouble. Three years ago, they had locked a dozen chickens in the schoolhouse over the weekend. The teacher was met with a big surprise and an even bigger mess on Monday morning before class. Ben, Wally, and Simeon smoked like chimneys, trespassed in people's barns, stole eggs from chicken coops, and then threw those eggs at passing buggies and cars. They had taken the deacon's buggy for a joy ride and crashed it into a ditch. They showed up at gatherings only to loiter on the fringes and play their horrible music or steal all the eats.

Of course, Ben's reputation was so damaged, he got blamed for just about everything that went wrong in the community, even things he didn't do. When the Sensenigs' woodshop had been broken into last October, David immediately blamed "the bishop's son and his two wild friends" even though Ben and his family had been in Ohio for a wedding.

"You warm enough, Winnie?" Ben said, tucking the

blanket around Winnie's legs. He kissed the top of Winnie's little bonnet and turned his face toward the fire. His intelligent eyes reflected the firelight, and Linda found it impossible to look away.

The first time she had invited Ben to go skiing with her was partly because she felt sorry for him but mostly because she wanted to teach him a lesson, to humble him a little, to make sure he knew he wasn't as special as he thought he was.

But the better she knew him, the more she realized she'd been completely mistaken. Ben didn't need a dose of humility. He already thought he was completely unworthy of anything good. Ben didn't believe he was special at all. He thought he wasn't good enough. For anybody. He worked hard to hide his insecurity behind that wounded pride and resentful temper, but he was just a vulnerable boy who sought to cover up his pain by proving everybody right. He didn't have to try to be a better person or make better choices when people didn't expect anything of him. It was so much easier to live life without the burden of high expectations, or any expectations for that matter.

Linda's heart hurt. Ben was so completely wrong. He didn't think much of himself, but Linda was constantly amazed at his wisdom, his sensitivity, and his strong will. If that strong will could be channeled in a productive direction, there was nothing Ben couldn't do if he put his mind to it. Like the smoking. How many people who tried to quit smoking actually accomplished it on their first try? That Ben had been able to resist so far told Linda a lot about his true character.

Ben whispered something in Winnie's ear and pointed to the fire. No man who was *gute* with children was completely hopeless. It was plain he adored Winnie, and Winnie loved him. He was also very attentive to his *mammi*, and he listened patiently to Cathy whenever she wanted to tell him about her health history.

Linda had told him he was touchy, overly sensitive, as if it were a flaw in his character. But being sensitive meant he was attuned to the needs of people around him, like his *mammi* and Winnie. It meant he had compassion when someone got her face smacked with a tree branch or smashed her finger while rowing a canoe. It meant he appreciated someone's buying him a new hat or making him a sandwich.

Even though her first invitation to go skiing had been more of a challenge, a way to cut his pride down to size, that wasn't how Linda felt now. Linda would rather spend time with Ben than anybody else, including her family or Ashley.

She caught her bottom lip between her teeth. She wouldn't tell Mamm, but Linda liked Ben. A lot. She found herself often thinking about him when they were apart and even more when they were together. She loved the way his mouth curled into a reluctant smile when she said something funny but he didn't want her getting a big head. She loved how he hated essential oils but was good-natured about trying them. She loved that he liked her cookies. She loved that he only spoke when he thought he could say something intelligent or insightful. And she loved that he was willing to give up smoking just to be able to beat her in a race, even though he would never beat her. She was just too fast.

A burning log crackled and slipped from the top of

the pile, sending sparks dancing into the darkening sky. "Oooh," Winnie exclaimed, pointing into the air.

Levi grinned at Winnie and poked his stick at the fire. "I think that counts as another word. She's up to twelve."

As if her *dat* had asked her to show off her vocabulary, Winnie turned her cherubic little face up at Ben. "Dee, Beh. Dee."

Linda laughed. "I have no idea what she said, but she sure is cute."

Esther looked especially pretty in a royal blue dress with a match tucked behind her ear. "She said, 'Sing, Ben.' She loves to hear Onkel Ben sing."

Linda raised an eyebrow in Ben's direction. "Does she? I'd like to hear that."

Ben looked down and shook his head, but she caught the hint of a smile on his face. "I only sing for cows and small children."

"Sing the railroad song," Esther said. "Winnie loves that one."

Cathy sat up straight. "I always enjoy a good railroad song."

Ben glanced at Linda, his smile an uncomfortable fit on his face. "The Amish don't believe in solo singing, Cathy. They think it tempts members to be proud."

Linda pressed her lips together. Ben talked about the Amish as if he weren't one of them. She tried not to let it bother her.

Cathy blew a puff of air from her lips. "It's not showing off to do a favor for an old lady who might not have many years left to hear you sing. Do you know 'I've Been Working on the Railroad'?"

Ben chuckled softly. "I don't know that one."

"If you're worried about standing out," Levi said, "we'll all sing with you." He settled into his camp chair. "In our heads."

"Very funny," Ben said, shooting a dagger at Levi with his gaze.

"Dee, Beh," Winnie coaxed again.

Ben tightened his arms around his niece, and he curled his lips in surrender, as if he couldn't say no to that face. "Okay. Which railroad song do you want? I know several." Cathy opened her mouth, but he motioned in her direction. "Except 'I've Been Working on the Railroad.'"

"You choose," said Esther.

"Okay then, but you all have to do the actions." Ben put his palms together, fingers pointing away from him. "Rub your hands together like this."

"What does this have to do with a railroad?" Cathy said.

"When you rub your hands together, it makes the sound of a train chugging up the hill."

Cathy rubbed her hands together and frowned. "No, it doesn't."

Winnie giggled, pulled her hands from under the blanket, and clapped them together. It was plain she'd done this one before.

Ben rubbed his hands together and began to sing. "*Little red caboose, chug, chug, chug. Little red caboose, chug, chug chug.*" He sang softly, obviously a little self-conscious, with his focus squarely on Winnie. Winnie's eyes lit up like fireworks as he held her protectively in his arms. Linda had never seen anything so tender in her whole life.

Cathy leaned closer to Linda. "You're not rubbing your

hands together. It doesn't make any sense, but we need to follow instructions."

Linda put her hands together, but her thoughts were so scattered, she couldn't even concentrate on something as simple as actions to a children's song. Every moment she spent with Ben Kiem was bringing her closer to the truth. He had taken up residence in her heart, and try as she might, she couldn't make him leave. In truth, she didn't want him to leave. But what did that mean? Should she do something about it or just ignore it? But how could she ignore it? It was the only thing she could think about.

"*Toot, toot*," Ben sang, pumping his hand up and down like he was pulling the cord attached to the train whistle.

Winnie clapped her hands in delight. "Toot," she said.

Levi beamed. "Good work, Ben. You get an extra marshmallow for teaching my daughter two new words tonight."

"That was fun," Cathy said, as if she was talking about a colonoscopy. "What other railroad songs do you know?"

"I think one is enough, don't you?" Ben said.

Esther settled deeper into her chair. "Of course not. I want to hear every train song you know."

Cathy nodded. "I want to hear 'I've Been Working on the Railroad,'" she said, either forgetting she'd already asked or just being her own persistent self. She must have really adored that song.

"Dee, Beh."

Ben stifled a smile. "Okay. But don't say I didn't warn you." He tugged Winnie closer and stared into the fire as he started to sing Johnny Cash's song, "Life's Railway to Heaven." "*Life is like a mountain railway, with an engineer that's brave. We must make the run successful from the cradle to the grave.*"

Linda held her breath. The Amish knew how to sing. Everybody sang from the day they were old enough to talk. They sang long, solemn hymns in church worship and songs that taught moral lessons in school. Even their weekly gatherings were called singings. The ability to sing was almost a birthright among the Amish. But Linda had never heard singing like Ben's. His voice was low and smooth, like chocolate from a fountain—thick, warm, and sweet. She could have listened to him all night long. No wonder Winnie loved to hear him sing. Hearing him was like watching a stunning sunset or tasting strawberries for the first time.

"I know that one," Cathy said, as if she was irritated no one had asked her. She joined Ben on the chorus, and she had a nice soprano voice—not as silky or attractive as Ben's—but in tune and sufficient for the song.

Ben's beautiful voice made Linda smile. Cathy's enthusiasm about the song made Linda laugh. "That was *wunderbarr*. No wonder Winnie loves it."

Cathy seemed very pleased with herself, even though the compliment was for Ben. "Thank you. We sound pretty good together, though Ben needs to learn to sing softer so you can hear the soprano part."

Ben grinned at Linda. "I don't doubt that I do."

"We should do some singing together," Cathy said. "I have a whole book of duets on my piano at home."

Ben bounced Winnie on his knee. "I don't mean to offend you, Cathy, but that would not be my idea of fun."

"Of course it would be fun. Young people these days have no idea what fun really is." Cathy poked at the fire.

"At least you're smart enough to quit smoking. You wouldn't be able to sing like that if they had to cut out your vocal cords."

Ben's smile faltered. "It would be proud if I cared about my singing voice. But Lord willing, I won't lose my vocal cords anytime soon."

He glanced past Linda, who was wishing very hard he'd look into her eyes again. Slowly, tensely, he stood up, shoved Winnie into Linda's arms and stepped out of their circle of chairs.

Linda wrapped her arms around Winnie, who didn't appreciate being handed off and showed her displeasure with a high-pitched scream. Linda stood up and stepped to Ben's side trying to figure out what he was up to.

Without releasing his gaze from the darkness outside the reach of the campfire, Ben held up his hand, motioning for Winnie to stay quiet. Of course, Winnie was a toddler and had no idea what Ben wanted her to do and no inclination to be obedient even if she knew. She fussed louder and reached out for Ben even as he pushed her away from him.

"What is it, Ben?" Levi said.

Ben took a slow step forward and nudged Linda behind him as if he wanted to protect her.

Protect her from what?

Then Linda saw it. She sucked in a breath as every muscle in her body tensed and an invisible hand clamped around her throat. A black bear, barely visible in the dim light, stood not twelve feet away, gazing at them curiously as if they were animals in the zoo. Linda's heart hammered against her chest. "A bear," she whispered.

Levi leaped to his feet, and Ben motioned for him to

stay where he was. "Don't make any sudden moves." Without looking behind him, he slid to his right, putting himself more fully between Linda and the bear. Then he raised his hands and waved them slowly above his head as if trying to flag down a car on a dark highway. "Hey, bear," he called, his voice loud and commanding. "Get out of here. Get out. Go on. This is our campsite. Go find your own."

Levi and then Esther stood up and waved their arms in the air too. Levi yelled at the bear to go away, and Esther called out things like, "Don't even think about stealing one of my marshmallows," and "Don't make me come over there, because I *will* spank you."

It would have been almost comical if it hadn't been so terrifying. All Linda could do was clutch Winnie in her arms and pray that she and Ben could protect Winnie if the bear attacked.

Winnie stopped struggling and watched her parents and *onkel* with fascination. They must have looked very strange to an eighteen-month-old. Her eyes widened as she gazed past Ben and saw the bear. She pointed her little finger and gave her interpretation of a dog barking. It was cute, but her parents were too frightened to notice.

Linda kept her eyes glued to the bear, which stood breathlessly still with her nose in the air, as if Ben, Esther, and Levi were highly entertaining. Then, as if she'd seen enough, the bear turned around and lumbered away among the brush and boulders until she was out of sight.

Ben's shoulders drooped as he let out the air he'd been hoarding in his lungs. He turned around and without warning, gathered Linda and Winnie into his arms. Linda was surprised by the gesture but not opposed to it, especially since Ben's embrace was warm and tender, as if it was the most natural thing in the world for him to do. "Are you okay?"

Linda suddenly lost the ability to speak, but whether it was from the shock of seeing a bear or the utter pleasure of being held by those strong arms, she didn't know. All she could do was nod.

That didn't satisfy Ben. He tightened his arms around her and Winnie. "It's okay. It wouldn't have hurt us."

Linda nodded a second time. She of all people knew that very well. Black bears as a rule weren't all that aggressive, and they scared easily, especially in the face of a big group of people. She'd been startled, because encountering a bear was always unnerving, but that wasn't why she couldn't speak.

Esther practically snatched Winnie from Linda's arms, but Ben didn't release his hold on Linda. He pulled her closer, and she could feel his heart beating against her cheek, though she had no idea how her face ended up pressed against his chest. It was probably improper and inappropriate, but this was an emergency situation, after all, and if there ever was a time to hold tight to a handsome and protective boy, this was it. She'd just been through something terrible. Any girl would be a fool to refuse comfort from someone who wanted to give it. She should definitely pretend not to feel his hard muscles beneath his shirt, and she was absolutely certain that she should ignore the enticing scent of cedarwood and orange oils on his neck. And above all, she should definitely put him out of her mind and not let thoughts of him keep her from getting a *gute* night's sleep tonight.

"Cathy? Are you okay?" Levi said.

Linda reluctantly pulled herself from Ben's arms and turned to see Cathy lying on the ground in a fetal position. Esther nudged Cathy with her hand. "Cathy. Cathy, it's okay. You don't have to pretend you're dead. You're safe."

Cathy opened her eyes and reached out her hand. Levi pulled her to her feet and led her to her camp chair. Her legs were definitely wobbling as she sat down. "Don't you people ever read the signs? When you see a bear, you're supposed to play dead. That way you won't get eaten."

Ben glanced at Linda and brushed his hands together, as if to wipe off any idea that he had even thought about touching her. "You only play dead when it's a grizzly bear. With a black bear you make a lot of noise."

Cathy swatted away whatever knowledge Ben wanted to share with her about bears. "You always play dead with a bear, and I figured if you all got eaten, there'd need to be somebody left to put out the fire."

Winnie, oblivious that anything of importance had happened, pointed to the bag of marshmallows Levi still had clutched in his hand. "Beh. Beh," she said, which seemed to be her word for anything sweet.

Linda felt her face get warm. Where were her thoughts taking her? Did she really put Ben in the same category as a warm toasted marshmallow? *Nae*, Ben was in a category all by himself. Toasted marshmallows were sweet, sticky, crunchy, and delicious. Ben was something extraordinary. She couldn't put her finger on it, but she knew she wanted to solve the mystery of Ben Kiem. It would be a very agreeable search.

Levi nodded at Ben, and there was some sort of unspoken agreement between them. "I think we've had quite enough of the outdoors. Let's go home."

Cathy frowned. "Are you sure? I'd like to hear more railroad songs."

Levi folded up a camp chair and slid it into its bag. "I'm sure. That's enough excitement for one day."

For sure and certain Levi was right about that. Tonight, Linda had experienced enough excitement for an entire year, and it had nothing to do with a campfire, a bag of marshmallows, or a black bear.

It was all Ben's fault.

Chapter Nine

Wally whistled and snapped his fingers in front of Ben's face. Ben slapped his hand away. "What is wrong with you?" Ben growled.

"Nothing's wrong with *me*," Wally said, pulling a cigarette from the pack and offering it to Ben. "No charge."

Simeon rolled his eyes and lit his cigarette, letting it dangle from his fingers as if it was part of his hand. "Since when did you become such a do-gooder, Wally?"

Wally glanced resentfully at Ben. "Since one of my best friends won't even have a smoke with us. Look at him. He's not even really here. Like as not he's thinking about somebody else when he should be paying attention to his friends."

Ben raised an eyebrow. "Don't be so touchy."

"Then don't be so righteous. Have a smoke with us."

Ben waved away Wally's offered cigarette. "*Nae*. It's been six weeks. I got through the hardest part. I don't want to have to start all over again. The headaches are wonderful bad."

Wally's eyes narrowed to slits. "Then don't ever quit again."

To Wally, it was so easy. If it was hard to quit smoking, just don't ever stop. "I'm saving forty dollars a week," Ben said. Wally wasn't always the most rational thinker, but he definitely understood the cost of a pack of cigarettes.

"You can get them cheaper at Walmart," Wally mumbled.

Simeon took a drag on his cigarette and stared at Ben. "What Wally is trying to say is, you're no fun anymore."

Ben swallowed hard. He didn't know what to say. If Wally and Simeon rejected him, he'd have no friends. He couldn't make new friends. Nobody else in the *gmayna* liked him.

Ach, *vell*, maybe Linda liked him. That thought sent something warm and sweet pulsing through his veins, until he realized that the only reason Linda liked him was because she didn't really know him. The more time they spent together, the less she'd want to be his friend.

Ben sat down on the bench and propped his hands on his knees. He couldn't go back to smoking. He hadn't felt this healthy in years, ever since he'd started sucking that poison into his lungs. He still had bad days, when his head ached or the need for a cigarette nearly overpowered him, but he could also breathe better, and the coughing had lessened considerably.

But the fact that he was trying to quit made his friends feel threatened, like he was judging them merely because he chose not to smoke. He understood how they felt. If Wally had been the one to quit, Ben would have felt the same about him, like he was betraying his friends. Like he didn't belong anymore. And that was the problem. Wally and Simeon were the only ones who didn't care how bad or irresponsible or unrepentant he was. He would never suggest they quit, because they'd tell him he was being preachy, but he'd feel a lot more part of the group if the other two quit smoking. He had to prove to Linda that he was smart because she thought it was dumb to smoke.

Wally propped his foot on the end of the bench. "You're turning into one of them."

"One of who?" Ben said, even though he knew exactly who Wally was talking about. All those righteous people in the *gmayna*. All those people who were too busy judging him to treat him kindly. All those forgiving Amish who never let you forget your sins. A cold, hard fist clamped around Ben's heart. Members of the *gmayna* still talked about the unfortunate incident, even though it had happened eight years ago. Ben was still known as "the boy who stole that music box," as if it was a nametag he had to wear for the rest of his life. No one liked him. No one wanted to associate with him except Wally and Simeon and only because the community hated them as much as they hated Ben. He felt like one of those lepers they were always talking about in the Bible. Everyone avoided him, except for people like his parents who were trying to reform him, make him change his ways, and even change who he was.

But in the last few weeks, it had been different. Linda didn't treat him like a leper. She treated him like a regular person, a friend she could be straight with, a boy she enjoyed hanging out with. She certainly didn't try to tiptoe around his feelings, especially when she thought he acted stupidly. She was always brutally honest, so he always knew exactly what she thought of him even if he didn't always like what she said. If she hated him, he'd know it.

And it had sure felt good to hold her in his arms, like she fit there. Like maybe she didn't mind being there. Ben swiped his hand across his mouth. He didn't need those thoughts crowding into his brain.

"You care more about Linda Eicher and your new friends than you do about us."

Ben threw up his hands. "What new friends? Linda and I have been hiking and snowshoeing a couple of times. And we go with her *bruder* and some *Englischers* and an old lady."

"You said you were going to start smoking again as soon as you beat her in snowshoeing. Now the snow's all gone."

Now wasn't a *gute* time to smile, but Ben could barely contain himself when he thought of Linda and how strangely adorable she looked in hiking boots and a Plain dress.

They'd been hiking twice since the snow had melted, hiking with Ashley, Dylan, and Cathy. Hiking wasn't as physically taxing as snowshoeing, but Ben still found himself breathing hard, even going as slow as they had to with Cathy in tow. But the longer he went without a cigarette, the better he felt.

Ben smiled to himself. He was better at canoeing because his upper body was stronger than Linda's. The whole day on the river she had smiled at him several times and hadn't once laughed at him, even though they'd done a lot of laughing. *Ach*, nobody could make him laugh like Linda Eicher could. Not even Simeon and Wally.

"Well, Ben?"

Simeon glanced at Wally. "He's not paying attention again."

"I was too. I haven't beat Linda at snowshoeing, so I'm not going to start smoking yet." They wouldn't like that excuse, but it was the best he could do.

"You're being so weird about Linda Eicher," Wally said. "She's ugly and skinny and has the loudest laugh I ever heard, like a duck. Her *mamm* gives me the evil eye at *gmay*."

Ben bristled like a porcupine. He didn't want to feel protective of Linda, but all he'd wanted to do that night they saw the bear was hold Linda tight until his heart stopped pounding. He had wanted to keep her safe, even though she probably knew ten times more about bears than he did. Up until now, there had been three people he'd allowed himself to feel protective about—Esther, Nanna, and Winnie. Esther would do anything for him, even when she didn't want to. Nanna refused to judge him, and Winnie loved him because she didn't know any better. Anybody else would just end up letting him down or making him feel foolish in the end. Hadn't it been that way with Magdalena?

Simeon took a drag on his cigarette. "She's looking for a *gute* Amish husband. Why is she wasting her time with you? Why are you wasting your time with her?"

Ben honestly could not answer that question. He went hiking and canoeing with Linda because he wanted to prove something to her so she wouldn't be so smug, but he was also beginning to enjoy every minute he spent with her. It was risky to feel that way, because for sure and certain, she'd drop him like a hot potato as soon as she got what she wanted from him. But what *did* Linda want from him? She didn't need a hiking partner. She'd done just fine with Ashley and Dylan before Ben ever showed up, and Ben seemed to slow her down, if anything. She could hike with Cathy if she was desperate.

Was Ben Linda's project? Was she trying to make him change his ways and repent? Was she still trying to teach him a lesson for hitching a ride behind her buggy? Or maybe she truly enjoyed spending time with him.

Ben's heart raced at that possibility. She laughed and smiled at him, and he hadn't imagined the way she'd leaned into him that night with the bear. But that couldn't last long. Linda didn't truly know the kind of person Ben was. If she did, she'd find other boys to spend time with, other boys more worthy of her. That thought made Ben's stomach hurt. Sooner or later, Linda would grow tired or frustrated and move on to some other boy, a boy who didn't smoke. A boy who could beat her up the hill or, better yet, carry her up the hill. A boy who hadn't ruined his future at the age of fourteen.

Wally tossed his cigarette butt on the ground. "Are you too righteous to have a little fun?"

"Of course not," Ben said. He wasn't righteous at all.

Wally picked up the canvas bag he'd brought with him. "*Gute*, because it's time we kicked up a little dust around here." He pulled some old clothes from the bag.

Ben couldn't muster any enthusiasm. He used to think Wally's ideas were exciting. Now they just felt like too much work and too little fun. Still, if he wanted to prove he was still Wally's friend, he'd go along and pretend to be eager about it. "What do you want to do?"

"Nobody ruins my boom box and gets away with it. We're going to teach Old Man Bateman a lesson."

With his shirt soaked in sweat, Ben tore off his gloves and threw them on the worktable. He marched out of the barn, turned on the hose, and let it run over his head as he scrubbed his fingers through his hair. The icy water stole his breath as it trickled down his neck. Ben ran the hose over his sunburned arms and splashed water in his face. He took a long drink but couldn't taste the water on his tongue. All he tasted was shame and anger and defiance.

He was angry at Wally and Mr. Bateman, Dat and Mamm and the *gmayna*, angry at the whole world. He didn't know where he belonged anymore, and the loneliness overwhelmed and frightened him. He needed to belong, even if it was in a group of three pathetic Amish boys who smoked behind the barn and set people's property on fire.

Ach, he was so mad at Wally right now, even though Wally was one of the only two friends he had in the world. Wally's little prank had gone horribly wrong, and Ben bore the brunt of Dat's displeasure and the community's indignation.

Dat had been so mad at him, he had assigned Ben the farm's most back-breaking chores to accomplish all by himself in the glaring sun and oppressive heat of the day. He'd shoveled coal, mucked out the barn, hoed their half-acre garden, and as an added bonus, Dat had ordered him to move the entire wood pile three feet to the north, just so he'd have more time to think on his sins.

He didn't get breakfast or supper, and dinner wasn't looking so promising either.

Ben ran his fingers through his wet hair. What did he care? In fact, he was glad Mamm and Dat were so mad at him. They usually didn't care about him at all. At least today they felt some sort of intense emotion for their worthless son. At least they were hurting as badly as he was. *Ach, vell,* probably not. They weren't hurt. They would just throw up their hands, agree that Ben was a hopeless case, and concentrate on their other children that they might still be able to save.

But what about Linda?

Ben clenched his teeth. This was all Wally's fault. Why wasn't Dat mad at Wally?

Wally had been wonderful mad about his boom box. Ben just hadn't realized how mad. He had come up with this *deerich* scheme to get revenge on Mr. Bateman by burning a scarecrow in his yard. It was the stupidest of all stupid ideas, but Wally had been wild about it. They stuffed an old pair of Wally's trousers and an old shirt with straw, used a cardboard box for a head, and finished it off with Ben's straw hat that Zoe had run over with her truck. They hung it in Mr. Bateman's cherry tree and set it on fire. What they hadn't realized was that a breeze would carry sparks to Mr. Bateman's tool shed and start it on fire too.

It had been a big hullabaloo, though Wally, Simeon, and Ben were long gone before the shed fire even started. The fire department came and put out the fire, but not before the shed was completely destroyed, along with many of Mr. Bateman's tools.

Neighbors, including most of Mr. Bateman's Amish

neighbors, gathered to watch the firefighters put out the fire and then helped clean up the mess. The scarecrow was just a pile of ashes, except for Ben's old hat, which had blown off the scarecrow's head before it caught fire. Mr. Bateman's wife had found it stuck in one of her rose bushes. There was a big outcry when everyone realized someone from the Amish community had set the fire.

No one had seen Ben and his friends do it, but because the *gmayna* hated Ben and Wally and Simeon so much, no one, *no one* doubted they had done it even though there was no evidence to prove it. They assumed Ben and his friends were guilty simply because there was no one else in the *gmayna* so rotten and incorrigible as they were. The thought that no one even hesitated to accuse him pressed into Ben's chest until he couldn't breathe.

Ben knew better than to lie to his *dat*. He knew better than to lie to anyone. But to protect Wally and Simeon, he hadn't confessed either. He didn't care that people thought he was guilty. He wanted people to hate him. If they hated him, they wouldn't try to change him. He'd never disappoint them. Dat had paid Mr. Bateman enough to get his shed rebuilt, and Ben would be paying Dat back for years. It was that or get kicked out of the house.

Ben turned off the hose and slapped the water off his arms. Apparently, Linda had wanted to beat him up the hill in snowshoes to prove she was a better person than he was. Or maybe she liked some friendly competition and knew Ben would be easy to beat. Why had she invited him to go skiing that first time? What did she want from him?

Did Linda know about the fire? Of course she knew about the fire. News spread in Amish country faster than pink eye. Did she blame him? His stomach clenched.

Something very deep inside him hoped she wouldn't believe it, that she would think better of him, even though he had given her no reason to, even though he was actually guilty.

For sure and certain, she wasn't going to show up tonight for their trip to the sand dunes. And Ben didn't care one bit. She was as petty and self-righteous as everyone else in the *gmayna*, and he didn't want to go to the sand dunes with her anyway.

"Ben?" Mamm stood on the back porch with a half a sandwich in each hand.

"What?" Ben snapped, his voice harsh and cold as ice. He shouldn't be so hostile. It looked like maybe Mamm was going to feed him.

Mamm raised an eyebrow to indicate she didn't appreciate his tone. "Maybe you shouldn't talk to me like that when I took the trouble of putting dill pickles in your tuna."

He bowed his head. "Sorry, Mamm. I really like dill pickles."

She melted into a smile, even though it was tinged with pain, pain that Ben had put there. She came down the steps and handed Ben both halves of the sandwich. "Eat. You haven't had a thing but water all day, and though I know Dat wants you thinking on repentance, it's hard to repent on an empty stomach."

Ben pressed his lips together. He didn't want to repent. He wanted to stay ferociously angry at Gotte, his parents, and the world in general. But then he thought how he didn't deserve such kindness from his *mamm*, and they both knew it. He was too hungry to be proud. He polished off the first half in four bites. The second one in three.

Mamm's eyes grew wide. "I should have made a few more."

"That was nice of you," Ben said, which was all the humility he could muster at the moment.

"You need your strength to climb the sand dunes tonight."

"I'm not going." No doubt Linda wanted to stay as far away from him as she could, just like everyone else.

"Of course you're going. Linda is waiting out front."

Ben frowned. "She's here?" He hadn't expected that in a million years.

Mamm suddenly looked oppressively sad. "Maybe she doesn't know about the fire."

Of course she knew about the fire, and she was going to give him a lecture about it. Or laugh at him. She probably couldn't wait to get him alone so she could make fun of him for being so foolish.

Ben glared at his *mamm*. "Maybe she doesn't assume I'm guilty, like everyone else in the district." That was completely unfair of him, because he *was* guilty.

Mamm gave him a wan smile. "*Ach*, Ben. Are you going to look me in the eye and tell me you weren't involved?"

He had to turn away from her piercing gaze. "I'm not saying anything about it."

She cupped his chin in her hand and gave him a look so full of affection it almost choked him. "Despite everything you've done, you would never lie to me. *Denki* for that."

The emotion on her face broke his heart. Ben took a step back, and Mamm dropped her hand to her side. "Where did you say Linda was?"

"She's standing on the front porch."

Ben didn't want to face Linda, but neither did he want to see his *mamm* like this, broken, disheartened. Ben had shamed their whole family. Of course Mamm was upset. "I'll go talk to her."

With water still dripping from his hair, he tromped around to the front of the house where he found Linda sitting on the front porch wearing her black bonnet and a wide smile. The smile took his breath away, and then suspicion settled into his chest. He'd burned down Mr. Bateman's shed. Why was she smiling?

"I'm not going," he said, folding his arms across his chest and giving her an I-couldn't-care-less-what-you-think look.

"Of course you're going," Linda said, not the least bit intimidated or repulsed by him. "Don't be such a baby."

Chapter Ten

The Sand Dunes National Park on a warm summer night was the most glorious place in the world. Nothing soothed Linda's troubled soul like sitting out under a sky dense with stars, listening to the wildlife, and feeling the soft breeze caress her face. But she feared that nothing would lift her spirits tonight. There was just too much pain and unhappiness in the world.

"This fried chicken is delicious," Cathy said, polishing off her second piece. "Not as good as mine, but most people don't know a thing about frying a good piece of chicken. Buttermilk is the secret. Without buttermilk, you might just as well boil it for all the flavor you'll get."

Ben didn't say anything, but he had already eaten three pieces of chicken, one biscuit, a heaping helping of chowchow, and three deviled eggs. It was a *gute* bet he liked the chicken even without buttermilk.

"Can I have a cupcake?" Nora said. She hadn't eaten much of anything, but she was always hungry for something sweet.

"Take three more bites of chicken," Linda said. It was what Mamm did with Nora at every mealtime. No matter how much she had or had not eaten, Mamm always wanted three more bites from Nora.

Cathy, Elmer Lee, and Linda's little sister, Nora, sat on one side of the picnic table while Linda and Ben sat on the other side. Ben had been extraordinarily quiet in the car and even less talkative during their picnic dinner. He seemed to resent that she'd made him come, though he'd gotten in the car willingly. Of course, it might have been because she'd called him a baby and accused him of being afraid she'd beat him to the top of the sand dunes. Ben couldn't resist a challenge to his manhood.

Maybe he'd gotten in the car because she'd promised him dinner. He ate as if he hadn't tasted food for days. At least his broody irritation hadn't killed his appetite.

And maybe he wasn't resentful. Maybe he was just ashamed of himself for burning down Mr. Bateman's shed. Despite what Mamm thought, Ben did have a conscience, and he couldn't be proud of what he had done. His silence might have been a sign of his remorse rather than his annoyance. Neither of them had said a word about the shed incident, but Linda was going to get an explanation before the night was over and help Ben come up with a plan to make it right.

Linda sighed. Was this the best or worst possible time to come to the sand dunes?

She, Ben, and Cathy had planned this trip before the fire, before the whole *gmayna* had turned on Ben, before Mamm had forbidden Linda from even sneezing in Ben's direction ever again. *Trying to bring Ben back to the fold is one thing, Linda, but I won't stand for you putting your own soul in danger. He doesn't need to be your project anymore. Let his parents take care of it.*

Linda wasn't one to disobey her *mater*, but she was nineteen years old and she'd always been a relatively compliant child, so Mamm really had nothing to complain about. Linda was in *rumschpringe*, and she was technically allowed to push some boundaries, even if Mamm didn't like it. Mamm had huffed and puffed about her taking Ben to the sand dunes for quite some time, but Linda had been insistent. And if it made Mamm feel better to believe Linda was trying to save Ben's soul, then Linda wasn't going to enlighten her.

Mamm had finally calmed down when Linda agreed to take Elmer Lee and Nora with them. And Cathy always came along. She was like a cocklebur stuck to Linda's stocking—but a cocklebur with a car who didn't seem to mind driving Linda and Ben everywhere.

Linda had insisted again and again that Mamm had nothing to fear. What could Ben possibly set fire to at the sand dunes?

Linda shuddered. She didn't want to think about that tonight. She wanted to enjoy the Ben Kiem she knew— the Ben who sang songs to his niece, the Ben who was disciplined enough to give up smoking. The Ben who willingly, cheerfully stirred cookie dough and whose smile could steal her breath with its brilliance. The Ben she knew would never set fire to someone's property. Linda tried to swallow past the lump in her throat. She hadn't wanted to believe it, but she'd seen the hat, smashed flat with incriminating tire marks on the brim. If Ben hadn't started the fire, he had been there, and he had participated willingly in destroying someone's property. The fact that Linda didn't want to believe it didn't make it false.

Linda handed Nora a cupcake. "The sun's already gone down. We need to clean up and get to the dunes before it's too dark to see our way."

Elmer Lee fished in his pocket and pulled out a small flashlight. "Just in case we need it."

Linda growled. "I told you no flashlights, Elmer Lee. It will ruin your night vision, and you won't be able to see the stars as well."

"I've got to have a flashlight or I'll trip over my own feet," Cathy said. "I won't be able to drive you home if I break my hip. I brought two flashlights, twelve hundred lumens each."

There was no arguing with that, even though Linda knew for a fact that Cathy had two titanium hips and wouldn't break either of them ever again. Fortunately, Linda had already made a plan. Maybe it was inappropriate, but she wanted to be alone with Ben. Maybe he would slip his arm around her while they gazed up at the sky. Maybe she'd have a chance to breathe in his enticing smell or smooth her hand along his jawline. Maybe he'd sing her one of those *Englisch* love songs he listened to on the radio.

Of course, with the way he was acting right now, she'd be lucky if he didn't venture off by himself and get lost in the foothills. Nothing killed the romantic mood like a search and rescue.

Ben surprised her by helping her clean up the food and then giving her a genuine smile. "*Denki* for dinner. I was starving."

She returned his smile. "I could tell. Have they stopped feeding you at your house?"

His smile faded. "*Jah*. I guess they have."

Linda's heart lurched. She'd been making a joke. Was starvation part of his punishment? In that case, she'd take him a meal every day. Ben deserved to be well fed, even if he was a *dumkoff* when he was with Simeon and Wally.

Elmer Lee offered Cathy his arm, and Nora held Cathy's hand. Elmer Lee and Nora were on "Cathy duty" tonight, and they were participating cheerfully because Linda had offered to do their chores for a whole week. In exchange for *not* filling Mamm in on the details of their visit to the sand dunes, they got donuts for a whole month. Linda felt crafty and devious and adventurous all at the same time. She would never lie to Mamm, but what Mamm didn't know about Ben couldn't make her angry or anxious. She was better off blissfully ignorant.

Besides, Cathy wasn't going to make it very far up the dunes, and it wasn't likely she would stop talking so they could hear the owls and the coyotes. Linda wanted Ben to have the whole experience—watching the stars, listening to the sounds of the night, feeling the darkness envelop him like a blanket. It was the most peaceful place on Earth, and from what Linda could see, Ben desperately needed some peace.

Cathy tromped toward the dunes flanked by Elmer Lee and Nora. "I haven't been here since I came with Esther's sister, Ivy. Ivy got a little impatient about leaving, and I had to throw my car keys into the sand to get her to stop pestering me. It took us almost an hour to find them. I think she learned her lesson."

Ben glanced at Linda and smiled. If nothing else, Cathy gave them a reason to share secret smiles with each other. Linda couldn't be irritated about that.

Linda nodded curtly at Elmer Lee, and he nodded back, a sign of the agreement they'd made earlier.

Elmer Lee turned on his flashlight, even though it wasn't all that dark, and directed the light on the path in front of Cathy's feet. "Thank you kindly, young man," Cathy said. "As soon as we get there, I'll tell you all about my gout."

Linda pulled off her shoes and stuffed them in her bag.

Ben studied her bare feet. "Should I take off my boots?"

"*Jah*. Ashley says the sand on your feet is therapeutic."

"What does that mean?"

"It's *gute* for you."

Ben puckered his lips as if he'd just licked a lemon. "Like essential oils?"

Linda laughed. "*Jah*. Like essential oils."

Even though he was skeptical about essential oils, Ben took off his boots and slung them over his shoulder with his fist wrapped around the laces. Linda draped her blanket over her arm. Her heart lodged in her throat as she reached out, boldly took Ben's hand in hers, and pulled him in the direction of the sand dunes. By the look on his face, he was obviously surprised, though he tried to hide his shock by turning his face away and studying the distant hills as if he might find something interesting up there. But he didn't run away screaming. He didn't even pull his hand away.

Linda thought she might faint with relief or leap for joy. She didn't know what he was thinking, but he hadn't let go of her hand. That had to be a *gute* sign.

Leaving Cathy and her attendants behind, Linda tugged

Ben up the first sand dune and on to the next one. Ben glanced behind him. "What about the others?"

"We've got to get away from the flashlight. It's not as good if you have a flashlight."

"Okay," Ben said. It sounded like a question.

Was he suspicious, curious, or reluctant? *Ach, vell,* she wasn't going to turn back now. "How far do you want to walk?" she said.

He tensed. "How far do you want to go?"

She pointed to one of the peaks in the distance. "I can still beat you up that mountain and back without breaking a sweat, but I don't want to tire you out."

His lips curled into a tentative smile. "I'm in better shape than I've ever been. You'll never beat me again."

Linda laughed. "*Ach,* you can tell yourself that if it makes you feel better."

He grunted but didn't argue. He was probably already planning their next hike. She hoped he'd plan a hundred hikes. She'd go on a hike with him every day for the rest of her life if he asked.

Linda glanced behind her. They were already well away from the crowds, and they had left Cathy, Elmer Lee, and Nora far behind. "We don't want to go too far, or we might get lost in the dark."

His eyes danced in amusement. "You should have brought a flashlight so we could find our way back."

"No flashlights. It's just not right." Linda led Ben up and down two more dunes until they were far enough away to suit her. Darkness descended suddenly, and Linda was grateful for the tiny flashlight she had hidden in the bottom of her bag. Despite all her protests, they'd need to find their way back to Cathy's car.

Linda pulled the blanket from the bag, and Ben helped her spread it on the sand. She'd chosen a lap quilt so Ben would have to sit close. No king-sized quilts allowed tonight. She wanted to do some cuddling. She sat down and gave Ben her best smile, though it was too dark for the look to have the impact it would have in the sunlight, or at least the impact she hoped it would have. Was she overconfident? Was she fooling herself to think Ben was as interested as she was?

Ben hesitated for the briefest of moments before sitting next to her, leaning back on his hands, and stretching his long legs out in front of him. Linda couldn't ignore the ribbon of warmth that threaded through her veins whenever she was within arm's reach of him. Tonight he was silent and distant, but she was acutely aware of the tension of the muscles taut across his shoulders and the warmth radiating from his body.

"Okay. What now?" he said.

Linda laughed. "Are you expecting a show?"

"I'm expecting something. You've gone to a whole lot of fuss if all we're going to do is sit in the sand and listen to each other breathe."

She leaned closer and nudged him with her shoulder. "*Ach, du lieva.* You always want to be entertained. Can't you just sit still and ponder?"

He drew away from her. "Ponder what?"

"Don't be so touchy. You can ponder life or the stars or guess how many grains of sand are in the sand dunes."

He raised an eyebrow. "Sounds fun."

"It is." She leaned her head back and closed her eyes. "Close your eyes and just take a few deep breaths." It was obvious from the silence beside her that Ben was watching her as if he feared she was a little touched in the head. She curled her lips upward. "Just do it, Ben. Have I ever led you astray?"

"Like with the essential oils?"

Without opening her eyes, she cuffed him on the shoulder. "*Jah*, like with the essential oils. They worked, didn't they?"

"I walked around smelling like a flower shop."

Linda took a deep breath. "Close your eyes. It's all part of the experience." She peaked out of one eye. Ben closed his eyes, but a deep worry line creased his brow. It was too much to hope he would relax, but at least he was trying. "What do you hear?"

"I can hear Cathy talking."

"You cannot."

"It carries over the distance."

Linda couldn't resist. She shifted so she was touching shoulders with him. "*Ach*, *vell*. Try not to listen for Cathy. What else do you hear?"

He blew a breath from between his lips and paused. The pause lasted for more than a minute. "I hear an owl, I think."

"Me too."

A high, short bark sounded in the distance. "That must be a coyote."

"I think so."

"Do you hear those screams?" he said. "That is a herd of elk. I didn't know they had elk here."

"For a boy who doesn't like the outdoors, you seem to know a lot about the outdoors."

"What makes you think I don't like the outdoors?" he said.

"That first day of snowshoeing, you acted like you were allergic to fresh air."

He grunted. "I didn't want to be there. I didn't want to snowshoe. And you made me feel like a *dumkoff*."

"I'm sorry I made you feel like a *dumkoff*." She smiled though he couldn't see it. "But seriously, you were acting like one."

"I suppose I was." He was silent for a long time. "It wonders me why you asked me to go again. Wasn't once enough torture?"

"You wanted so badly to beat me in a race. You even quit smoking. I had to give you another chance. And each time I win is more fun than the last."

"Ha ha. Your winning streak is about to come to an end."

Linda savored the sound of his low, silky voice. "I accept your challenge. Maybe we can convince Cathy to stay in the car next time so we can have a real race."

"Do you see any possible chance of that?"

"Not really." Linda tapped his bare foot with hers. The contact sent her pulse racing through her veins like a raging river. "I've changed my mind about you being a *dumkoff*. You saved me from a bear."

"I didn't save you. I just waved my arms and talked the bear into going away."

Linda pulled her legs into her chest and wrapped her arms around her knees. "You stepped in front of me so the bear would eat you instead of me. A whiner would never have been that brave."

He turned his face toward her. "You think I'm a whiner?"

She laughed. "*Used* to think."

"Oh, *sis yuscht*. If I need a list of my faults, I'll ask my *dat*, not you."

How could she talk Ben out of his bitterness? "I'm not listing your faults. I'm just pointing out how much I've changed. And I'm making a mess of it, but I want to thank you for saving my life."

"I didn't really save your life."

"*Jah*, you did, and I'm grateful." Linda hooked her arm around his elbow. He probably thought she was forward and reckless, but he was just so irresistible, and she had ignored his enticing scent for as long as she could.

She couldn't see him very well in the dark, but she felt him. It seemed like his entire body was clenched like a fist. She was making him uncomfortable, but now it would be even more awkward if she disentangled her arm from his. So, she panicked and, in a moment of insanity, rested her head on his shoulder as if she'd done it a thousand times.

For a brief, incredibly uncomfortable moment, she held her breath. He was probably holding his breath too. He was so stiff, she might as well have been resting her head on a boulder wearing a shirt.

Ummm. What should she do now?

She could pretend to want a good look at the stars, release his arm, and lie on her back. But would he feel obligated to lie down too? Would that be even more awkward than sitting here like this? Linda couldn't imagine anything more awkward than what she was already doing, trying to get cozy with a fence post.

After the worst ten seconds of her life, Ben suddenly softened. Or maybe he just surrendered to his terrible fate. He tugged his arm from hers and slid it around her back, pulling her close as he had that night they saw the bear. With her heart banging against her chest, Linda snuggled deeper into his embrace, sliding closer and nestling her head against his neck. *Ach*, he smelled so good.

"So, uh, how do you know so much about the outdoors?" she said, doing her best to keep her voice from shaking. "Like what to do when you see a black bear or how to recognize what a herd of elk sounds like."

"Our whole family used to go camping almost weekly during the summer months. Dat loved to fish and hike. But then he got his calling as bishop and didn't have time for it anymore. Dat and I used to go fishing together. Sometimes Levi would come. Now Dat mostly ignores me, unless I'm working with him on a bathroom remodel or doing something he doesn't approve of. Then he yells."

"It must be hard to be the bishop's son."

He stiffly rubbed his hand up and down her upper arm. "I don't know. When he's not working our business or our farm, he's helping someone in the *gmayna*. I like it better when he doesn't focus his attention on me, so I don't mind when he's gone."

Linda pressed her lips together. Ben was stuck in a hole he had dug for himself—as if he wanted to live in that hole instead of climbing out and setting his face toward the heavens. Why did he choose that tight and meager life, when there was so much more to him that he refused to see? Why did he hang out with Wally and Simeon and paint ugly pictures in the snow and burn down sheds? It was as if he was trying to be a person he wasn't, as if he was determined to prove he was hopeless.

Linda lifted her head and pointed to the sky. "You asked for a show. Look at the sky."

Ben looked up, and she sensed when he riveted his attention to the heavens. The Milky Way was a sparkling cloud of stars overhead, and the brighter stars were like beacons for weary travelers. "*Ach, du lieva,*" he said. "I didn't know."

They sat without speaking for several minutes, straining their ears for the silent symphony of the stars. They both caught their breath when two shooting stars flashed across the sky, one right after the other. "This is why you don't turn on a flashlight," Linda said.

He pointed to the east. "Look at that star. It's so bright."

"I think it's a planet. And do you see the Big and Little Dippers?"

"Of course. Every camper worth his salt can find those."

She laughed. "Sorry to insult your camping knowledge."

"One time, it was just Dat, me, and Levi camping, and Dat showed us all the biggest constellations. That was before he stopped loving me and before I stopped trying to make him love me."

Linda couldn't let that falsehood stand without a fight. "Of course your *dat* loves you. What a silly thing to say."

He didn't like it when she called him silly. She used the word purposefully in an attempt to light a fire under him. His anger was better than this self-inflicted hopelessness that he wore like a heavy winter coat.

He didn't take the bait. Instead, he sighed and slid his arm off her shoulder. "I've done too many bad things for anyone to love me. I know what I am. Might as well accept it."

Linda found herself getting angry at Ben's lack of emotion. "Accept it? And then what? Go on living in this tiny little world you've created for yourself?" She grabbed his hand. "You are not worthless, Ben. You have so much love to give. I've seen how you treat Winnie and your *mammi*. You put up with my essential oils and my snow-shoes and my teasing."

"Not cheerfully."

"You're fiercely loyal to Esther and Levi, and whether you want to admit it or not, you put yourself between me and that bear. You were more concerned for my life than your own. And no one who can sing like you can be all bad." Her voice cracked into a thousand pieces, but she pressed forward because she had to make him understand. "And because . . . *ach*, I love you, Ben. It's crazy and I can't believe I'm saying this, but I love you."

A full year of silence.

Linda's heart pounded in her ears. What had she been thinking? You don't tell someone you love him unless you know he loves you back. But she'd been caught up in the moment and the beauty of the stars and had just blurted it out. She rarely thought about what came out of her mouth before she said it. It was definitely an affliction.

She couldn't see his face very well, so all she could do was guess at his reaction, but her heart sank when he slipped his hand from hers. "Why do you say that?" he said in his low, husky voice.

"Because it's true."

"I don't believe you."

How in the world could she be in love with someone this irritating? "You don't believe me?"

"What about the fire? Didn't you hear about the fire?"

"Of course I heard about the fire. Everybody heard about the fire. But that doesn't matter to me, Ben. I know you, and that is not who you are."

He turned his face from her and stared into the darkness. "You don't know me. The people who really know me know that this is exactly who I am. They don't expect anything better, and that's fine with me. It makes my life a whole lot easier not having to live up to expectations."

"But you quit smoking. You sing railroad songs. You're doing better, so much better than you were a few months ago. You could go apologize to Mr. Bateman. Tell him you didn't mean it and then offer to pay for the damage. A group of us are going next week to help the Batemans rebuild that shed. You could be in charge of the whole thing, show people that you've changed. You can change, Ben. You already have."

After a long, uncomfortable pause, Ben laughed softly. But there was no happiness in it. "I can't believe I've been such a fool. All this time I thought maybe you didn't mind me so much, that maybe you wanted to be my friend because you enjoyed spending time with me. How could I have been so stupid? I'm not your friend. I'm your project."

Linda's mouth fell open. "What do you mean I'm not your friend? I . . . I just told you I love you." She nearly choked on *love*. Why had she let it escape from her lips in the first place?

"You don't love me. You're just saying that because

you want to change me. I don't wonder but Mammi or Levi put you up to this." By the light of the stars, she saw him take off his hat and run his fingers through his hair. "*Ach.* You almost had me fooled."

"I don't want to change you. I like you just the way you are."

"Who could like me the way I am?"

"I do." Linda turned to face him and clutched his arm as if to stop him from jumping off a cliff. "But Ben, there's so much more to you than hanging out with Wally and Simeon and playing pranks and damaging property. I like you as you are, but you can change. You can make your life into something beautiful and useful instead of just one big waste of time."

"So why are you wasting your time with me?"

"I already told you."

"And I already told you I don't believe you. Everybody in the *gmayna* would be so impressed if you were the girl who got Ben Kiem to mend his ways, maybe talked him out of jumping the fence."

"I don't care what the *gmayna* thinks," Linda said between clenched teeth.

"Maybe you think you're being noble, but it's pretty low to lie to me about how you feel just to convince me to change."

"I'm not lying, Ben. I love you." Though right now, she was this close to changing her mind. Ben was the most aggravating, stupid boy in the whole world. "This whole 'I hate myself' attitude is starting to get on my nerves."

"You really sound like a girl in love." The words were bitter poison from his mouth.

"Well, maybe you need to quit wallowing."

He stood up, and she could almost hear his spine snap into place. "Wallowing? Is that what I'm doing? Do you know what my *dat* said to me this morning? He said he is ashamed to call me his son. He said I am going to kill my mother with all the worry. That's something every boy wants to hear, that he is going to send his mother to the grave. Did you hear the things people said about me after what happened at school? *Ben Kiem is a very bad boy. There is no hope for such a wayward child. Ben Kiem is evil to the core.*"

Linda lowered her head. She'd never said anything bad about Ben, but she'd gone out of her way to avoid Ben through the years because she didn't want to be seen as a girl who flirted with evil. Or the girl who would even consider it.

"Parents wouldn't let their *kinner* play with me. I was ashamed and lonely. Wally was the only friend I had, and he befriended me to make his parents mad." He turned his back on her. "Do you have any idea how the teacher treated me for the rest of the year?"

"Magdalena?"

"Magdalena. She was sweet and kind to everyone except me. She even made an effort with Wally, but she hated me, and she made sure everyone knew it. I had embarrassed her deeply, and she wasn't going to just let it go. She shamed me in front of the class daily and told my parents I was *dumm* and lazy. When she wasn't sneering at me or telling me how stupid I was, she ignored me as if I was a bad smell that hung about the classroom."

Linda didn't know what to say. It had all been so horrible, and yes, Ben had been ostracized. Linda's practical side wanted to tell him to quit whining, but the sympathy washed over her. Ben had been fourteen years old, and the *gmayna* should have shown more kindness.

"Magdalena was right about me. I can't change, and if I did, no one would believe it was true. I'm the boy everybody whispers about behind their hands, the one who can't be saved. The whole community would be better off without me. So excuse me for wallowing, but considering who I am, you shouldn't expect any better."

He seemed determined to cast himself in a bad light, as if to convince her to stop loving him, but all it did was make her feel worse and worse for how the community had treated him, how she had treated him. "I'm sorry, Ben."

"Don't say you're sorry. You're trying to make yourself feel better, and it doesn't change anything. If you want the truth, here's the truth. I thought you were my friend, but I should have known it was a lie. People have tried a lot of things to change me, but it is especially cruel to pretend to love me so you can save my soul."

"I would never do that."

He snatched his boots from the ground. "Whatever obligation you felt for me, you don't have to feel it anymore. You don't have to go hiking or canoeing or snowshoeing with me ever again. You can tell my *dat* and anyone else who wants to know that you've done your duty."

"Ben, it's not like that."

"Just leave me alone." He marched in approximately the same direction from which they had come, but he was going to get lost without a flashlight.

"Wait, Ben. Let's go together."

"I'll find my own way home. Don't wait for me."

Linda scooped up the blanket as quickly as she could

and stuffed it into her bag before remembering that she needed the flashlight from the bottom of the bag. She yanked the blanket out of the bag, fished around for the flashlight, and turned it on. By the time she had put the blanket back in the bag and picked up her shoes, Ben had disappeared. She hurried in the direction he'd gone, but she soon lost track of his footprints. "Ben," she called, knowing full well he wouldn't answer.

Linda squeaked in frustration, kicked at the sand, and plopped down on the ground, sitting cross-legged like a bird on her nest. She sat in the dark listening to the buzz of a thousand crickets and her sharp, frustrated breathing. Ben was a whiny *dumkoff*, and she was glad to be rid of him.

That thought lasted about as long as it took a star to shoot across the sky.

She would never, ever be glad to be rid of Ben. Despite her recklessness in declaring her feelings out loud, she had meant every word.

She loved Ben.

The thought terrified her, made her body ache with longing. Even if her love had been the most powerful force on Earth, it couldn't compel Ben to love her back. It couldn't make Ben see the truth about himself, and it certainly couldn't change him. Linda blinked away any hint of a tear. There was no point in crying for someone who didn't deserve to be cried about. How could she have let herself fall this hard?

If only she could muster her practical side right now, she could talk herself out of caring for him. Practical Linda would never fall in love with someone like Ben. He was irresponsible, reckless, and liked to set things on fire.

It would never work between them, her wanting to be baptized and him wanting to jump the fence. He didn't believe in essential oils, she used them instead of doctors. He couldn't make it up the smallest hill without gasping for air, and she had hiked two of Colorado's tallest mountains.

She had a small, uninspiring voice. When Ben sang, the birds stopped chirping just to listen. Linda had no patience for mistakes and no sympathy for foolishness. Ben gently tended to people's tiny scratches and gave people second and third and fourth chances. Plus, he had literally saved her life.

Nae. They were not well suited at all.

There were dozens of practical reasons why she should feel nothing for Ben.

And none of them mattered.

She loved him. She wanted to be with him. She had made some terrible mistake, and she couldn't make it right. Even the brightest night sky was no match for the darkness that penetrated Linda's heart.

All she could feel was a breathtaking, gut-clenching pain.

Chapter Eleven

Ben, Wally, and Simeon sat at the picnic table farthest from the pavilion where fifteen or sixteen of *die youngie* were talking and laughing and having what looked like a grand time trying to ignore the three Amish boys smoking on the other side of the park. There was a volleyball game going, and someone had set up croquet, though no one was playing.

Though he tried not to stare or even look at her directly, Ben's attention was riveted to one particular girl in a lavender dress that he was sure brought out the color of her eyes, though he wasn't close enough to know for certain. Of course, anything Linda wore made her eyes look a brilliant blue, like the clear sky on a cold day. He envied every person she talked to, watched her eat a cookie, and smiled to himself when he realized she was wearing hiking boots instead of flip-flops. Was that the only pair of shoes she owned? How would she play volley-ball in hiking boots?

Maybe she'd play barefoot.

Ben's face got warm remembering the feel of Linda's bare foot brushing against his that night at the sand dunes.

At the slightest touch, his heart had done a backflip and his stomach had performed a somersault. *Ach*, what a *dumkoff* he'd been. It had all been part of Linda's plan to make him her project, and he'd almost fallen for it.

He took a drag on his cigarette, coughed like he was going to hack up a lung, and tried his best to pretend Linda wasn't less than a hundred yards away, looking so beautiful that his throat went dry. He didn't care what Linda was doing. She wasn't a part of his life anymore, and he was going to cut her out of his heart, even if it killed him.

Ben leaned forward and propped his arms on his thighs. Why did he even come to gatherings anymore? Everybody hated the sight of Ben, Wally, and Simeon at any youth gathering, and it was pretty clear people would rather they stayed away, especially after the fire. Three old ladies and the two ministers had given him lectures after *gmay* on Sunday. Everyone had glared at Ben the entire service, except the babies and toddlers who were too young to know better.

Even now, *die youngie* under the pavilion were giving Ben and his friends sideways glances. Some of the boys looked downright hostile. Linda was completely ignoring Ben, or maybe she hadn't noticed he was there. Ben ran his hand down the side of his face. Of course she'd seen him. He was smoking like a chimney, and he and Wally had been purposefully laughing hysterically to draw attention to themselves. Ben's throat was already raw from laughing like a hyena. That's what he got for trying too hard.

Wally liked to go to gatherings, even though he never played games or ate pretzels or talked to anybody. He wanted to make all the self-righteous young people uncomfortable and angry. He wanted everyone in the *gmayna* to hate him so he felt justified in hating them. It made sense to Ben. Linda would say it was childish. And that's why Ben was glad she wasn't in his life anymore. When he was in the middle of it, he hadn't realized how often he had made decisions based on what Linda would think of him. What a *dumm* way to live his life. He didn't owe Linda an explanation for anything, and now he didn't have to care what she said. It was better if she hated him. Then he wouldn't have the pressure of trying to live up to her expectations. It was *wunderbarr* to be so free again.

But making everybody hate him got old after about ten minutes, and Ben would rather be anywhere but here. Every smile Linda gave to someone else, every move she made, felt like a knife twisting in his gut. The raw ache of Linda's deception nearly suffocated him. He had let himself trust her, but she was just like everybody else—only interested in him as a charity project. Well, now she knew there were some projects doomed to failure from the very beginning.

"What are we doing here?" Ben said. "I'm not having any fun."

"My *dat* made me come," Simeon said.

Ben threw his cigarette on the ground. "Well, he didn't say you had to stay, did he?"

"I guess not."

Ben glanced at Wally. "Let's go find something better to do than watch *die youngie* play volleyball."

Wally didn't seem in a big hurry to go anywhere. "Zoe said if she got off work early, she'd come pick us up."

In the distance, Linda fell to the ground trying to hit the volleyball. Ben growled under his breath as he watched Freeman Sensenig grab Linda's hand and help her up.

Ben clenched his fist, remembering how good it felt when Linda put her hand in his and dragged him up and down the sand dunes. His hand had tingled for hours afterward. No matter what Wally said, Ben was never coming to another gathering ever again. "How long do you expect us to wait?"

"What's your rush?" Wally said, realizing he was getting under Ben's skin but probably not understanding why. "It's a nice night out here."

An invisible hand tightened around Ben's throat as Linda and Mary Ann Miller left the volleyball game and walked straight toward them. What did she think she was doing? Hadn't he made it perfectly clear he didn't want her to bother him ever again?

Even though he didn't care one whit what Linda thought of him, his heart beat the wild rhythm of a freight train barreling down the track. His palms got sweaty, and his hands shook. He had been right about one thing. That dress did make her eyes seem extra blue, extra blue and extra piercing, as if she was looking into his soul. Did she like what she saw there? Not likely. Without taking his gaze from her face, he stood up and stuffed his hands in his pockets.

"Look, Ben. It's your girlfriend," Wally said.

"I told you, she's not my girlfriend," he muttered under his breath. "I don't even like her." Which was a very big lie, but if he told it to himself enough, he might start to believe it.

"Hey, Simeon," Mary Ann said, raising her hand in a half-hearted wave as she and Linda got closer. "*Hallo*, Wally and Ben."

"*Vie gehts*?" Simeon said. Simeon wasn't inclined to be flippant like Wally or mute like Ben.

A painful emotion flashed in Linda's eyes. Ben didn't like it. Linda should always be smiling. He'd never forget the day they'd spent in the canoe on the river. Combined with the sunlight sparkling off the water, her smile had practically blinded him. That's how he'd always think of Linda, even if she had just been pretending.

Just as suddenly, the pain disappeared from her eyes, replaced with an awkward smile stretched across her face. Linda seemed less certain of herself than she usually was, but she was still Linda, not inclined to let anyone intimidate her. "We came to see if you'd like to play volleyball. We need more players."

Wally snickered. "Volleyball is *dumm*."

Linda raised an eyebrow. "If you think it's so *dumm*, why are you sitting here watching it?"

Wally frowned and squinted into the setting sun. "What do you care?" The irritation rose off Wally like steam. *Ach, du lieva*. If someone didn't know Linda well, they'd think she was poking fun at them. But that was just Linda's way. If she thought something was ridiculous or didn't make sense, she couldn't keep her mouth shut. Of course it took next to nothing to set Wally off. He was angry at everybody and everything. "It's not your private park. We can be here if we want to."

Linda nodded. "It's okay. I understand why you'd be afraid to play."

Ach. She was up to her old tricks. But not even Ben was *dumm* enough to fall for that again.

Wally glared at Linda through the smoke of his cigarette.

"We're not afraid. We just don't want to play. Volleyball is a stupid game."

Wally didn't scare Linda. "For sure and certain, you wouldn't be able to keep up, not with your lungs full of smoke." She gave Ben a pointed look, and try as he might, he couldn't hold her gaze. He'd started smoking again because that was what Wally and Simeon wanted, but he knew how foolish he must look to her. He felt foolish too. All those headaches and suffering for nothing.

A fire started somewhere in Ben's gut. Pulling back his shoulders, he met her gaze. He didn't care what Linda thought. "We like to smoke," he said, because he had to say something, and he couldn't think of anything clever.

"I'm glad for that," Linda said. It sounded more like an accusation than the truth. Though her smile stayed glued in place, the light in her eyes went out, almost as if her feelings were hurt.

Mary Ann's smile faltered as she glanced at Wally. "*Ach, vell.* We just wanted you to know you're invited."

Simeon turned out to be braver than Ben ever could be. "We should go play. It might be fun." His gaze shifted from Wally to Ben and back again. "Just while we wait for Zoe."

"We don't want to play," Wally said, as if that ended the discussion.

Simeon swallowed hard. "I do."

A fire flared in Wally's eyes. It went out as quickly as it had ignited. He sat down on the top of the picnic table and pulled a new pack of cigarettes from his pocket. "Go ahead. Nobody's stopping you."

Simeon stood up and gave Wally a doubtful look. "Just until Zoe comes."

Mary Ann and Simeon turned to go. Linda wasn't finished. She frowned in Ben's direction. "We searched for you for over an hour. Even Cathy hiked the sand dunes with us trying to find you."

Ben looked anywhere but into Linda's eyes. He didn't want to see the pain of that night reflected back at him. "I told you I'd find my own way home."

"I didn't want to leave without you." She waited for him to say something. He didn't. "We were worried. We drove to your house, but you weren't there. I went back the next morning. Your *mamm* said you'd come home a little before sunrise."

It wasn't like Linda to worry. Ben didn't like it. "I hitchhiked. A trucker dropped me off outside Monte Vista." It had taken almost two hours to walk home from the highway, but not long enough to clear Linda from his head. There probably weren't enough years for that.

"You hitchhiked? That was *dumm*."

"Smarter than walking all the way."

"Dumber than just getting a ride home with me and Cathy."

She had a point there, but that night no one could have paid him enough to get in a car with Linda Eicher.

Wally, who had been trying to convince Simeon that Simeon wouldn't have fun playing volleyball, suddenly turned on Linda. "You think you're smarter than everybody, but Ben is smarter than the whole *gmayna* put together. I'm sick of you putting him down. You think you're better than us, but you're just a preachy, stupid, ugly girl who isn't better than anybody."

In one long stride, Ben was face to face with Wally.

Wally grunted when Ben jabbed his finger into Wally's chest. "That's too far, Wally. Just shut up about it."

Wally's eyes nearly popped out of his head as he raised his hands in surrender, his cigarette lodged between two fingers. "Okay, okay. But she shouldn't put you down like that, like you're manure stuck to the bottom of her shoe."

Ben's throat burned with anger. "She's not putting me down. She's speaking the truth, and I deserve it." Especially after how he'd treated her. Especially because he wasn't even worthy to breathe the same air as Linda.

Linda stepped forward and laid a gentle hand on Ben's arm, which was still pressing into Wally's chest. "Wally is right. I'm too opinionated and harsh, and I'm sorry."

"You should be sorry," Wally said. "You've done nothing but make Ben miserable."

The earlier pain he'd seen in Linda's eyes returned full force. Ben had to grab the edge of the table to keep from reaching out and pulling her into his arms. The sooner she dealt with the pain and realized she couldn't fix him, realized that he couldn't be fixed, the better for both of them.

A giant red pickup truck roared into the parking lot, drawing everyone's attention. The driver, Zoe, killed the engine, and the birds started chirping again. Zoe and her friend Mack jumped out of the cab of the truck and slammed the massive doors behind them.

Wally grinned smugly. "Here they are. Too bad you can't play volleyball after all, Simeon. Maybe another time."

Zoe and Mack caught sight of Wally and Ben and practically sprinted across the grass to their picnic table. Linda and Mary Ann linked elbows and took a few steps back to make room for Zoe's entrance, which was like a bulldozer driving into a church service.

Zoe threw herself into Ben's arms, wrapping her hands around his neck and her legs around his waist. He had to brace himself hard against the table to keep them both from toppling to the ground. He glanced at Linda before he remembered that this was exactly the thing he needed to do to make her hate him. More than that, this was exactly the kind of thing a boy as wicked as Ben Kiem would do. It was perfect, no matter how offended Linda was.

But she didn't look offended. She looked stricken, devastated, completely off balance. His heart crashed to the ground. He didn't want Linda to feel bad. He wanted her to get angry. Anger and disdain were better than this look of wounded betrayal.

Zoe jumped out of Ben's arms and patted his chest. "You ready for some fun, Bennie?"

Bennie. That was what Zoe called him. To Ben, it was like fingernails on a chalkboard. He faithfully kept his gaze away from Linda and forced a smile. "What are we going to do?"

"It's not too early to go bar hopping." Zoe was just blowing smoke. There was only one real bar in Monte Vista, and Alamosa was too far to drive if Zoe got drunk by the end of the night.

Instead of running the other way as fast as she could, Linda seemed eager to meet Zoe. She stuck out her hand. "I'm Linda, and this is Mary Ann."

Zoe looked at Linda's hand as if no one had ever wanted to shake hands with her before. "Um, hi," she said, sliding her hands into the back pockets of her tight jeans.

An amused grin sprouted on Linda's face. It was the

first genuine smile Ben had seen from her today. She pointed to her own cheek. "You have a makeup smear right there."

Zoe did indeed have a smudge of black makeup in a line down her cheek. She turned to Ben. "Do I?"

Ben nodded. "Yeah. A big one."

Zoe hissed a few bad words, pulled a thin mirror from her pocket, and looked at herself. She tried to wipe away the smudge with her fingers, and when that didn't work, she had the nerve to grab Ben's sleeve, leaned over, and wipe her face with that. Zoe's makeup was as thick as tar. Would it come out in the wash? *Ach*, *vell*, he'd never liked this shirt anyway.

Linda turned her whole body away from Zoe, as if she was suddenly very interested in the outcome of the volleyball game on the other side of the park. Ben pressed his lips together. She wasn't looking at volleyball. She was laughing. She pressed her hand to her mouth as her shoulders shook violently. At least she wasn't laughing out loud.

Ben studied his shirt and the black smudge on Zoe's face that now looked like a bruise. He was torn between being annoyed about his shirt and wanting to laugh himself. Zoe wouldn't take the laughing too well. He couldn't very well claim to be laughing *with* her and not *at* her. Linda used to say that, and Ben had never believed her.

Wally lit another cigarette. "Let's get out of here."

Zoe kept wiping at her face, slowly moving the black tar into a line at her jaw. "You know you can't smoke in my truck."

Wally scowled. "We're sitting in the back anyway."

"You'll be sitting in the back," Zoe said. "Ben is going to sit in the front with me."

Wally glared at Ben and puffed slowly on his cigarette. "Then I guess I don't have to worry about it."

On one hand, Ben didn't appreciate Zoe singling him out. Wally was interested in Zoe, and it was obvious he didn't like the attention Zoe paid Ben. On the other hand, if Zoe's attention irritated Linda, all the better. But Linda wasn't even watching how Zoe curled her fingers possessively around Ben's arm or how she pressed her body against his. Her gaze was squarely and faithfully focused on the volleyball game.

"Come on, Zoe," Mack whined. "I want the AC."

Zoe puckered her lips. "Too bad. It's my truck. I get to decide."

Linda finally turned around. She had managed to quell her laughter, but she grinned like she couldn't help it even though it hurt. Her smile was wide and unhappy, as if Ben's behavior amused and pained her at the same time, as if there was so much about Ben's life she could laugh and cry about. "Have fun bar hopping."

Mary Ann raised her eyebrows in Simeon's direction. "Are you sure you don't want to play volleyball? We need another player, and you're the best player I know. Freeman thinks he's too *gute* for us and hogs the ball."

Simeon adjusted his hat and looked at his feet. "I think I'll stay here, Ben. They really need another player, and I don't want to sit in the back of the truck. Go without me. I'll see you tomorrow."

Wally's eyes narrowed to slits. "It wonders me why we wanted you to come anyway." He put his arm around Zoe, and they took a few steps toward the truck. "Have a good time," he said over his shoulder. "Oh, wait. You're playing volleyball. It's impossible to have a good time."

Ben followed Wally, Zoe, and Mack toward the truck, resisting the urge to glance back at Linda. He simply didn't care what she was thinking or how she looked.

Linda must have run out of self-control. Her outburst of loud and unapologetic laughter made them all turn around.

"What's so funny?" Wally hissed.

Linda pointed at Mack. "Your pants," was all she said.

Ben felt his face get warm. Mack liked to wear his pants loose, with the waistband down below his hips and his underwear in full view. With the crotch of his jeans almost to his knees, it looked like he'd have a hard time running a race. Or kneeling down. Or bending over.

Ben knew enough to be embarrassed, but it didn't seem to bother Mack. He smiled. "Pretty sweet, huh?"

"Pretty sweet," Linda said. Was she laughing *with* Mack or *at* him?

And why did Ben have the sneaking suspicion that Mack wasn't the only one she was laughing at?

Chapter Twelve

Linda dragged her feet across Esther and Levi's front lawn, even though she had promised herself she wasn't going to sulk.

She wasn't one to wallow, not in self-pity, not in regret, not in a broken heart. There was nothing wrong with her that couldn't be fixed with a little determination and a heavy dose of practicality. And being practical meant no wallowing. Linda had no sympathy for sentiment, not even her own. It was silly to spend one more minute of regret on a boy who was determined to ruin his life.

Why waste time helping someone who didn't want your help? Why waste time with a boy who was never going to change, didn't want to change, and hated you for suggesting he could change?

There were lots of other fish in the sea—Freeman Sensenig for one, who had asked to drive her home from the last gathering. She hadn't especially wanted to ride home with Freeman, but after watching Ben get into that truck with Raccoon Girl and the boy who couldn't keep his pants up, she'd sort of snapped. Freeman had asked, and in a moment of insanity and pique, she'd said yes.

Ach, she was going to have to break up with Freeman, and they weren't even a couple.

Cathy followed Linda to the porch. "I'm not going to be much use today. I have a bunion that's been giving me trouble, so standing on my feet for this apricot thing is going to be impossible."

Cathy kept calling it "this apricot thing." Esther had invited Cathy and Linda over to can the apricots she'd picked from the tree in her backyard, which seemed like a complete waste of time. Who ate canned apricots? They were slimy and mushy. Better to make four-dozen apricot pies and be done with it. "Thank you for driving me, Cathy. It's called a frolic, and you don't have to stay if you don't want to."

"Of course I have to stay. How else will I hear the gossip about you and Ben?"

Linda pressed her lips together in a hard line and reluctantly knocked on the door. Cathy might not have a gall bladder, but she had *gute* instincts. Linda suspected that Esther hadn't invited her to a canning frolic because she needed help with her apricots. Linda had been invited because Esther wanted to talk about Ben, and Linda would rather eat a whole quart of apricots than relive that horrible and unnecessary part of her life. "There's nothing to tell, Cathy. He's not interested in me or anything I might have to say to him."

"Nonsense. He looks at you like your teeth are made of diamonds. Or, I guess Amish people don't care about diamonds. He looks at you like your teeth are made of whoopee pies." She frowned. "That doesn't really make much sense, but you know what I mean."

Esther opened the door, threw her hands in the air, and

squealed in delight as if she hadn't seen Linda or Cathy for years. The bodice of her apron was lined with at least ten colorful fabric clips, and a magnetic lid lifter was tucked behind her ear.

Linda grinned. "You look like you're ready to can and quilt."

"Of course," Esther said. "Around here, I have to be ready for anything." She pulled the lid lifter from her ear. "I found this in the bottom drawer this morning. I didn't want to forget where it was."

"What is it?" Cathy said. "I'm more of a quilter than a canner."

Esther handed it to Cathy. "It has a magnet on the end so you can get canning lids out of the hot water after you sanitize them. It saves your skin from getting scalded."

Cathy gave the lid lifter back to Esther. "I'm afraid I won't be able to help with the canning. I'm just here to gossip."

Esther's eyes flashed with amusement, and she glanced at Linda. "Gossiping is half the fun of a frolic."

"It's a sin to gossip," Linda murmured. She definitely did not want to be here.

Cathy nodded. "Then we won't gossip. Heaven knows, I've got enough sins to answer for, especially for that lost month in Las Vegas."

"Las Vegas?" Esther said.

Cathy stepped into Esther's house. "I was young and stupid, and it was more than fifteen years ago. I'm over it."

"So you were what, sixty-eight?" Linda asked.

"Yes," Cathy said. "That has to be my excuse."

Cathy was in her eighties, but she still didn't consider herself old. Linda wanted to be just like her, except not quite so grumpy. But without Ben, Linda didn't see how her life could be anything but miserable. Linda cleared her throat, pasted a smile on her face, and resolved to never think of Ben Kiem again. She was too practical to let this nonsense with Ben turn her into a sticky puddle of apricot jelly. She was already over him. Over and done.

"Where's Winnie?" Linda asked.

"She's taking a nap. Lord willing, she'll sleep until we finish."

They went into Esther's kitchen where three bushels of apricots sat on the table. Esther plucked an apricot out of the basket and took a bite. "Levi helped me pick yesterday. Cathy, what if Linda washes them and you can cut out the pits and put the fruit in bottles while you sit at the table?"

"Okay," said Cathy, "but if I get tired, I'll just sit here and watch the two of you work."

"Fair enough."

Linda ran water over each apricot and put them in a bowl at the table for Cathy. Cathy picked up the first apricot and studied it. "Do these need to be peeled?"

"No," Esther said. "Their peels are thin enough. We're going to bottle some and make the rest into apricot jelly. Won't that be nice?"

Cathy scrunched her lips together. "I don't approve of jelly as a general rule. Do you have a sugar-free recipe?"

Esther shook her head. "It's terrible without sugar. Sorry."

"If you want to kill your husband with diabetes, apricot jelly is the way to do it. Of course, I don't think you should want to kill your husband at all, but that's just my opinion."

Esther smiled playfully. "I agree with that."

Esther washed bottles then set them upside-down in a

pan of shallow water boiling on the stove. Once the bottles were sterilized, she put them on the table for Cathy to fill. Linda didn't know why she was surprised at how fast Cathy could fill a quart jar with fruit. Cathy had many talents and skills. At that age, you knew how to do a whole lot of stuff.

Once all the apricots were washed, Linda heated up a concoction of water and sugar and poured it into Cathy's full bottles. Then Esther used her magnetic lid lifter to transport a lid from the boiling water onto the jar and screwed it tight with a band. It was an efficient, well-organized process that kept their hands busy and their minds free. The perfect activity if you wanted to visit.

Which was a bad thing, because Esther wanted to visit. "So, Linda, have you seen Ben lately?"

Cathy plopped an apricot into the jar. "The last time I saw him was at the sand dunes. He just up and walked away from Linda. It was the middle of the night. We looked for him for an hour, even though I told Linda if we left him at the dunes all night, it would serve him right. But Linda wanted to look. We never did find him."

"Oh, dear," Esther said. "I'm sure you were upset."

"I was irritated," Linda said. She wouldn't admit to being upset, and never in a million years would she admit to being devastated, especially not to Ben's sister-in-law. "It was rude of him to just walk away like that. We spent all that time looking for him."

Cathy popped half an apricot in her mouth. "I should have asked him to carry a whistle. We could have followed the sound of his blowing."

"Ben didn't want to be found. For sure and certain he heard us calling his name. He just let us go on calling."

Linda glanced at Esther who was staring at her with a funny look on her face. She shouldn't have said anything. Surely Esther noticed the way her voice cracked when she said Ben's name.

Esther set another quart jar in the boiling water. "So you took him to the sand dunes, and he just walked away from you."

"And we couldn't find him in the dark," Cathy said. She drew her brows together. "Do you think he's still out there?"

"No," Linda said. "He hitched a ride partway and walked the rest of the way home. I saw him last week at the park. He's fine."

The corners of Cathy's mouth drooped. "I can't imagine he's fine. At the very least, he's sore from walking home. He probably got a bad case of athlete's foot for all the trouble he put us through."

Esther set two more bottles on the table. "I'm sorry about that."

"It's not your fault," Cathy said.

"I feel responsible for him. He's related to me."

Cathy was never one to spread sunshine and rainbows if a storm cloud was available. "Kind of unfortunate for you, but I suppose you can't pick your relatives. Ben is handsome, but handsome will only get you so far when you're an idiot. And he can sing, but having a good voice and having good sense aren't the same thing. I'm not sure why Linda still wanted to take him to the sand dunes after he burned down that barn."

It felt as if a horse was stomping on Linda's chest. Was taking Ben to the sand dunes a good decision or the worst one she'd ever made? "It was a shed, not a barn, and we shouldn't gossip."

"We're not gossiping," Esther said, her piercing gaze glued to Linda's face. "We're sharing, and there's nothing in the Bible against sharing our news and our feelings."

"I'll tell you how I feel." Cathy pointed her knife at Linda. "Linda wanted to take him to the sand dunes even after he burned down that garage. And then he ran off, and I hiked all over kingdom come looking for him. I got two mosquito bites and stepped on a frog. I feel betrayed and a little nauseated, but the nausea is mostly from the sound the frog made when I squished him. I don't know how Linda put up with Ben as long as she did."

Watching Linda out of the corner of her eye, Esther set the first full bottle into the hot water bath. "You're . . . uh . . . you're not putting up with him anymore?"

How did she answer such a question?

I don't want a boyfriend who sets things on fire.

I'm devastated, but I don't want to tell you I'm devastated because being devastated over Ben Kiem is about the dumbest thing a girl could do.

I'm going back to my practical life where nothing exciting ever happens and where Ben and his charming smile can't hurt me.

Linda retrieved a knife and sat down at the table. "Ben doesn't like hiking as much as he used to."

Esther grunted. "He's more interested in girls who drive red trucks."

The pressure on Linda's chest increased, but she tried not to feel anything. She didn't care one whit about the girls and the trucks Ben spent time with. "Oh. Have you met Zoe?"

"Saw her through the window. That girl can't keep her hands off of Ben, and that tongue . . ." Esther made a face and shuddered, and her gaze flicked in Linda's direction. "I'm sure you didn't hear me say that." She slammed the lid onto the pot. "I just don't understand it."

Linda shrugged. "He's still in *rumschpringe*."

Esther shook her head. "That's no excuse for terrible behavior. You're in *rumschpringe*, and you're still capable of being sensible."

Cathy nodded. "I told you, just because he's handsome doesn't mean he has any good sense."

Esther propped her hand on her hip. "He's started smoking again."

"I know." Linda didn't want to talk about it anymore. All the progress Ben had made, all the promise he'd shown in trying to improve his life was gone. And Linda refused to mourn for what might have been.

"*Denki* for being kind to Ben, even if he didn't appreciate it."

Esther made it sound like Ben had been some sort of charity project. Ben had accused Linda of the same thing, as if she only spent time with him because she wanted to change him. Linda didn't want to change Ben. She loved him, or used to love him, just as he was. She wanted him to find enough self-respect to change on his own.

She hadn't "put up" with Ben. Their first snowshoe trip hadn't been all pies and cakes, but every outing after that had been sheer pleasure. Ben was kind and attentive and so fun to be with. She cherished every minute they'd spent together, even if the good times were distant memories.

But she wasn't going to wallow. What was done was done, and it was time to move on from this silly fascination with Ben Kiem. Maybe it hadn't even been love. Maybe she'd just been swept up in the excitement of being with someone so unpredictable and different.

Would telling herself that make it easier to get over him?

"I never thought of Ben as a project, if that's what you're saying."

"I never believed Ben was your project," Esther said.

"Ben did." A less practical girl might be less practical about it, but Linda was extremely practical, and she would never, ever again tell a boy she loved him. It made her vulnerable, and practical girls could not afford to be vulnerable.

Esther opened her mouth and promptly shut it again. "*Ach.* I see." She strangled the kitchen towel in her hands. "So do you think you can give him another chance?"

Linda stared at Esther in disbelief. Another chance? Absolutely not. How could Esther even ask such a thing? The first time had been painful enough. She didn't want to offend Esther by saying what she really thought of that plan, and she certainly didn't want Esther to know how the question had upset her. She took a deep breath. When in doubt, always answer a question with another question. "What do you mean by another chance?"

"Do you think you'll maybe take him hiking or canoeing again?"

Cathy saved Linda from having to vehemently refuse to even talk to Ben again. "Why would she do that? I can't spend my days traipsing all over the country looking for Ben every time he runs off. Until he can act like a civilized human being, Ben isn't getting in my car."

Linda had never been more grateful to have Cathy on her side. She swallowed past the lump in her throat.

Esther's frown etched deep lines into her face. She stood quite still for a few seconds then grabbed Linda's hand. "Linda, I see an apricot Levi missed on the tree out there. Will you come and help me pick it?"

Oy, anyhow. "Uh. Just one?"

"*Jah*. You can hold the ladder for me so I don't fall."

Linda was trying to figure out how to say no when Esther stuffed the ticking kitchen timer in her pocket and pulled Linda out the back door. She led Linda to the side of the house nowhere near the apricot tree, stopped short, and folded her arms. "What did you do?"

Ach, *du lieva*. Apricot day had been a wonderful bad idea. "Do when? What do you mean?"

"You were helping him. He was doing better." Esther exploded like a firecracker. "Then you took him to the sand dunes and something changed. What did you do?"

Linda bit down on her tongue to keep from bursting into tears. Of course, biting down on your tongue made it hard to talk, but it was better to be angry than weepy. "It's not my fault."

"Everyone was upset about the fire. I know it was a terrible thing, but you shouldn't cut Ben off just because he made a stupid mistake. He trusted you. You should have been a better friend."

"You don't know. And don't yell at me."

Esther held up her hands. "You're right. I don't know." Huffing out a breath, she leaned against the house as if she were trying to push it over. "I'm sorry. I have a very bad temper, and when someone I love gets hurt, I get testy."

Linda kept her mouth shut. It was all so unfair.

Esther pressed her fingers to her forehead. "I shouldn't make assumptions, but Ben won't talk to me. It sounds like I'm making excuses for Ben, which I'm not. Setting that fire was a terrible thing, and people were justifiably upset. I just thought you'd be a little more thoughtful with your response."

"You don't know how I responded."

"Please, tell me what happened. Did you tell Ben you didn't want to see him anymore?"

Linda was tempted to let Esther go on believing that she had been the one to reject Ben. The other way around was so much more humiliating. She folded her arms and looked away. "Is that what you think?"

"Ben's been hurt before, when he was younger. I don't know the details, but Levi says he took it very hard. I don't know what happened between you, but it's obvious Ben is extremely upset about it."

Linda wasn't going to embarrass herself by telling Esther everything. "He told me that his *dat* hates him. I told him that was silly. He doesn't like it when I call him silly. He thinks he's a lost cause. We argued about that for quite some time."

"*Ach*. Poor Ben."

"It frightens him to think he has to live up to anybody's expectations. So he doesn't even try. I encouraged him to apologize to Mr. Bateman and help rebuild the shed. He accused me of trying to change him. He thinks the only reason I invited him to do things together is because I've turned him into a project. He can't imagine he could be anything other than a project."

Esther's expression softened. "*Is* he anything other than a project?"

"You can believe what you want."

"Forgive me. I've been elbow deep in apricot fumes all morning."

Linda took a deep breath. She couldn't be mad at Esther. Esther was incredibly protective of her *bruder*-in-law. Her loyalty was something Linda loved about her. "Ben wasn't a project. I would never treat anyone that way."

"Do you love him?" Esther asked so softly, Linda barely heard her.

"It doesn't matter."

Esther laid a hand on Linda's shoulder. "It matters very much."

Ach. Wasn't it enough that she'd already made a fool of herself in front of Ben? Did she have to do it in front of his whole family? But it was too late. Anything she said to avoid the question would be a lie. "I told him I loved him, and he didn't believe me." She wrapped her arms around her waist. "We argued about that too."

"*Ach.* Poor Ben."

Poor Ben? What about poor Linda? She'd handed Ben her heart, and he'd stomped on it like it was a poisonous spider. Didn't she deserve a little sympathy too? "*Jah.* Poor boy has suffered so much."

Esther obviously heard the tinge of spite in Linda's voice. "I'm not making excuses for him. Ben is responsible for his poor decisions, but you were closer to him than almost anyone. I know you understand why I feel sorry for him."

Linda was honest enough to acknowledge the truth of Esther's words. "I suppose I do."

Esther sighed. "Ben has a very low opinion of himself. He doesn't think he's worthy of love and won't accept it when it's given to him. He gets into trouble because it's easier than trying to fulfill his *dat*'s expectations."

"*Jah*," Linda said. "He justifies himself by blaming the *gmayna*. He uses our disappointment to justify doing nothing or doing bad things. If no one thinks well of him, he doesn't have to live up to anything."

Esther gave Linda a sad smile. "You told him you love him, and he didn't take it well. He doesn't believe anybody could love him. In fact, he's worked hard to make himself impossible to love. So he thinks you're lying to him."

"As if I'm playing a trick on him to force him to mend his ways."

Esther picked up a stick from the grass and started whacking it against the side of the house. "So now he's going to prove to you and everyone else that he can't change, that he's as bad as we all think he is. He wants it to be perfectly clear that he will not be tricked or manipulated into changing."

"This might sound strange, but I don't want him to change. He needs to repent of some bad behavior, but I like the person he is way down deep inside."

Esther snorted. "Very deep. And I know what you mean, because I love him too, but he has lost himself somewhere among the cigarettes and the boom boxes and the girls with black lips."

Linda would have laughed if she hadn't been so close to tears. "Raccoon Girl."

"Levi tried to talk to him this morning about the big red truck and Wally and the smoking, but Ben wouldn't listen. He says he's never been happier, even when it's obvious he's the most miserable boy in Colorado."

Linda's heart felt like a stone in her chest. "He's never been happier because things are easier. He doesn't have to be afraid of failure because he won't try. He's quite comfortable thinking everybody hates him because then he doesn't have to work for anyone's approval."

Esther broke her stick in half and then snapped each half in half again. "So." She tossed her sticks to the ground. "So. What about you and Ben?"

"What about me and Ben?"

"Have you given up on him?"

Linda blinked back the angry tears that threatened to overtake her. "What do you want me to do? I *cannot* save Ben, and it's unfair of you to place that responsibility on me."

"I only meant—"

"He despises me, Esther. You should have seen him at the last gathering. He can't stand the sight of me, and all I did to deserve it was tell him I love him." She slapped away the tears on her cheeks. "Loved him."

Esther draped her arm around Linda's shoulder. "I'm sorry. You're right. None of this is your fault. I'm just so frustrated with him. He's as stubborn as a mule."

"I'm sorry about Ben, but I have to protect my own heart. Giving him another chance is like sticking my finger in a rat's nest over and over again. Soon I'll run out of fingers."

"That happened to my *dat*'s *bruder*. We called him Onkel Six Fingers." Esther gave Linda a sideways grin, and they both laughed.

"I'd be wonderful foolish if I let Ben break my heart again. He doesn't love me. And I have decided that I don't love him anymore."

"*Ach*, Linda, you're wrong about one thing. Ben loves you something wonderful."

Linda stopped with the tears and grunted her disagreement. "That is the most ridiculous thing I've ever heard. Besides, I'm looking for someone a little smarter than a boy who sets things on fire and has to buy a new hat every week. I don't want anything to do with him, and I'm sure he feels the same about me."

Esther grimaced. "Oh, dear. I may have done something we'll both regret."

"What's that?"

Esther didn't need to answer. Linda heard the obnoxious roar of a truck in the distance, and her stomach sank to her toes. She didn't even have to look to know that it was a giant, red pickup truck with air conditioning and stereo sound.

"Esther," Linda hissed.

"I thought if you and Ben could just talk about it . . ."

Like two shy schoolgirls, Esther and Linda peeked around the corner of the house. Linda's least favorite truck barreled down the road and skidded to a halt behind Cathy's car. They could hear the bass of the stereo vibrating through the closed windows. Esther turned to Linda, clenched her teeth together, and squeezed her eyes shut. "I should have told you he was coming. And he's brought that *Englisch* girl and her truck. Oh, *sis yuscht*. I'll have to be nice to her."

Linda simply couldn't abide another encounter with Ben and Raccoon Girl. She backed herself against the side of the house. The bricks were lumpy and uncomfortable. "I'm staying put. Will you send Cathy out after Ben goes in? He needn't know I was even here." Linda drew her brows together. Was there any evidence that she'd been in the house?

Esther eyed her doubtfully. "You don't think Cathy will say something?"

Linda blew air from between her lips. For sure and certain Cathy would say something. She peeked around the corner again. Ben and Zoe were getting out of the truck, Ben, hatless, with that shock of thick, light brown hair and an I-couldn't-care-less look on his face, and Zoe, with black lipstick and a silver chain around her waist. Ben wasn't even pretending to be Amish anymore. He wore a black T-shirt with some sort of weird dragon-looking thing on the front and a pair of baggy jeans that he'd probably purchased at the second-hand store. Thank Derr Herr Ben hadn't taken fashion advice from Mack. Ben's waistband was positioned securely at his waist. Linda wasn't surprised by his clothing choices, but seeing Ben dress *Englisch* made her heart hurt all the same.

Linda lost her ability to breathe. Every time she saw Ben, she was reminded all over again how handsome he was and how much she loved him. Well, used to love him. She wasn't about to give her love to someone who refused to love her back.

As much as she wanted to avoid another unpleasant encounter with Ben, she also didn't want to behave like a coward. What would she do if she were a girl who was completely over Ben and wished him nothing but the best and actually felt grateful he didn't return her love? What would she do if she had nothing to be ashamed or embarrassed about and didn't care whether Ben dated a girl with black lipstick or no lips at all?

Linda stepped out from behind the house, steeled herself

against Ben's handsome face, and strode purposefully toward Ben and his girlfriend. Ben furrowed his perfectly straight, thick eyebrows and took a step back. Did he think she was going to tackle him?

Ben looked past Linda to Esther who was close behind. "What's she doing here?" he asked. Oy, anyhow. Had Linda ever heard a more hostile tone?

"I invited her over," Esther confessed.

"I don't want her here."

There was no confidence booster quite like two people talking about you as if you weren't there. Linda swallowed hard and smiled for all she was worth. "*Hallo*, Ben," she said. "*Vie gehts*?"

Zoe puckered her lips into a pout. "Hey. It's not polite to speak a different language. I can't understand you."

Linda kept her smile going, even though her face hurt from the effort. "Uh, sorry. It just means 'How's it going?'"

Zoe checked her fingernails. "Oh. Okay, I guess."

Esther finally caught up to Linda. "Ben. You brought a friend. Is she staying for dinner?"

Ben looked at Zoe. "We're not staying. I just came to get my paycheck from Levi." In spite of everything, Ben still worked with his *dat* and Levi remodeling bathrooms and kitchens. His *dat* hadn't fired him yet.

Esther gave Ben a look of profound disappointment. "*Ach*, Ben, you know Levi does the checks on Monday. He'll give it to you on Tuesday at work."

Ben kicked at the grass with a ratty blue tennis shoe. "I was sort of hoping he could write my check early, so I have money for the weekend."

"Why don't you stay for dinner, and you can talk to Levi about it?" Esther said.

Zoe made a sour face and shook her head. "Bennie and me are meeting Mack and Wally at Dairy Queen in fifteen minutes."

"Not without money." Ben glanced at Linda and quickly looked away. At least he had the good sense to be embarrassed about it.

"We're having yummasetti," Esther said.

Yummasetti was a traditional Amish dish that very few Amish made anymore. Maybe Esther wanted to remind Ben of his roots and tempt him with something truly delicious and fattening.

"I'm not staying," Linda said, in case that made a difference. If Ben didn't have any money, he'd need to rely on the kindness of people like his sister-in-law if he didn't want to starve.

Ben pressed his lips together and studied Linda's face for what seemed like three weeks. Then his gaze flicked in Esther's direction. "Good," he said.

That one word felt like a stab to the heart.

Ben finally pulled his gaze from Esther's face. "We've got to go."

"Come on, Ben," Esther said. "I've got a whole pan of yummasetti in there, and Levi will get fat if he has to eat it all."

Ben scrubbed his fingers through his hair and looked at Zoe. "You don't have to stay."

Esther seemed very enthusiastic about the possibility of Zoe not being there. "Yes, of course. No reason to stay."

Zoe seemed as excited about coming to dinner as Esther was to have her. "I don't really like Amish food. No offense."

"Oh?" Esther said, not seeming the least bit concerned

that Zoe wouldn't like the dinner she cooked. "Well, maybe you'd prefer the McDonald's in Alamosa."

Zoe opened the passenger side door of her truck and pulled out a brown paper bag. "It doesn't matter. I'll drink if I don't like the food."

"*Ach*, I'm sorry," Esther said, "but we don't allow liquor in our house."

Zoe laughed as if only she was in on the joke. "Oh, yeah, sure. It was worth a try. Right, Bennie?" She smiled at him, but Ben was as stiff as a board and as red as a beet.

"I'm serious, Zoe. You don't have to stay," Ben said. Maybe Linda was imagining things, but it sounded like he was begging her to leave. "You can come back and get me later."

Cathy came limping around the side of the house. That bunion must have been acting up. "What happened to you two? It doesn't take that long to pick one apricot."

Esther grinned sheepishly. "Sorry, Cathy. We got sidetracked."

Cathy's mouth fell open when she caught sight of Zoe. "I guess you did get sidetracked." She held out her hand, and Zoe actually shook it, as if maybe Cathy had caught her by surprise. The feeling was probably mutual. "I'm Cathy Larsen. Are you Ben's latest girlfriend?"

Zoe leaned against the bed of her truck. "Yeah," she said, smiling as if Cathy had challenged her to a fight. "Me and Bennie are tight."

"Bennie? I like it. Sounds like an Elton John song." Cathy tilted her head to one side. "Is that eye makeup hard to get off at night?"

Zoe flipped her hair out of her eyes and watched Cathy closely, as if she was waiting for Cathy to attack. "No."

Cathy frowned. "I was allergic to my eye makeup. My eyes puffed up like two balloons. So I got eyeliner tattooed on my eyes. See?" She leaned her face close to Zoe, who took a step back before peering at Cathy's eye tattoos.

"Wow, okay," Zoe said. "I've heard of people doing that."

"It's very convenient," Cathy said, "but when your skin droops, so do your tattoos. Let that be a lesson to you. Don't get a tattoo anywhere that's going to droop, and when you get to be my age, everything droops."

Zoe brightened. "Bennie's got a tattoo. It's a skeleton hand just below his right collarbone."

Whatever smile Esther was holding onto faded to nothing. There just weren't any words.

Cathy studied Ben's shoulder, probably hoping to see something beneath his black T-shirt. She shook her head. "It's definitely going to droop."

Linda wanted to cry as much as she wanted to laugh. She was hurt and confused and so mad at Ben she could barely breathe. But the whole situation was wildly, painfully funny, and if she didn't laugh, she'd burst into tears. When she decided to laugh, it was completely out of her control. She barely had time to turn around before the laughter burst from her lips. She clapped her hand over her mouth, but everyone knew exactly what she was doing. Ben was probably furious. He didn't like to be laughed at. But there was nothing Linda could do. If he didn't want to be laughed at, he shouldn't have gotten a tattoo that was going to droop someday.

The timer in Esther's pocket dinged loudly. "*Ach*," Esther said. "The first batch is done."

Linda took a deep breath, got control of herself, and turned back around as if nothing had happened. She was sorry to leave Esther with all those apricots, but she refused to stay, especially since Ben was looking at her as if she'd just run over a cat with her buggy. "Cathy and I have to go."

"We do?" Cathy said.

Linda smiled sweetly at Zoe. "But you should stay for dinner." Esther twitched beside her. "We haven't finished canning the apricots yet. You'd be a great help."

Esther understood and nodded enthusiastically. "You and Ben could both help. Only one more bushel to get in bottles."

Zoe pulled her phone from her back pocket. "It's getting late. Bennie and I should get going."

Esther curled her hand around Ben's right shoulder. Did the skeleton beneath his shirt cross her mind? It definitely crossed Linda's. She cleared her throat and looked away. "Won't you stay for dinner?" Esther said. "Winnie would love to see you. You haven't been around for a while."

Zoe took Ben's arm in both of her hands and dragged him away from Esther. "Come on, Bennie. It's a Friday night. Let's get out of here."

Ben resisted for a few seconds then gave in. Without looking at Esther, he said, "I've got to go. Tell Levi I need to talk to him. And give Winnie a kiss for me."

Esther sighed. "Be safe."

Without making eye contact with any of them, Ben climbed into the truck and slammed the door behind him. He didn't buckle his seat belt.

They could hear Zoe's truck long after it disappeared down the road.

Linda stretched a wide smile across her face, but there

wasn't much hope of cheering Esther up, or herself for that matter. "Well, at least now we can help you finish the apricots."

"And join us for dinner," Esther said.

Cathy's gaze was riveted in the direction the truck had gone. "Mark my words, that tattoo is going to droop. I hope I'm around to see it."

Chapter Thirteen

Her pillowcase was wet again, both sides. For a girl who prided herself on being sensible and unsentimental, she certainly cried a lot. At least she did when no one could see or hear her. Linda's family certainly didn't suspect anything was wrong, except maybe three days ago when Mamm looked at her funny and asked her if she was coming down with something.

Linda got out of bed, tiptoed down the hall, and pulled a clean, dry pillowcase from the closet. She had to be extra quiet because the linen closet was right outside Mamm and Dat's room, and she would be mortified if they woke up. Linda went back to the room she shared with Nora and changed her pillowcase so she could sleep without her cheek getting soggy. That was, if she could sleep at all.

This was getting silly—all this lost sleep over a boy. And not just any boy, but Ben Kiem, the wildest and stupidest boy in the district. She should be relieved that Ben didn't want anything to do with her. She should thank him for rejecting her. He'd saved her from a future of certain heartache.

Why couldn't she have fallen in love with Freeman Sensenig? Or even Simeon Beiler. Ever since that night at the park when Simeon had decided to join them for volleyball instead of go with Ben and Wally, Simeon had stayed securely attached to Mary Ann and the rest of *die youngie* who did normal things like play croquet and go to *singeons*. Simeon was even trying to quit smoking. He'd asked Linda for some essential oils to help him with the headaches.

Why couldn't she have fallen in love with him? *Ach, vell,* she would have had to compete with Mary Ann, and Mary Ann was prettier and more deserving.

Ben had not attended church this morning, and because he was the bishop's son, there was gossip. Everyone felt sorry for the bishop and his wife. What a misfortune to have a son like Ben! The rumor was that the bishop had finally kicked Ben out of his house. Nobody was sure where he was staying now, except Linda, who was certain that Esther and Levi had taken him in. Levi was a faithful *bruder*, and Esther had a soft spot for Ben. Esther's own wayward sister had lived with her for many weeks.

But if Ben was living with Esther and Levi, they were keeping it a big secret. They probably wanted to avoid the gossip and the condemnation they would surely get if people knew that someone as bad as Ben Kiem was sheltered in their home. But Linda suspected that's where Ben was by the stiff way Levi held himself during services and the way Esther avoided everyone's gaze and tried to act normal. It was hard to believe everything was normal at Esther's house when she had showed up to church with a celery stick tucked behind her ear.

There were rumors that Ben and Wally got drunk every

night and went around looking for mischief. Angry, profane words had been spray-painted on the Palmers' barn a few days ago. The Gregersons' house had been broken into last week, but nothing had been stolen but some food from the fridge. Of course no one knew for sure if Ben and Wally were responsible, but when things went bad in the community, they were the first ones blamed. Most people, even Linda, had no doubt Ben and Wally were the culprits for everything bad that went on. Who else could it be? It wasn't like Ben was hiding his wickedness. He wanted people to think he was the worst kind of person.

Well, he'd succeeded.

Linda lay back down and pounded her pillow to soften it up. Oh, how she wished she didn't care. How she wished her heart didn't ache every time she heard Ben's name or saw a red truck. *Ach*, how she wanted to be that practical, unfeeling girl she had always believed she was. But as Mamm said, "If wishes were horses, beggars would ride." She had to quit wishing for things to be different than they were and start trying to change them. And that meant no more crying into her pillow at night or thinking about Ben during the day. That meant dating a boy she could actually marry and moving on with her life.

Linda bolted upright when someone tapped softly on her bedroom window. What in the world? Pulse racing wildly, Linda glanced at Nora sleeping peacefully, got out of bed again, and pulled the curtains aside.

She wasn't sure what she was expecting on the other side of the pane, but it wasn't this. Cathy held the flashlight of her phone pointing upward below her chin, and the effect was terrifying. She looked like a ghost or some sort of eerie spirit. She turned her phone around so Linda could read the screen. "Come with me right now," it said.

Linda paused and glanced behind her. Was she dreaming? It didn't feel like she was dreaming. The wood floor was cool on her feet, and she could still smell the freshly laundered pillowcase she'd been resting her head on.

Cathy turned her phone around and typed something else. She wasn't very fast, but Linda couldn't complain. Linda didn't know how to text at all. Cathy showed Linda the screen again. "Ben is in trouble. We need to help him."

Linda's heart lodged in her throat. She swallowed hard three times, but she couldn't get rid of that suffocating feeling. How did Cathy know Ben was in trouble? Was there really anything they could do to help? Was Linda going to start being realistic and practical or not? Because if she was, that meant forgetting any feelings she ever had for Ben and letting him suffer the consequences of his own actions. He was just another boy in the *gmayna*, and he should go to his family and friends for help, not a girl he barely knew.

Linda stood at the window in her nightgown, struggling to breath and struggling to be sensible. She didn't owe Ben anything, and he had no hold over her.

Ach. If only that was true. Ben had an iron-fisted grip on her heart. It was why she cried herself to sleep every night and why she would go and help him now. Ben might hate her, but she couldn't refuse help to someone who needed her. She could sort out the consequences and the heartache later.

Linda nodded at Cathy and shut the curtain. Her pulse pounded savagely in her ears as she got dressed, being careful not to wake Nora. In a moment of good sense, she jotted off a quick note to Mamm in case she wasn't back before morning. That was the responsible and practical thing to do. Ben might not care how many people he hurt, but Linda did. Mamm would be worried sick if she woke up and Linda had disappeared.

Linda sneaked out the back door and around to the front of the house where Cathy was parked in her car with the engine running and the lights turned off. "I'm sorry to wake you," Cathy said, sounding extraordinarily annoyed, "but Ben woke me up, and I wanted to share the joy."

"What happened? Where is he?"

Cathy put the car in drive, turned on her headlights, and pulled onto the road. "His chickens have finally come home to roost."

"What? What about chickens?"

"He's at some house in Monte Vista. A friend of Zoe's. He didn't say, but it sounds like things there are getting out of control. Zoe won't leave, so he asked me to come and get him."

Linda couldn't understand it. Ben usually would have simply walked home. That's what he did from the sand dunes. "Is he hurt?"

"I don't know, but don't get your hopes up. He sounded slightly drunk."

Linda folded her arms and stared out the window. "My hopes up about what?"

"Hopes that he's changed or suddenly grown a brain."

"Don't worry. I've given up hope where Ben is concerned."

Cathy nodded. "It's best to be realistic."

Realistic. That's exactly what Linda wanted to be. Still,

the thought of him in trouble felt like a hundred-pound weight around her neck. "Let's get this over with."

"I agree. I get precious little sleep already as it is."

"Why did Ben call you?" Linda said.

Cathy shrugged and squinted into the darkness. "He has my number memorized, and I might be the only reasonable person he knows who also owns a car."

Linda frowned. "Why did you invite me?"

Cathy glanced at her phone and turned onto a side road. "That was pretty clever of me, don't you think, using my phone to communicate through the window? I didn't want to wake your mom. She never would have let you come."

"But why me?"

"Well," Cathy said, as if it were the most obvious thing in the world, "of course I asked you. We're a team, like Sonny and Cher or Siegfried and Roy. I saw them in Vegas, though I don't usually talk about that dark time." She scrunched her lips to one side of her face. "My husband offered to come, but it takes thirty minutes to get his walker and him in the car, and Ben would have been waiting until Christmas. Lon used to be an EMT, and he has his very own police scanner. He agreed to listen on the scanner and let us know if there's trouble."

A police scanner? Surely Ben wasn't in that kind of trouble.

Cathy turned down another street. "I didn't want to go alone because an eighty-three-year-old woman should not be on the road by herself after midnight. I came to you because I didn't want to burden Ben's family with this. Esther and Levi need their sleep, and Ben's dad would probably do a lot of yelling. Ben doesn't need more yelling." Cathy gave Linda a grumpy, sleepy smile. "I want Ben to see a friendly face."

Linda felt the compliment thread its way up her spine. "I don't know if Ben wants to see me."

"He doesn't think he does," Cathy said. "But you are truly the only person he wants to see. I still don't think he's good enough for you, but he does have good taste."

Cathy glanced at her phone one more time. Linda didn't like that it took her attention from the road, but she wasn't about to tell Cathy how to drive. Lord willing, they wouldn't get into an accident.

They came to a house with a waist-high hedge lining the front and sides of the yard and an orange mailbox to the side of the driveway. Four cars were parked on the street side of the hedge. It looked like a party.

Linda gasped. Cathy's headlights shone on a solitary figure sitting on the ground next to the mailbox, holding his head in his hands. "I think it's Ben," she said, pointing out the window.

Linda jumped like water on a hot skillet when Cathy's phone rang. Cathy pulled up next to Ben and answered her phone. Linda rolled down her window. "Ben?" she said.

Ben looked up, revealing a bloody lip and a huge purple bruise on his swollen cheek. His eyes narrowed to slits. "What are you doing here?"

Linda tamped down her anger and reminded herself she was only here because Cathy shouldn't be out on the road by herself at night. It had nothing to do with Ben. She gave him her fakest smile. "Nice to see you too."

Ben stood up, but he looked a little unsteady on his feet. "Go away. I don't want you here. I'll walk."

She needed to hang out with Ben more often. This kind of behavior made her less and less likely to feel any sadness at all for what she had lost. "You can walk if you want, but in your state, you'll probably get lost and fall in a ditch."

"I'm not drunk, if that's what you think."

She looked straight ahead out the windshield. "I'm sure I don't care."

"Just go away," he said, tapping his hand on the roof of Cathy's car.

"We came all the way out here. You might as well get in. It would be silly to walk home when you have a perfectly *gute* ride."

"I don't care what you think."

"*Gute*, because what I'm thinking isn't very nice."

Ben walked in front of the car and stumbled into the street. Linda didn't know if he was drunk or hurt, but he had to have been in a very bad way to call Cathy for a ride. Cathy said Ben needed to see a friendly face. She didn't need to chastise him. He was already fully aware of how foolish he looked. Would it kill Linda to show him a little sympathy? Maybe a little kindness? Convinced that it actually might kill her but she should do it anyway, Linda heaved a sigh and jumped out of the car. "Ben, wait. Please come with us. We'll take you home. We need to take a look at that ankle, and I've got some wonderful *gute* essential oils we can put on that lip."

Ben turned, and the lines around his eyes softened. For a brief moment, she saw the Ben she used to love. His lips twitched upward. "Don't even think about it."

Cathy rolled down her window. "That was my husband.

The police are on their way. They think someone is selling drugs in there. Get in, Ben, and let's get out of here."

Ben caught his breath and snapped his gaze toward the house. "They *are* selling drugs in there. I knew I had to get out, and I made some people mad. Zoe wouldn't take me home."

"Let's go," Cathy said. "Lon says we've got about ten minutes."

"I've got to get Wally first."

Cathy shook her head. "There's no time."

Linda pressed her lips together. "Wally made his choice. He'll learn from the consequences. We need to go."

Ben scrubbed his fingers through his hair. "I've been stupid. Wally's been stupid, but I can't leave him. It would kill him to get arrested."

"Might do him some good," Cathy said.

"No!" Ben said, his eyes wild with fear. "We've got to get Wally out of there."

Linda thought she was going to be sick. "Ben . . ."

Ben scrubbed his fingers through his hair. "If you have to go, go. I won't leave without Wally."

Linda glanced doubtfully at Cathy. "Okay. Go get him. We'll wait."

Ben sprinted toward the house, limping painfully as he went.

Linda got back in the car. "We will wait, won't we, Cathy?"

Cathy grunted. "I suppose, but if I get arrested, I'm holding you responsible."

In horrible suspense, they watched the clock on Cathy's dashboard. Dread grew like toxic mold in Linda's chest. "It's been five minutes."

Cathy checked her phone. "He said it was a party. Maybe he stopped to eat a piece of cake."

Linda wasn't quite sure what came over her, but she jumped out of the car. "I'm going in," she said.

Cathy slid out her side, a little slower than Linda, but no less determined. "I'm going with you."

"No, Cathy. It's not safe."

Cathy came around the car and started up the driveway. "I've been in worse situations."

When all this was over, Linda would love to hear all about those worse situations, but right now, she had to concentrate on not passing out from fright. Not waiting for Cathy, she marched up the driveway, climbed the front steps, and threw the door open. She definitely interrupted something. Maybe a dozen young people sat or stood in the front room, and they all turned when she burst through the door. A stocky, scowling man clutched Ben's T-shirt collar, and Ben's hands were likewise wrapped around the other man's collar. Zoe looked as if she was trying to stop a fight, with her arm and shoulder sort of wedged between the two of them, but it wasn't going to do much good when push came to shove.

"Linda, get out of here," Ben yelled.

"I'm not leaving without you," Linda said, with more courage than she felt. Her knees wobbled, and she seriously thought she would fall over before she could find her way back out the door. She looked around the room. Wally stood against the far wall next to a painting of some trees, looking like he wanted to be anywhere but there. "Wally," Linda said. "We're going. Come with us."

"Oh, look, it's Wally's Amish mommy come to fetch

him home," someone said. "Have you got to milk the cows, Wally?"

Wally squared his shoulder and put on that bravado he wore like a tight pair of pants. "I already told Ben. I'm not going anywhere."

Zoe grunted and shoved the stocky man away from Ben. "Just let him go, Kevin. He doesn't have to stay."

Ben's breathing was labored and angry. He held out his hand to Wally. "Come on, Wally. Let's go."

Wally folded his arms across his chest and shook his head. "I'm staying."

"Young man, you should be ashamed of yourself."

Linda turned around. Cathy stood in the threshold, fierce in her fluorescent purple sweat suit, glaring at Wally with all the force of her eighty-three-year-old stink eye.

The room fell silent, either from fear or complete shock. "Linda and I went through all the inconvenience to come out here and pick you up, and you're not going to give us any trouble." She looked at each person in the room as if she was staring into their souls. "You should all be ashamed of yourselves. What would your mothers say about your behavior? God doesn't take kindly to children who break their mothers' hearts."

Still, nobody said anything. Cathy pointed at Wally. "You should be grateful you have friends who care enough about you to want to help. And you should be especially grateful to me. I had to walk all the way up the driveway on a sore bunion just because you're too stubborn to know what's good for you. Now, show some respect for an old lady, and get in my car."

Linda couldn't hide her complete surprise when Wally lowered his head, stuffed his hands in his pockets, and shuffled to the front door. Cathy moved aside and let him out.

Cathy pointed at Zoe. "You too, young lady. You're too nice a girl to be caught up with this crowd."

Linda didn't believe that Zoe was too nice a girl for anything, but Zoe bit her bottom lip, nodded at Cathy, and followed Wally out. Linda never would have believed it if she hadn't seen it. Ben purposefully shoved his arm against the stocky man's shoulder as he passed, but the stocky guy was probably too befuddled to take offense. Cathy had given quite a performance.

Linda was already dumbfounded, but she was shocked to the point of dizziness when Ben took her hand and tugged her forcefully out of the house. But she didn't have time to be irritated or confused or pleased or whatever she might have felt, because a police car with flashing lights pulled up to the house and parked directly in front of the driveway.

Ben's eyes went wide. "Wally, Zoe, go. Go!"

Wally and Zoe took off down the porch steps and sprinted across the lawn in the opposite direction of the police car. Wally cleared the side yard hedge in a single bound. Zoe sort of shoved through it to the other side. Ouch. That had to hurt.

Linda's heart beat so fast, she could barely speak. She pushed the words out anyway. "Ben, you have to go."

"I'm not leaving you," he said, a determined desperation in his voice.

That declaration comforted and terrified her. Ben would somehow protect her. But that made no sense. He couldn't protect her. He was going to get arrested, and it would be her fault. Thank Derr Herr, her practical side crashed through her fear. "We came all this way to help you. Go now!"

Cathy came out of the house and shut the door behind her. She saw the police car. "Well, shoot." She shoved Ben down the stairs. "Get out of here."

Ben's eyes were wild with fear. "I won't leave you."

"Run, Ben," Cathy growled. "Linda is Amish. They won't bother her. And the police do not arrest women my age. They don't think we're capable of committing crimes. It's pure ageism, if you ask me."

The conflict on Ben's face was heart wrenching. This was the Ben Kiem she had fallen in love with. The boy who was so loyal he willingly sacrificed everything for his friends. The boy who cared so deeply that it terrified him.

Linda wrapped her fingers around Ben's arm. "We'll be okay. Please go."

In his eyes, she saw the painful moment when he made his decision. Despite his injured ankle, he took off across the yard and leaped over the hedge like Wally had done. Half a second later, the police got out of their car and headed up the driveway.

Cathy nudged Linda. "Let me do the talking. I've always been able to negotiate myself out of a speeding ticket."

Linda nodded. She couldn't have said a word if her life depended on it.

Cathy waved the policeman closer. "Officer, I'm glad you're here. I was just about to call the police. There's some sort of loud party going on in there, and my friend and I came over to complain about it."

The police officer tipped his hat. "You live around here, ma'am?"

Cathy paused as if she didn't understand the question. "Not exactly. Linda and I were in the neighborhood. That's my K-car parked out front."

The officer scratched his head. "Yeah. We noticed it. I can't believe any of those are still on the road."

"They don't make 'em like they used to," Cathy said.

The police officer nodded. "Thank goodness." He glanced at his partner. "Well. Okay then. Thank you, ma'am. Now I need to ask you to go back to your K-car and go home. We'll take care of it from here."

"Okay," Cathy said, "but the party's over."

"Don't you worry about that, ma'am. We'll check it out."

"But the party really is over. They're all gone, except for maybe the cat. I think I saw a cat curled up on the couch. That would explain why my eyes are itchy and my nose is running. I'm allergic to cats. And pollen. I wish I would have known that before I knocked. I never would have gone in."

The officer's eyes nearly bulged out of his head. "You went in the house?"

"Yes. I told you, I came over to complain about the noisy party. I told them the police were coming, and they all cleared out the back."

"What? Jack, check in back."

The other policeman ran around the side of the house. Linda held her breath when he ran past the place where Ben had jumped the hedge, but Lord willing, Ben and his friends were long gone, probably in Zoe's big red truck.

Looking slightly irritated, the officer clenched his teeth. "Ma'am, thank you for all your help. You can go home now."

Cathy frowned, and a deep, wrinkly line appeared between her eyebrows. "Don't you want to take my statement?"

"If we need to talk to you again, we'll just look for the K-car. I think you own the only one left in Colorado."

Cathy shrugged. "Okay. I'll do anything I can to be helpful."

The policeman gave Cathy a politely annoyed smile. "Next time you encounter a noisy party, just call the police. We don't like it when our senior citizens put themselves in danger."

Cathy's nostrils flared, but she seemed perfectly calm when she replied. "I'll remember that, Officer. Thank you for your help." She linked her elbow around Linda's arm and pulled her over the sidewalk and down the driveway. She leaned her mouth closer to Linda's ear. "See what I told you? Ageism is alive and well. I would have given that boy a piece of my mind, but he let us go and didn't catch Ben, so I have to be satisfied."

Linda couldn't relax. She glanced back at the policeman. "Did you really tell them the police were coming?" she whispered.

Cathy shrugged. "I did. I hate the thought of drug dealers not getting their just desserts, but the one guy had a gun. He could have shot us or the police. He could have shot Ben, but he didn't. I guess you could consider it a thank-you gift. Besides, if they'd gotten arrested, they might have taken it out on Wally or Zoe later, and neither of them deserve that, even though they've been pretty stupid."

"Why did you ask Zoe to come with us? She's the one who brought Ben here."

Cathy put her arm around Linda. "We girls have to stick together. Girl power, and all that."

Linda didn't know what girl power was, but she liked the idea of women watching out for each other. And she liked the idea of Cathy being leader of the Girl Power Club.

At the end of the driveway, Cathy eyed the orange mailbox. "Broncos fans," she said. "They should know better."

Back in the car, Linda suddenly felt extraordinarily weary, as if she'd climbed Mount Elbert three times in one day. She leaned her head back against the seat and tried to figure out exactly where things had gone horribly wrong. She kept coming back to the day Ben Kiem had hitched a ride on the buggy for a skiing trip. Did she regret that memory or cherish it? Did it matter? Ben had taken enough of her peace, her happiness, and her life. She wasn't going to let him take any more of it. She was done with him.

Being the practical and sensible girl she was, she pulled Ben Kiem from her heart and left her feelings on the side of the road next to the Denver Broncos mailbox.

Goodbye, Ben, and good riddance.

Cathy started the car and pulled onto the road. A movement across the street caught Linda's eye. Ben stood in the shadows of a juniper bush, arms folded, gaze riveted to Cathy's car as they drove away.

Linda blinked back the tears. Ben was still watching out for her.

But she wasn't going to let herself care.

Chapter Fourteen

Walking was no way to go places, even if you were Amish. But when your friends ditched you and you refused to be in the same car with Linda Eicher, you didn't have much choice but to walk, even if putting weight on your ankle took your breath away and your lip was swollen to the size of a cherry.

The sun was just rising over the horizon when Ben finally turned down the road to Esther and Levi's house. Were they going to be happy to see him or mad he'd stayed out all night? Would they be glad he hadn't died in some ditch or mad that he'd left without telling them where he was going? He didn't know, and while he cared deeply about Levi and Esther, he was almost numb to their reaction. He was tired and in pain, and as long as they let him sleep there, even for one more night, he'd be grateful. It was definitely more than he deserved.

How had he sunk this low?

He hissed when he stepped on a pebble and his ankle buckled. Right now, he'd be grateful if he made it to Esther and Levi's at all.

He shuffled to the side of the road when he heard a car

behind him, but instead of driving by, the car stopped right next to him. He groaned inwardly. It was Cathy Larsen, no doubt come to scold him about his life.

She rolled down her window. "You look like something the cat dragged in."

"Thank you," he said, because he didn't have the energy to be rude, especially not to Cathy, who had really come through for him last night.

"Get in, and I'll take you the rest of the way."

Ben never wanted to do anything more in his entire life. His whole body ached, and his ankle was on fire. But he'd been humiliated enough for a lifetime. He didn't need Cathy to make him feel worse. "I'll walk."

Cathy rolled her eyes. "If you're trying to prove your manhood, don't bother. I've seen you at your worst, or at least, I hope last night was the worst I'm ever going to see from you. You went pretty low, and I should know. I watch *Law and Order*."

"I don't need you to preach to me."

"I'm not preaching. And you could do permanent damage to that ankle if you keep walking on it. I should know. My husband has two pins in his elbow."

Ben took a step forward, and the pain shot up his leg. He gasped. For some reason, the possibility of a ride made it impossible for him to go farther on his own. Whatever pride he had left died on the side of the road. He raised his injured leg and hopped to Cathy's car.

He got in the back seat because it was too hard to hop all the way around the car to the passenger side. As soon as he got in and shut the door, Cathy drove forward. It was only another quarter of a mile, but the ride was a tremendous blessing all the same. He should probably thank her, but all he could do was close his eyes and try to push the pain from his mind. There was so much pain, and his ankle was the least of it.

Cathy pulled up to Esther and Levi's house, turned off the engine, and got out. Was she coming for breakfast? *Ach*, if she got in the house, he'd be forced to sit through one of her lectures. Ben slid out of his seat and limped around the side of the car, bracing himself against it so he wouldn't fall over. "Cathy, you don't need to see me to the door. I'm fine."

"I'm not here to see you to the door. I'm here to make sure Esther and Levi know what you've done. I've got a feeling you won't tell them on your own."

Ben sighed and shook his head. "Please don't. I've hurt them enough already."

Cathy squared her shoulders and made the most of her five-foot height. "You sure have. I was beginning to wonder if you can't think of anyone but yourself, but then last night, you proved me wrong. You're not completely hopeless, and I'm willing to give you another chance."

"What do you mean?"

Cathy pulled her purse from the passenger seat of her car. "It would take all morning to write you out a list of all the stupid things you've done." She pinned Ben with a pointed look. "Breaking Linda's heart would be on the top of that list."

Ben's gut clenched. He'd broken Linda's heart? *Nae*, that couldn't be true. Linda hated him, at least she did now.

"But Esther and Levi will want to know that you stood by your friends last night. You saved Wally and Zoe from possibly going to jail, even though they didn't appreciate it at the time."

Ben lowered his head. "Thank you for talking Wally into leaving. He's the only friend I have left."

"That's not true, even though you think it is. Wally is the only friend you haven't pushed away with your stubborn pride. I swear, Ben, you can be so thick."

"I'm not worth your time, Cathy."

Cathy snorted. "Well, mostly that's true. But Linda told me how you refused to leave her after you all got out of the house."

A lump lodged in Ben's throat. "She didn't deserve to be caught up in all that."

Cathy raised an eyebrow. "At least we can agree on something." She turned and walked up Esther's sidewalk. "Linda says she has some essential oils for your face, though I don't know that anything will help. You'll never be quite as handsome again. Smoking does that to you."

Ben had nothing to say to that. What did it matter how he looked when his soul was so ugly? "Don't bother Linda. I don't like essential oils anyway, and she shouldn't waste her time."

"Don't I know it," Cathy said.

Ben followed Cathy to the porch, hopping all the way. "I think they're asleep. Why don't you come back another time?"

"Another time?" Cathy said. "It's almost seven o'clock. They're up."

Ben opened the door and met a very angry Esther standing in the hall. She propped her hands on her hips and glared at Ben as if she was trying to catch his shirt on fire. A small wire whisk was tucked behind her ear, like she'd been whipping up some cream and had to find a place to put the whisk to answer the door. When she caught sight of his face, a look of sympathy traveled briefly across her features before disappearing altogether. She scowled harder. "Where have you been? We've been worried sick."

"You should have been," Cathy said. "Ben got himself into a lot of trouble."

Levi came into the front hall, took one look at Ben's face, and pulled him in for a bracing hug. Esther had a temper. Levi was usually more sympathetic. "*Mein bruder*," Levi said, squeezing Ben so tightly, he nearly crushed the wind out of him. "*Ach, mein bruder*. What happened?"

Esther seemed to grow impatient with Levi's show of affection. She raised an eyebrow. "And where have you been?"

Cathy bustled into the house, nudging Levi, Ben, and Esther aside on her way to the kitchen. "Make some room, make some room. You don't want to smother him before he's had a chance to explain." Was she taking his side now? Ben would never be able to understand Cathy Larsen.

"*Jah*," Levi said, patting Ben on the shoulder. "*Cum reu*. You need some strong *kaffee* and a *gute* breakfast."

"I think what he needs is a kick in the *hinnerdale*," Esther said.

Cathy grunted in amusement. "Believe me, he's been kicked just about everywhere else."

Ben hissed as Esther laid her hand on his bruised cheek. "*Ach, bruder*. When are you ever going to learn?" Ben didn't think he could feel any lower than he already did. He didn't deserve Esther's tenderness. She didn't need to treat him kindly. It only made him feel worse.

Esther took his hand and led him down the hall to the

kitchen. He held his breath and tried to walk normally, but his ankle ached so badly, he couldn't help but limp. "*Ach*, what have you done to yourself?" Esther said. "I refuse to give you more stitches."

Winnie sat in her highchair eating scrambled eggs, spoon in one hand and a fistful of eggs in the other. "Beh!" she cried when she saw him. Ben did his best to smile, but his heart wasn't in it. He wasn't good enough for Winnie. He wasn't good enough for any of them.

"A very big *Englischer* stepped on my ankle," Ben said, easing into a chair at the table. "No stitches needed."

Esther scooted another chair next to him and sat down. She pulled his leg onto her lap and pushed up his pant leg. "*Ach*, *du lieva*, Ben. It's swollen like an overgrown zucchini."

"He stepped pretty hard."

"Levi, can you hand me a bag of frozen corn from the freezer?" Levi did as he was told then pulled up a chair on the other side of Ben. "Would you like to sit down, Cathy?"

"Of course." Cathy sat next to Ben, and Levi sat next to Winnie. *Ach*. That was all he needed, all these eyes staring at him, wanting an explanation, when he was eager to crawl into a hole and never come out.

Esther set the bag of corn on Ben's ankle. He grimaced. Cradling his foot in her hands, Esther stood slowly. Then she set his foot gently on the chair. She turned and grabbed some supplies from that one well-stocked drawer she'd used a dozen times when she needed to tend to Ben's injuries. She came at him with a wet rag and some soap, and he pulled his face away before she did something he'd regret.

"Ben," Esther scolded. "We have to clean this up. Your lip is bleeding, your cheek is bluish purple, and your eye is almost swollen shut. Let me help you."

Ben surrendered and held still while Esther tortured his face with a wet rag. "Now," Esther said softly, "you had best tell us what happened."

Cathy huffed out a breath. "Some Denver Broncos fans were doing a drug deal. Ben wanted to leave, but Zoe wouldn't take him home. So he called me."

Esther looked at Cathy as if she had a carrot sticking out of her ear. "He called you?"

"I'm the only person he knows who owns a car and likes a little adventure. *And* I haven't had my bunion surgery yet, so I can still drive. And I have a police scanner."

Levi chuckled, glanced at Ben, and took a swig of the small glass of milk on the table that Ben suspected was Winnie's. "Why don't you tell us what happened. Is it possible the police will show up this morning?"

Ben's embarrassment was profound, but it looked as if Cathy was going to take the long way around the story, and Esther was getting more and more agitated. "Zoe took me and Wally to a party. But it wasn't a party. There were two men selling drugs, and I knew I shouldn't be there."

Cathy nodded at Levi. "He's not as dumb as most people think."

Ben sighed. He was dumber. "I tried to get Wally and Zoe to leave, but Zoe has a crush on one of the guys, and Wally wasn't thinking straight. The one man, Kevin, punched me in the face a couple of times when I tried to leave, and the other one stomped on my ankle. I borrowed Zoe's phone and called Cathy, because I couldn't walk and

I wanted to get out of there. They finally let me out of the house."

"*Ach*, how terrible," Esther said.

Cathy nodded to Esther. "But here's where it gets really good."

Or really bad. "When Cathy got there, she said the police were coming." He decided not to mention Linda.

"Lon has a police scanner."

"I couldn't leave Wally in there. I don't know what he would do if he got arrested. So I went back in to get him, but he wouldn't come out. Cathy came in and convinced Wally to come with us. She even got Zoe out of there." Ben glanced at Cathy. "I'm wonderful grateful."

"Sometimes a grandmother figure is what you youngsters need. But that's not all. The police came, and Ben refused to leave Linda. He was worried about her."

Esther's eyes grew big. "You dragged Linda into this?"

Ben drew back when she pressed his lip too hard. "That wasn't my fault."

"I invited Linda," Cathy said. "She wasn't much help, except she ruffled Ben's feathers a bit. I always like to see that. And she convinced Ben she'd be okay, so he finally jumped over the hedge. I talked the police out of arresting us, and then we came home. We had to leave Ben there because the police would have been suspicious if we picked up a stranger on our way out of the neighborhood."

Esther dabbed at Ben's lip with her rag. "*Ach*. When will you learn, Ben? You can't play with fire and not get burned."

"Do you have to pile my sins on my head? You said you wouldn't mention the Bateman fire again."

She sighed. "I'm not talking about the Bateman fire. I'm talking about your life."

Levi looked at Ben, his eyes full of tender emotions. "You're safe now, and it's over. We will speak no more of it."

Esther turned and looked at Levi as if she wanted to argue, but Levi just pinched his lips together and raised an eyebrow.

Esther heaved a great sigh. "Oh, alright. Fine. We won't mention it, but please, please don't put us through that again. Neither of us slept a wink last night for worrying about you. I was forced to take out my pickleball paddle and pound it against the house just to make myself feel better."

Cathy nodded at Ben. "Remember that when you think what you do doesn't hurt anybody else."

There was a firm knock on the door, and Esther left to answer it. Esther said hello, and someone gave a soft reply. Ben's heart galloped around his chest. Though he couldn't tell what they were saying, it only took him half a second to know it was Linda at the door. Her voice was like a familiar song he knew by heart. He tensed. Lord willing, Esther wouldn't invite her in. He didn't want Linda to see him like this, and for sure and certain, after last night, Linda wouldn't want to lay eyes on him again.

A lump of regret and longing lodged in his throat as he strained his ears to hear what they were saying. His heart sank when he heard Linda step into the house and Linda and Esther walk slowly down the hall. Linda didn't smile when she saw him, but she didn't look away either, as if she just didn't care what he thought anymore, as if she'd grown indifferent in six short hours. She looked tired, but she was still the most beautiful girl Ben had ever seen.

"You're up early," Cathy said. "Especially after our adventure last night."

Linda seemed to try harder for Cathy. She smiled, but her smile was anything but natural. "It was quite an adventure." Her gaze flicked in Esther's direction. "I suppose Ben told you all about it."

Esther pursed her lips. "I'm sorry you were involved."

"Well, I can't say it was fun, but I can say I've never done anything like that before. My heart has never pounded so hard, like it was clawing to get out of my chest." She held out her hand. "Look, I'm still shaking."

"That's the adrenaline," Cathy said. "It can last for hours."

The thought of Linda in danger made Ben physically ill and struck him dumb.

"I'm sorry Ben put you through that," Esther said.

Linda gave Esther a small smile. "Cathy invited me, and I chose to go."

Esther frowned. "For sure and certain you didn't know what you were getting into."

"Cathy said Ben was in trouble. That's all I needed to hear." Linda's face turned red.

Ben felt the warmth of Linda's meaning like a mug of hot chocolate on a chilly night. The sensation spread from his chest through his entire body. She couldn't know what those words meant to him. She cared about him. On some level, deep or shallow, she cared. "You . . . you probably weren't expecting a fistfight or the police or Kevin."

"Or the Denver Broncos mailbox," Cathy added.

The ghost of a smile traveled across Linda's face. "I definitely wasn't expecting Kevin."

"I'm sorry," he said softly.

"I made the choice. I faced the consequences." Something like painful resolve flashed in her eyes.

After an awkward pause where Ben and Linda stared at each other for what seemed like three weeks, Linda turned away from him and squared her shoulders. Whatever had just passed between them disappeared like morning mist. Linda fished in her bag and pulled out two small bottles. "I brought some essential oils for Ben."

Essential oils. It had always been a joke between them. Ben longed to say something about peppermint or lavender or anything that would make Linda smile for real. But he couldn't think of one thing. There was too much pain between them to find anything funny in their situation. He swallowed hard. He couldn't pretend that he wasn't the one responsible for that pain. Everything was his fault, but that didn't mean he knew how to fix it.

Linda handed the oils to Esther. "This is frankincense for the bruising. And this is myrrh for his cut lip."

"It's Christmas in July," Cathy said.

Linda glanced at Ben's leg, which was propped on Esther's chair. "I should have brought something for his ankle."

Esther shook her head. "Frozen corn will do the trick."

"I'm . . . it's okay. I'm fine," Ben said.

Esther and Linda both paused and looked at him as if he was making a nuisance of himself. Esther set the oils on the table. "Would you like to stay for breakfast, Linda? We're having eggs and Raisin Bran."

"*Denki*," Linda said. "But I don't want to keep Freeman waiting. He was so kind to bring me."

Levi furrowed his brow, which was exactly what Ben would have done if he hadn't been trying to hide his emotions. "It's kind of early for a buggy ride," Levi said.

Linda seemed to want to look anywhere but at Ben. "*Ach*, I know. He comes every morning to help me with my chores. Mamm pays him extra money to care for our horses."

How long had this been going on? It couldn't have been more than a few weeks. Linda hadn't mentioned Freeman once in all the time they'd spent together.

"Still," Cathy said. "That's going the extra mile to bring you here to Esther's house on an errand."

Linda cleared her throat. "After what happened last night, Freeman told me he'd take me anywhere I wanted to go, day or night. I think he's a little overanxious."

Cathy scrunched her lips together. "You don't need Freeman. I'll always take you wherever you want to go."

Jah. Linda should listen to Cathy. Ben ground his teeth together. He was the one who should be watching out for Linda, not some lovesick Amish boy who didn't know a snowshoe from a water ski. Did Freeman know how to scare a bear away? Did he even know the first thing about paddling a canoe?

Linda glanced at Ben and quickly looked away. "I have to go. Tell me how those essential oils work out."

"*Denki* for bringing them," Esther said. She and Linda walked out of the kitchen. "Come anytime," he heard Esther call. That was just wishful thinking. Ben had a feeling that as long as he was living here, Linda would refuse to cross Esther's threshold.

Like a winter avalanche, something big and wide shifted inside Ben. Here he was, *again*, sitting in Esther's kitchen while she fussed and worried over him as if she truly cared about him, as if she loved him in spite of all the bad things he had done. Levi had welcomed Ben into his home as if Ben had never made a bad decision in his life, as if the things he'd done hadn't irreparably hurt his family. Linda brought him essential oils as if she still considered him a friend, and she had looked at him like maybe she had spoken the truth when she'd told him she loved him.

Esther came back into the kitchen and poured herself a bowl of Raisin Bran, watching Ben out of the corner of her eye the whole time. "Such a nice girl, that Linda."

"I always hear good sense from her mouth," Levi said.

Cathy folded her arms. "I know Freeman very well, and he's a good sort of man. Anyone willing to drive Linda over here at seven in the morning sounds like he's dedicated."

"Freeman doesn't know how to ski," Ben murmured. It was the worst thing Ben could say about him. Freeman was Ben's superior in every way, and the truth felt like a hot coal against his skin.

The avalanche inside Ben's head finally buried him. He needed Linda like he needed to breathe, and he'd pushed her away and said a thousand terrible things and given her every reason to hate him. All because he was too afraid of loving her. Ben slid his leg off Esther's chair, propped his elbows on the table, and buried his face in his hands. "Freeman deserves her. I never did," he moaned. Great sobs wracked his body, and he lost himself to despair.

Chapter Fifteen

"Beh? Beh? Onkel Beh." Someone had taken Winnie out of her highchair, and she was standing next to Ben where he sat at the table. Watching Ben curiously, she patted his leg and babbled in her own special language, half *Deitsch*, half gibberish.

"She said *onkel*," Levi whispered, as if not wanting to interrupt the conversation between his daughter and his *bruder*.

Ben couldn't resist those wide, curious eyes. He took a deep breath, wiped his cheeks, and lifted Winnie onto his lap. Winnie turned around to look at him, took his face between her chubby hands, and kissed him on the nose. "Owie," she said, tapping her finger to the bruise on his face.

Esther, Levi, and Cathy sat around the table staring at him unapologetically, like he hadn't just made a fool of himself. Levi tilted his head as if studying every line of Ben's face. "Freeman Sensenig never got a kiss from Winnie. She saves them for only a handful of very special people."

"That doesn't make me special," Ben said. "Winnie just hasn't met Freeman yet."

Esther scolded him with her eyes. "It makes you very special to me. How many people love my daughter the way you do?" Esther's eyes softened at the corners. "You are the most frustrating boy I know. Next to Levi, of course."

Levi chuckled and tipped his head in her direction. "*Denki, heartzley.*"

"I want to understand," Esther said. "Why did you reject Linda? At the sand dunes, she told you she loved you, and you accused her of pretending. Why did you say all those *hesslich* things to her?"

"And then you ran off, and we spent an hour looking for you," Cathy said, as if Ben hadn't heard it at least six times already.

Esther reached out and squeezed Ben's arm. "Did you really think Linda chose you as a project?"

Ben lowered his eyes. He didn't believe that then, and he certainly didn't believe that now. But the truth was harder to explain, even harder to make them understand.

Levi's low voice felt like a warm blanket around Ben's shoulders. "Ben doesn't want to be hurt again."

Ben took a deep shuddering breath and tightened his arms around Winnie.

Cathy narrowed her eyes. "Did your last girlfriend dump you?"

"Nothing like that," Levi said. He glanced at Esther with a sad smile on his face. "Ben fell in love with his schoolteacher."

Ben squeezed his eyes shut in an effort to block out the memory. It had dogged him for eight years.

"Oh, dear," Cathy said. "That sounds like a recipe for disaster."

Ben pressed his fingers to his forehead. Cathy had no idea.

"Everybody in the community knows about it," Esther said.

"They don't know the whole story." Levi searched Ben's face. Ben looked away. He didn't care who knew. Levi took Ben's avoidance as permission to tell. "The teacher, Magdalena, probably didn't realize what she was doing, but she singled Ben out his last year of school. Some of *die kinner* called him the teacher's pet. She praised his schoolwork when she should have been teaching him humility. She made him the teacher's helper and gave him the biggest part in the Christmas play."

Ben winced, feeling the pain all over again.

"Magdalena was pretty and sweet and gave him a lot of unnecessary attention." Levi cleared his throat. "I'm sorry, Ben. Do you mind if I tell this?"

Ben turned his face away. "It doesn't matter."

Esther patted him on the shoulder. "It's your story, Ben. Tell us what happened." The compassion in her voice nearly unraveled his composure, but Levi was going to sugarcoat it or get it wrong, and Esther needed to see once and for all what a hopeless boy he was. "It's foolish, but I loved Magdalena."

"It's not foolish," said Esther. "You were fourteen years old."

Cathy nodded. "Teenage boys are not known for rational thought."

"I wanted to impress her, give her a big gift for Christmas. I didn't have any money, and I couldn't ask *dat*. So I stole a music box from a store and gave it to Magdalena as a gift. It was pretty and played music. She loved it until she found out it had been stolen. Then she was furious. I embarrassed her in front of the whole community. I damaged her reputation as a teacher. The school board talked about firing her."

Levi sighed. "I'll not judge Magdalena, but she didn't show Ben forgiveness. She wanted revenge."

"Or maybe just restitution," Ben said.

"She made sure everyone knew what Ben had done, made sure people knew it wasn't her fault."

Ben pushed his fingers through his hair. "She made me sit in a corner for the rest of the school year. And she scolded the others if they were nice to me. She called me horrible names in front of the other children, making sure everyone knew that she felt nothing but disdain for me. She wanted to prove that she'd never liked me."

"I'm sorry," Levi said. "I didn't know that."

Ben couldn't look at anyone. "My friends weren't allowed to play with me. Their parents didn't want their children associating with a thief."

"Parents don't realize what they are teaching their children in the name of protecting them," Cathy said. "But I suppose we all do things out of fear that we regret later. Fear shouldn't be our reason for doing anything."

Ben drew his brows together. Sometimes Cathy said things that were worth paying attention to. "Wally was my only friend. No one liked him either."

"For a boy hungry for friendship and love," Cathy said, "Wally must have been a life jacket in deep waters."

Ben nodded. "He was." Despite all his faults, Wally had always stuck by Ben, until last night.

Levi's eyes pooled with tears. "Dat was harsh. Mamm

was heartbroken. I should have been a better *bruder* to you."

"You were always a *gute bruder*, Levi."

"I wasn't. You got into trouble because you were ashamed and hurt and you wanted to lash out and make people hurt as much as you were hurting. I had just started *rumschpringe*. I didn't want to be bothered with you. I was finding my own way and didn't like my little brother tagging along."

Ben eyed Levi as if he'd never seen him before. Levi thought Ben's fall was his fault? "I don't blame you, Levi."

"I blame myself."

Esther stirred her soggy cereal. "Linda didn't seem to care about your past."

"I guess not." They wouldn't stop staring, and Ben was too tired to hide anymore. He kept his gaze glued to Winnie's face. "I don't want to love her. Loving someone gives them permission to hurt you."

"Love is not a weakness, Ben," Esther said.

"It is when you get hurt. Sooner or later, Linda was going to realize that she didn't really love me. How could she love me?" He pointed to his swollen eye. "Look at me. No one could love this. No one could love who I truly am."

"Linda does."

Ben shook his head adamantly. "Not even Linda. And it was only a matter of time before she figured it out."

"So you accused her of making you her project so you wouldn't have to tell her the truth."

"I don't know what I did. I just had to get away from her."

Cathy acted as if she finally understood. "So you decided to speed up the process by hanging out with Zoe and spray painting Palmers' barn. You're just so dumb, Ben."

"Yes, I am."

Esther grabbed his hand as if to keep him from falling off a cliff. "No, you're not," she said, giving Cathy a reproachful look. "You're smart and sweet, kind and loyal. Can't you see that?"

"All I can see is that I've lost Linda, and I can't catch my breath because it hurts so much."

Levi stood and came around to Ben's side of the table. "I'm going to be a better brother to you starting now." Folding his arms, he leaned against the tabletop. "Linda still loves you."

Ben covered his face with his hand. "It's too late. I've made too many mistakes. I've said too many things I can't take back."

Levi planted a bracing grip on Ben's shoulder. "Did you hear me, *bruder*? Linda still loves you. That means it's not too late."

Ben blinked. "But how do you know?"

Esther burst into a smile. "It's obvious. She can't keep her gaze away from you. And she didn't need to bring those essential oils. You'll be fine without them."

Cathy nodded. "Much as I hate to admit it, Esther is right, though I wish Linda had more sense than that. She loves you, not Freeman, though he *is* my first choice. Last night she was so worried about you, she didn't care for her own safety. She ran into that house like she owned it. Didn't even bother checking for guns."

Tears rolled down Ben's face. "It's too late. I've made too many mistakes."

"No one can sink so low that the light of God's love can't find him," Levi said.

Ben shook his head. "There are so many sins laid to my charge. How can I hope to earn God's forgiveness?"

"You don't earn it, Ben. He gives it freely to the broken-hearted."

"Linda is always telling me I can't escape the consequences of my choices. The way I've treated her . . . there's no coming back from that. God might forgive me, but there's no reason Linda would. I've hurt her. She's smart enough to walk away. She doesn't need or want the pain I've caused her. I'm not worthy of her love. I don't know how to be the kind of man she deserves."

Esther took Winnie from Ben's lap and handed him a tissue. "Of course you do. You've always been that person, but you've buried him so deep, you don't think you can find him again."

Cathy scooted away from the table. "I'm not very impressed with you, Ben, but even I can see that you have some good qualities. You went back into the house last night to get Wally, even after he'd already refused to leave. Linda thinks you have a good heart, and I'm pretty sure she still loves you, or did until last night."

Ben fell silent. He barely dared hope, but hope was there, like a crack of light in a very dark place. If his foolishness hadn't driven Linda completely away, if she still felt a sliver of love for him, maybe he had a chance. Maybe he could quit trying so hard to convince everyone he was a lost cause and start trying to be someone worthy of Linda's heart.

Ben looked into the faces surrounding him. "Is there . . . do you think there's a chance for me?"

Esther smiled. "Of course."

Levi placed a hand on Ben's shoulder. "I want to help you. I want to be the *bruder* you needed eight years ago."

Esther bounced Winnie on her hip. "We all want to help you. We love you, Ben."

"I don't know why," he said, his voice cracking.

"Neither do I," said Cathy, "but for all your faults, you're irresistibly lovable."

Ben's heart tumbled all over itself. He loved Linda. He would let Gotte make him the kind of man Linda could love. His heart soared to the sky before crashing to the ground. "What if Linda marries Freeman before I can make it right?"

Levi sighed. "Then God has another plan."

"It would be wonderful *gute* if God's plan and my plan lined up."

Levi laughed. "I don't expect that happens very often, but God's plan is always the best one, no matter what."

Ben sighed. "I hope you're right." But if he couldn't win Linda, he didn't care about any other plan.

His love for Linda was the only thing that mattered.

Chapter Sixteen

Linda smiled so much her cheeks hurt. Dat always said that if you wanted to feel happy, you should pretend to be happy until you *were* happy. Usually if Linda was in a bad mood, smiling made her feel better, even if she didn't feel like smiling.

Today wasn't one of those days. She had whistled a painfully cheery tune while gathering eggs and mucking out the barn. She'd smiled all the way to work and all the way back. She'd laughed at customers' jokes, even if they weren't funny, and she'd spread extra jam on her roll at dinner even though Mamm gave her the stink eye.

Nope. She didn't feel any better. She hadn't felt better for weeks, and all the smiling was getting her was a headache and premature wrinkle lines around her mouth. She really should give up smiling altogether. There was nothing, absolutely nothing, to smile about.

And here she was again, at the only city park in Byler, hanging out with *die youngie* and trying not to think about Ben Kiem and his aggravatingly handsome face. She was also making an extra effort not to think about the way he'd refused to leave her, even when he thought he would get arrested, or the way he held her in his arms right after they saw the bear.

Linda sighed, popped the last piece of pretzel into her mouth, and squared her shoulders. She refused to think about Ben for one more minute. It wasn't practical, it wasn't healthy, and it was completely futile. Ben might as well have lived in another state or been born a hundred years before her. He was nobody she needed to worry about, and she was wasting her energy pining for him.

"Do you want to play volleyball, Linda?" Freeman said. "We could be on the same team."

She should be worrying about Freeman, who came every morning to help with the horses and looked at Linda as if she were a chocolate donut with sprinkles on top. *Ach.* Freeman was a wonderful nice boy, but she didn't love him. She knew what love felt like, and Freeman wasn't it. She pressed her lips together. She hadn't started out loving Ben either. Maybe she shouldn't give up so easily. Freeman might be the very man to help her forget Ben. It wasn't likely, but she should at least give the relationship half a chance.

"I'll join you in a minute," she said.

"Okay," Freeman said. "I'll save you a place next to me."

Ach. Who saved places in volleyball? Apparently Freeman, who was getting too attached to Linda when she didn't even know if she wanted him to. She didn't have the heart to play volleyball. She didn't have the heart for anything. Ben had completely ruined every good memory of snowshoeing, camping, and hiking she ever had.

A buggy crawled slowly up the road before pulling into

the parking lot. Ben and his little sister Ellen got out, and Linda almost lost her lunch. And her dinner. What was he doing here? Didn't he know he wasn't wanted?

He wore a cream-colored shirt with suspenders and dark trousers and looked very typically Amish. He would have fit in with any Amish gathering where people didn't know what he truly was.

Ben put his arm around Ellen and said something to her that Linda was too far away to hear. *Ach*, yes. This was Ellen's first time at a gathering. She had just turned sixteen. It looked like Ben was trying to reassure her. A lump stuck in Linda's throat. Ben was always tender and sweet like that with the people he loved. It was one of his best qualities. He smiled at Ellen like a protective big *bruder* and nudged her toward Linda and the other young people.

Ellen ambled over tentatively, finding one of her friends in the small group. Ben leaned against the buggy, seemingly content to watch Ellen, but making no move to come closer. Linda breathed a sigh of relief and ignored the feeling of profound disappointment she had no business feeling. She had moved on from Ben Kiem. No reason to feel disappointed, especially since he'd ruin everything if he stayed. Nobody liked him, nobody wanted him around, and nobody was sorry that he didn't want to be part of the group.

The thought made Linda a little sad until she remembered that Ben was responsible for his own choices. He had to live with the consequences.

When you pick up one end of a stick, you pick up the other end too.

Linda didn't notice that Ellen had moved in her direction until she was standing right next to her. "*Vie gehts*, Linda?"

"*Hallo*, Ellen. It's *wunderbarr* to see you. Is this your first gathering?"

Ellen nodded eagerly. "But I'm not nervous or anything. Ben said I'm the second prettiest girl here and not to worry."

A genuine smile tugged at Linda's mouth. "Second prettiest? What a thing to say."

Ellen blushed to her toes. "He says you're the prettiest, and I don't mind being second to you."

Linda's mouth went dry. "*Ach*. That is very nice."

"Ben is nice to everyone, even though Dat says . . ." Ellen lowered her eyes. "I love Ben. He's just been through a rough patch, as Nanna likes to say. But on Sunday he told the whole family he's sorry and said he'd do all our chores from now on to make up for what he's done. Henry and Martha Mae cheered until Mamm told them they weren't getting out of chores, even if Ben is sorry."

Linda furrowed her brow. "*Ach*. I see."

"Ellen," someone behind them called. "Come play volleyball."

Ellen's gaze flicked in the direction of the game. "I'm not very *gute*, but I like to play." She turned to go and then twirled back around. "*Ach*, I almost forgot. Ben has something to tell you, and he asked me to ask you if you wouldn't mind going over there and talking to him." She inclined her head toward Ben's buggy. "He doesn't want to impose—he said that three times. 'Be sure she knows I don't want to impose.' But if you will talk to him, he would be wonderful grateful."

Linda's heart leaped into her throat. She glanced at Ben, standing resolutely next to his buggy, as if the only reason he'd come was to talk to Linda. "What does he want to talk about?" Her voice sounded agitated, even to her.

Ellen shrugged. "I don't know. But he probably wants to apologize for something. He's been apologizing to everybody. He spent an hour and a half in Mamm and Dat's bedroom apologizing, and Levi says he went to that farmer down the road and apologized for the fire. Like I said, he's apologizing to everybody."

Linda didn't know if she believed it. Ben dug in his heels more often than he felt remorse for anything. Ben would rather blame someone else for his problems before he ever took responsibility for himself. Besides, the last person she wanted to talk to was Ben. Why would she want to stir up old memories that had taken her so much effort to bury? "Will you tell him he doesn't need to apologize to me? I'm fine. He can cross me off his list."

Ellen frowned. "He said you wouldn't want to talk to him, but he said to tell you that he'd follow you home and sit out on your porch until you talked to him. He says he's willing to sleep out there, and I don't know about you, but I'd rather not have a boy sleep on my porch. It would be strange."

So much for not wanting to impose. For sure and certain, Ben could be a *dumkoff* sometimes, like that time he quit cigarettes just because he wanted to beat her in a race. It was something she loved about him, even if she didn't love him anymore. "Okay. I'll talk to him," she said, if for no other reason than to get him to leave her alone once and for all.

"And remember, he said he doesn't want to impose."

Linda stifled a bitter laugh. Ben Kiem was the biggest imposition of her entire life.

"Linda, come play." Freeman motioned to her from the game.

Linda huffed out a breath. Boys! She was sick of the whole lot of them.

She thought about taking Ben a cookie or something from the eats table, but if he wanted a cookie that badly, he could just come over and get one himself. She glanced in his direction. Should she sneak behind his buggy, so no one saw her talking to Ben Kiem, the boy who burned down sheds and went to drug parties? Or should she march right over there so Ben knew she didn't really care what he thought about her?

She decided to march, to let Ben know how much of an inconvenience it was to go all the way across the park to hear what he had to say, which probably wasn't worth hearing. She didn't need or want an apology. Maybe she wouldn't even let him talk, just give him a piece of her mind or maybe a sermon on following the *Ordnung*. Then she could march away, and he wouldn't be able to catch her on that sore ankle.

Just in time, she reminded herself that Ben was simply another boy in the *gmayna*. She had no reason to be annoyed with him, no reason to feel hurt. She felt nothing for him but the general concern that every member of the body of Christ should feel for every other member. She'd forgiven him, and that was the end of it. But, oh, *sis yuscht*, how was she supposed to be indifferent when he was so handsome?

Even as handsome as he was, he didn't look very *gute*. There was a long, thin scab down his upper lip, and his cheek glowed purple with a tinge of yellow and blue, the lingering effects of the unfortunate incident last week. She pasted a smile onto her lips. A practical girl wouldn't be swayed by a few bruises and a pathetic face.

Slowing her pace, she stretched her smile tighter. *If you want to be happy, you have to act happy.* "*Hallo*, Ben. Ellen said you wanted to talk to me."

"I did," he said, his voice achingly deep and earnest. "I'm sorry to impose."

Too late for that apology.

"How are you?" he asked.

How are you? Surely that wasn't why he'd asked her to come all the way over here. "I'm fine," she said in clipped tones that hopefully broadcast her disinterest in anything he had to say.

He studied her face for what seemed like three years, his eyes deep pools of unhappiness. For a boy who had been so eager to talk, it seemed he had nothing to say.

She folded her arms. "Freeman really needs me in that volleyball game."

His eyes flashed at the mention of Freeman. It brought Linda a small measure of satisfaction even as she felt guilty for the emotion. It was wrong to use Freeman as a way to get back at Ben. It was all such a mess, and she wanted to go home and bury her head in her pillow. So, of course, she smiled like a cat.

"It's nice to see you, Ben. Your face is healing well, and it looks as if you didn't break your ankle. I'm *froh* for that." She turned to walk away. "Maybe we'll see you at *gmay* on Sunday." *Because I care about you as a member of the district, not for any other reason.* Hopefully, he caught the dismissal in her voice.

"Wait, Linda. Please wait." He took off his hat and scrubbed his fingers through his hair. "I just . . . I've rehearsed this in my head a hundred times, but there's so much to say and the words fill my mouth, but I can't speak."

The intensity of emotion she saw in his eyes nearly broke her heart. She remembered the first time she'd gone to Esther's house to pick up Ben for snowshoeing. She'd seen a boy who yearned for approval and ached for acceptance. She'd seen a boy who clutched his heart tightly to his chest, afraid someone would snatch it out of his hands and break it.

Linda pressed her lips together and looked away. She didn't care. She didn't care. "Ben, it's alright. I don't need an apology. I'm not going to pretend I wasn't upset, but you bear no responsibility for that. And everything turned out well. Please don't worry about it for another moment." The pained look on his face didn't go away. She sighed. What did he want her to say? "I need to get back." She glanced at the volleyball game. "But just so you know, you were never my project."

He nodded. "I know. I made that up to protect myself."

Well, at least he admitted it. "Okay. *Gute.* Take care of yourself."

"Wait, Linda." He reached out his hand as if to touch her but let it fall to his side. He was trembling. "Do you still feel the way you did that night at the sand dunes?"

She cocked an eyebrow and pretended to not understand the question. "Angry? Irritated? Glad I'd brought my flashlight?"

"You . . . you told me you loved me."

Nae, she wasn't going back to the sand dunes to sift through the memories. "That was a long time ago."

"Not that long."

She certainly wouldn't argue how long it had been. If she measured the time in sleepless nights and tears on her pillow, it had been a very long time indeed. "Did you have something you wanted to say to me?"

Ben limped a few feet closer, wincing with every step. "Linda, it's been so long since I've allowed myself to feel anything but anger and bitterness. But when I spent time with you, I finally felt like I could breathe, like I didn't have to play a part or meet your expectations. I didn't even know what had happened until I was in the middle of it. When I realized how I felt about you, it scared me. I was afraid that when you knew what kind of a person I really was, you'd reject me." He closed his eyes. "I couldn't go through that pain again, so I ran."

The memory of that night lodged like a shard of glass in her throat. "You said some very unfair things."

"I was harsh, and I hurt your feelings."

Linda shook her head. "It doesn't matter. It does no good to cry over spilt milk. I've forgiven you. You can forgive yourself."

"But that's just it. I can't forgive myself." He grabbed her upper arms and pulled her dangerously close. She was too stunned to pull away. "I'm tortured every day knowing what I've lost." He seemed to come to himself. Releasing her arms, he grimaced and stepped away from her. "I'm sorry. I shouldn't have . . ." He pressed his fingers to his forehead. "I love you, Linda, and I always will."

Linda's heart felt like a lumbering, heavy freight train thudding inside her chest. How dare he say this to her?

Didn't he know he'd burned all his bridges? Didn't he know she had been forced to move on without him? "I don't know that I believe you," she said. "When you love someone, you don't hurt them."

"I'm sorry I hurt you."

Ach. She shouldn't have said that. It made her look weak. "I didn't mean you hurt me specifically. I just meant that if you love someone, you should treat them better than you treated me."

"For sure and certain," he said. "I'm sorry."

"You don't have to apologize. I forgive you." She nearly turned on her heels and marched away, but she was honest enough with herself to know she didn't sound sincere or truly forgiving. And the look on his face was pure agony. She sighed and tried for a genuine smile, which turned out to be impossible. "Ben, I truly do forgive you. Please don't worry about it anymore."

"I do want your forgiveness, Linda, for sure and certain, but I also want your love." Pain and longing etched deep lines into his face. "I'm not asking you to wait for me. That wouldn't be fair, not after all I've put you through, but starting right now, I'm going to be a better man. I've stopped drinking. I've stopped smoking. I'm not seeing Zoe anymore, and I've apologized to my parents. Someday I'm going to be the man you deserve."

The fiery intensity in his eyes sent Linda's heart racing. A man like Ben, armed with virtue and purpose, would be formidable indeed. But she didn't dare count on him. In the past, his resolve had been as strong as tissue paper. "I . . . I don't know what to say, Ben."

"Say it's not too late."

"It's not fair for you to ask me that."

"You're right."

She couldn't stand the thought of hurting him, and she would never, ever be cruel, but she had to protect her own heart. Getting it stomped on once was enough pain for a lifetime. She looked down at her hands. "It just . . . it just hurt so bad. You went out of your way to do things to upset me. You wanted me to stop loving you, didn't you?"

"I wanted to prove that it was impossible to love me."

And that was why she couldn't assure him. Ben had proven himself unpredictable and reckless, and Linda couldn't count on anything he said, even if she used to love him. Even if he still had a large piece of her heart. "I worked hard to get over you," she said. "I'm sorry, Ben, but I have to be practical. I hope all the best for you, but I won't make a promise I can't keep."

"I wouldn't want you to." What little light he had in his eyes faded to nothing.

She glanced behind her. "I . . . I need to get back."

"I know," he said flatly. "An urgent volleyball game."

She had convinced herself that Ben couldn't hurt her anymore, but her heart ached so sharply she couldn't breathe. "May the Lord be with you," she said.

"I meant what I said. I'll be worthy of you someday, Linda, and I won't trouble you again until I am."

Linda turned and walked away before the tears began to flow. Ben certainly didn't need to see that. She certainly didn't need to look back.

Chapter Seventeen

"I shouldn't have come," Linda whispered, as she spread mayonnaise on a slice of bread.

Mary Ann rolled her eyes. "Nonsense. Surely it's not still awkward between you and Ben."

Awkward? Linda couldn't keep her gaze from straying to Ben every ten seconds, and Ben was completely ignoring her. It wasn't awkward. It was downright agonizing. If he loved her, why did Ben persist in avoiding her, going out of his way to stay at least twenty feet away from her at all times?

Linda immediately chastised herself for such a foolish thought. Of course she wanted Ben to stay away. She had to protect herself, and being around Ben was dangerous. And what did she expect? The last time they talked, she had given Ben a wonderful harsh set-down.

Linda and Mary Ann and a dozen other women, Amish and *Englisch* alike, stood under the Batemans' maple tree in an assembly line of sorts making sandwiches for the noon meal. Cathy was at the front of the line, putting slices of bread on paper plates, alternating between whole wheat and white. Linda was the mayonnaise spreader,

Mary Ann was in charge of mustard and horseradish sauce, which alternated between sandwiches. All the whole wheat sandwiches got mustard. All the white got horseradish. It was a *gute* way to keep the two kinds of sandwiches separate, but Linda felt bad for the men who preferred whole wheat with horseradish. They were going to be disappointed. Esther was on tomato and lettuce duty. Everybody got tomatoes and lettuce whether they wanted them or not.

At least twenty-five men and boys, Amish and *Englisch*, and a few *Englisch* women were working on erecting a steel building on Bateman's property. After Ben had apologized to him, Mr. Bateman had asked Ben if he could organize a group to build him a garage for his truck and tractor. Mr. Bateman had paid to have the cement poured, and all the neighbors had come together to put up the building. It was as close to an old-fashioned barn raising as it got. It was a community event.

Ben's ex-girlfriend Zoe was there too, though she didn't look at all comfortable. She was at the far end of the table, cutting sandwiches in half and setting them at the end of the table for easy pickup. While Ben hadn't ignored Zoe like he had Linda, there didn't seem to be anything particular between them. Cathy was the one who had invited Zoe, and she had come in her red truck and brought her hammer.

Linda gave into the temptation to glance in Ben's direction again. He was hefting long pieces of metal from the truck and stacking them into a pile to use for the support beams on the garage. He had always had strong arms and broad shoulders, but they were even more noticeable when Ben did heavy lifting. His muscles bulged under the weight of the metal beams, and sweat dampened the back of his shirt. It was impossible to look away. Good thing Linda could spread mayonnaise and gawk at Ben at the same time.

Cathy handed Linda a plate with two pieces of bread on it. "No offense, but you're being a little stingy with the mayonnaise."

Linda pulled her gaze from the activity on the other side of the yard and looked at Cathy. "If you put too much on, the sandwich gets gloopy."

"True, but your mayonnaise is about three atoms thick. Trust me, they'll like more than less."

"Okay. I'll put more on." Linda scooped another dollop of mayonnaise out of the jar with her knife and found Ben again in the crowd.

Cathy noticed where Linda's gaze had strayed. "Ben looks like a different person. I can't say anything about the state of his soul, but he looks much better, don't you think?"

Linda felt her face get warm. She looked away and concentrated hard on getting just the right amount of mayonnaise on the slice of bread. "Um, yes. He looks good." Good was maybe an understatement. A month ago, he wore the dull expression of someone who drank too much and abused his body with little sleep and lots of cigarettes. Now he was almost unrecognizable, tan and energetic, working twice as fast as some of the other men and looking half as weary. His brown eyes seemed to dance as he interacted with the others, giving them instructions and organizing their work. It was *gute* Linda had such strong resolve when it came to Ben, or his strong jaw, thick eyebrows, and commanding presence would have made her giddy.

Cathy squinted in his direction. "I know you and Ben aren't dating anymore, but I think we should invite him to go swimming. I really want to see that tattoo."

An *Englisch* girl down the line nudged the girl next to her and pointed to the group of working men. "I don't mind making sandwiches when I have a view like this."

Linda pressed her lips together. She could definitely watch Ben work all day long, no matter what he was doing. And it really wasn't right to feel that way. A practical and sensible girl would remember that she had moved on, that Ben was likely to break her heart again if she gave him another chance, and that it was better to marry a dependable, faithful Amish boy than one who would leave her at the sand dunes in the middle of the night. Besides, she'd told him to his face that she wasn't interested. She'd look flighty if she changed her mind. And Linda was anything but flighty.

Cathy handed Linda the last slices of bread. "I'm going to move to the other end of the table and help Zoe pass out chips. Be sure you mind your mayonnaise."

Linda smiled. "I will."

She and Mary Ann finished spreading mayonnaise and mustard while they watched the metal supports go up. Simeon worked alongside Ben, following him with metal for the pile, helping him when something heavy required two people to carry it. Simeon didn't have the same need to ignore perfectly nice Amish girls making sandwiches. He set down a metal support, looked up at Mary Ann, and waved. Mary Ann giggled and waved back with a paper towel in her hand.

"Simeon has changed," Linda said, nudging Mary Ann with her elbow. "It's all your doing. He likes you."

Mary Ann turned red as a beet. "Simeon wants to do what's right. He just needed some encouragement." She eyed Linda. "Ben has changed too."

Linda pulled her gaze from Ben. "He has, I guess."

"So why are you still avoiding him?"

"I don't avoid him. I'm just a girl going about my life. We don't really have much to do with each other, kind of like me and most of the boys in the *gmayna*." Linda watched Ben throw a beam over his shoulder and carry it up a ladder. She swallowed hard. Ben was not like most of the boys in the *gmayna*. "Besides, he acts like I don't exist."

Mary Ann snorted her disapproval. "Acts like you don't exist? He hovers around you like a moth to a light."

"He does not. He won't come within ten feet of me."

"It's not the distance that matters so much as the connection," Mary Ann said. "You pull him into your orbit like the Earth attracts the moon."

"I have no idea what you're talking about. I never was *gute* at science."

Mary Ann squeezed Linda's hand, getting a smear of mayonnaise on her finger. "Everything, *everything* Ben does is for you. Do you realize that?"

Linda's heart drummed an uneven rhythm. She didn't dare hope that was true, and even if it was, how long before Ben got bored with his life and ran off with Zoe or started smoking cigars? "Ben apologized to the entire *gmayna*, scrubbed spray paint off the sidewalk by the library and helped Jim Palmer bring in his hay. None of those things have anything to do with me."

Mary Ann nodded. "They have everything to do with how Ben feels about you. I've never seen a boy so single-minded in my entire life."

"He hasn't said a word to me for a whole month." But shouldn't she be happy about that? He was honoring her wishes and doing his best not to bother her. What more could she want?

"Well, you don't give him any encouragement. You've got to light a match if you want to start a fire."

Linda slumped her shoulders. "I don't want to get hurt again."

"That's silly, Linda. Isn't that why Ben broke things off with you in the first place? Because he didn't want to risk getting hurt again?"

Silly. Linda sucked in a breath as a memory hit her between the eyes. Ben hated that word. His disgusted expression at being called silly always made her smile.

Mary Ann spread the mustard on the final slice of bread. "You've got to take some risks. I can't believe I have to tell you that. You ski and hike and swim. You're braver than any girl I know."

Practical Linda warred with her sentimental side, but she didn't really have a sentimental side, so it wasn't much of a battle. Had Ben really changed, or was his transformation temporary? Did she truly want to give him another chance to break her heart? His change of heart certainly seemed more permanent this time. Esther had told Linda about the alcohol withdrawals, which sounded even worse than the cigarette withdrawals. According to Esther, Wally wouldn't leave Ben alone, harassing him all hours of the day and night, trying to get him to go out drinking or partying with him and his *Englisch* friends. But Ben hadn't gone out with Wally once, even though he didn't have any other friends.

Once the sandwiches were ready to go, Cathy whistled loudly to call all the men and boys to eat. Linda wasn't sure who had put Cathy in charge, but since she seemed so eager to do it, nobody protested. The entire group gathered, and Cathy said a blessing on the food. Everyone, men and women, lined up for a sandwich. Ben kept letting others go before him, and he was soon at the back of the line. Linda's throat got tighter and tighter the closer Ben inched toward her in the line. There were three boxes containing small bags of chips. Cathy assigned Linda the Cheetos box. Linda had never seen Ben eat a Cheeto. Surely he didn't like them. She wouldn't even have to talk to him.

"*Denki* for making lunch for us."

She'd been concentrating so hard on not watching Ben creep closer that she jumped out of her skin when she looked up and he was standing right in front of her. She yanked her arm out of the Cheetos box, bumping it hard with her elbow. It overturned and tumbled to the ground. Bright orange bags of Cheetos scattered across the grass in every direction.

"*Ach, du lieva*," Linda said. She couldn't have chosen a worse time to be clumsy. She knelt down, turned the box right side up, and started filling it with Cheetos bags.

"Here, let me help."

"No need. I can do it."

"I want to help." Ben got down on his hands and knees and crawled under the table to her side. Now he was eye level with Linda and so close she could see the faint growth of whiskers on his jaw.

He picked up a bag and handed it to her.

"*Denki*," she said, making the mistake of looking into his eyes. They were dotted with little flecks of gold and so deep she could definitely drown in them. *Ach*, she was going to faint. But she wouldn't faint because sensible girls did not faint.

He leaned closer, and time seemed to stop as they stared at each other. Then he reached out his hand and brushed his thumb tenderly down her cheek. She instinctively pulled away. He pointed to her face. "You, uh, you had a piece of grass right there."

"*Ach*. Okay. *Denki*," Linda said breathlessly. She hadn't been this close to Ben since she'd told him she loved him at the sand dunes. She reached under the table to pick up the last chip bag, lifted her head too fast, and banged it against the bottom of the table. She gasped and pressed her palm to the top of her head.

Ben wrapped his hands around her upper arms. "Are you okay?"

She couldn't speak, couldn't move. His touch was firm but gentle, his eyes full of concern. It felt so good to be this close to him again. So good and so perilous. His hands fell from her arms as she quickly shoved the last bag into the box. "*Jah*. I'm okay."

"Can I do anything for you?"

She gritted her teeth, unwilling to let his compassion steal her resolve. "*Nae*." She pushed the box of chips in his direction. "Um, well, take a bag of Cheetos, if you want."

A half-smile curled onto his lips. "*Denki*. I love Cheetos."

"I do too," she said, even though at that moment, she couldn't remember if she liked Cheetos or not. He turned to crawl back under the table to get to the other side. "Oh, uh, the white bread sandwiches have horseradish," Linda said. "The whole wheat ones are mustard. I know you like horseradish, so I wanted to warn you."

He gazed at her, his eyes shining. "You remembered."

"I . . . uh. *Jah*." Of course she remembered. How could she forget that day in the meadow at the top of Rock Creek Trail when he was so appreciative of the sandwich she'd made for him? How could she forget the way Ben had pressed forward even though his leg was bleeding? She'd always remember the way he looked at her when the valley came into view. *Jah*. She remembered all right. She'd never been happier than in the times she'd spent with Ben, and all she had left were memories, memories she wanted to pack in a box and forget. *Ach*, how she wished she could forget.

He stared at her as if he was going to say something then seemed to think better of it. He stood and walked around the table. He must have decided it was easier than crawling.

He got back in line and picked up a plate with a white bread sandwich. He smiled at Zoe and talked with her for a minute. Linda caught her bottom lip between her teeth. Did Ben still have feelings for Zoe? Did he ever have feelings for her, or was he just hanging out with Zoe to annoy Linda? It didn't seem like he had feelings for her now. He was polite and friendly but didn't betray any particular interest in her.

Ben didn't even so much as glance at Linda again. And suddenly she craved his attention so badly her stomach hurt. Why did she still feel this way? She should be over

Ben by now, and the way her heart fluttered and her thoughts raced wildly from one thought to the next almost made her wish he had ignored her altogether.

Once everyone was served, they sat on the grass under the shade of Bateman's two large trees and ate lunch. Linda steered clear of Ben's side of the yard, and sat with Cathy, Mary Ann, Zoe, and newly-married Mayne Schmucker.

Cathy twitched her lips in disgust. "I don't know why I took this sandwich. It's a gluten nightmare."

"I'm sorry, Grandma. I should have brought some gluten-free bread," Zoe said.

Mary Ann had only met Zoe once, that time in the park when they'd invited Simeon, Ben, and Wally to play volleyball. "*Ach*, is Cathy your grandmother?"

Cathy shook her head. "I've adopted Zoe as an honorary granddaughter."

"Both my grandmothers are dead," Zoe said. "Cathy agreed to be my grandma, and I really needed one that night at Kevin's house."

"We girls have to stick together," Cathy said.

Mayne eyed Zoe, sniffed once, and looked away. Zoe definitely wasn't the normal *Englisch* girl who came to these sorts of things. Mayne didn't understand how much Zoe had already changed. Her lips were a light shade of pink, and she'd done something different with her hair so it fell down over her ears in a more natural style. Her makeup was still dark and heavy, but she no longer had the thick black lines under her eyes.

"I like your hair," Linda said.

Zoe tucked a lock behind her ear. "Thanks. I'm growing it out and letting the natural color come in. I don't even exactly remember what my natural color is." She opened her bag of chips. "Linda, I wanted to thank you for coming with Cathy that night at Kevin's and for getting us out of there."

Linda shook her head. "I didn't really do anything."

"You cared enough to come. I was jealous that Ben and Wally had a community of friends who cared about them enough to come and get them. And then Cathy made me leave too, and I sort of felt like I had a family for the first time in my life."

Linda gave Zoe a tentative smile. Cathy was right. Girls needed to watch out for each other. Even though Ben had made a fool of himself with Zoe, Zoe was not Linda's enemy. "Zoe, I want to apologize."

"What for?"

"I called you Raccoon Girl behind your back. It wasn't nice."

Zoe smirked. "It's okay. I've heard worse. Besides, I get it. You were jealous."

Linda didn't dare comment on that. Of course she'd been jealous, but how did Zoe know? It was best to change the subject. "I haven't seen Wally for a while. Do you know how he's doing?"

Zoe crossed her legs and propped her elbows on her knees. "Not good. Ben's his best friend. They've always watched out for each other, like that night at Kevin's place. Even though Wally got mad at Ben for trying to protect him, he was grateful once he got out of there. But Wally feels like Ben has cut him off, abandoned him to be with the self-righteous Amish people." Zoe glanced at Linda and Mary Ann. "Sorry. That's just what Wally said. He's mad at Ben because Ben won't hang out with him anymore, and he's mad at Linda because he thinks it's all Linda's fault. Even I don't hang out with him very much. He likes to look for trouble, and he's so angry all the time."

Linda's heart sank. "He thinks it's my fault?"

"He needs counseling," Cathy said, squinting at the ingredients list on her bag of chips.

"Wally's looking to blame everyone but himself," Zoe said. "He'll get over it, but he sure misses Ben and Simeon."

Mary Ann kept casting longing glances in Simeon's direction. "Maybe we should go over and sit with Ben and Simeon." They were sitting by themselves apart from everyone else. "They look so lonely over there."

"This is a *gute* spot," Mayne said. "It's shady."

Cathy was oblivious to Mary Ann's eagerness. "They're fine. Ben's the broody, lone-wolf type. He likes being by himself."

Mary Ann frowned. "I don't think so. Ben doesn't want to make anyone uncomfortable, and Simeon doesn't want him to be alone."

"Why does he think he makes people uncomfortable?" Linda asked, even though she knew the answer as soon as the words came out of her mouth.

Zoe stretched her feet out in front of her. "It's not my place to tell you how to treat people, but he doesn't think he fits in anywhere, not even with you guys."

Mayne stuck her nose slightly into the air. "We can't just forgive them like nothing happened. They've got to prove themselves."

"*Nae*, Mayne," Mary Ann said, anger flashing in her eyes.

"That's exactly what we're supposed to do. Forgive them and never speak of it again. Forgive them immediately and completely."

Mayne sort of sputtered on her reply. "Well, I've . . . we've all forgiven them, but that doesn't mean we trust them. Ben was very nice to organize the *gmayna* to help build this garage, but he burned down Mr. Bateman's shed, and he's a liar and a thief."

Linda's chest tightened with indignation. A liar and a thief. Mayne was talking about something that happened eight years ago. Could she truly not let it go? This is how the *gmayna* had seen Ben for all these years. Ben had been rejected by the community, and he had made friends with Wally and later Simeon because no one else wanted anything to do with him. Ben and Simeon were trying to make amends for the bad things they'd done, but it was as if people in the district were waiting for them to mess up again. Was that happening all over again? How long would Ben keep trying to prove himself before he just gave up?

Linda couldn't breathe for the unfairness of it all.

Zoe picked at her fingernails. "With church friends like you, Ben doesn't need enemies."

Cathy shook her uneaten sandwich in Mayne's direction. "Do any of you people actually read the Bible? Haven't you heard the story of how Saul became Paul? From what I hear, all of you treated Ben like a leper."

Mary Ann nodded. "Yes, we did." Tears pooled in her eyes. "Everybody. Even me."

Cathy pointed her sandwich at Linda, but she was so

wholehearted about it, half of it broke off and fell in her lap. "Not everybody. Not Linda."

Mary Ann wiped her eyes. "You're right. Linda didn't treat Ben any different than she treated anyone else. She tried to help him."

"Ben was never my project," Linda said.

Cathy set what was left of her mangled and uneaten sandwich on her plate. "That's obvious. You would have given up a lot sooner than that if he was just your project."

Zoe eyed Linda. "You were always real nice to Ben. He said so."

Mayne glanced at Linda, confusion playing with irritation on her face. "So what is he to you?"

Linda was ashamed of herself. She was just as guilty as anyone else. But was she ostracizing Ben because she couldn't forgive him? Or because she was trying to protect herself? Ben had broken her heart. She still felt the pain like the point of a knife. But could she forget her pride and the pain Ben had caused her and just try to be his friend?

What *was* Ben Kiem to her?

She squared her shoulders and decided to be practical. There was no reason she and Ben couldn't be friends. She certainly wouldn't fall in love with him again. "You're right, Mary Ann. We should go and sit by Ben and Simeon. Simeon sneaked an extra cookie, and I want it."

Mayne's expression froze in place. "I'm very comfortable right here. I'll stay."

A line formed between Mary Ann's eyebrows. "*Ach*. Never mind. It looks like they're making some new friends."

Though she'd been determined not to look in Ben's direction, Linda turned around. In the course of five minutes, three girls from the *gmayna* and two *Englisch* girls had managed to sneak next to Ben and Simeon without Linda's noticing. They were making a lot of noise. How could you strike up a conversation and find things that funny to giggle about in a mere five minutes?

Ben and Simeon stood in the middle of the flock of girls, Simeon smiling and soaking up the attention, Ben more reserved, with a relatively pleasant look on his face. It was obvious that those girls, at least, didn't share Mayne's sentiments about Ben. Linda should have been glad that girls wanted to befriend Ben and Simeon. But she only felt extreme irritation, though she didn't know what else she should have expected. Ben was the handsomest boy in Colorado, probably the whole country. No matter how many people he'd offended, the girls were still attracted to him, even the *Englisch* girls. Linda's stomach hurt. Nothing *gute* would come of Ben associating with *Englisch* girls. How long before he was riding in their trucks and going to bars? He'd already been down that road with Zoe.

Linda swallowed past the lump in her throat. Ben was unpredictable and undependable. She was smart to protect herself.

There was another worry that Linda would never voice to anyone. In every way possible, Ben was superior to every other boy in the *gmayna*. How long before he realized it? Apparently, some of the other girls already had. How long before Ben forgot all about Linda in favor of another, prettier girl? The thought made her ill, even though it was what she told herself she wanted.

Cathy narrowed her eyes as she glanced at Ben, and the lines on her forehead folded on top of each other. "Well, okay then. I didn't want to have to try to stand up anyway. I deeply regret sitting on the ground in the first place."

Mary Ann looked like she was about ready to cry again. "We should have decided sooner. Now he'll think I'm just like Mayne."

Mayne gave Mary Ann a sour look. "What do you mean by that?"

Cathy patted Mary Ann's leg. "Don't you worry. Simeon hasn't been able to keep his eyes off you since he got here."

Mary Ann looked at Cathy as if she'd just offered to do all her chores for a month. "Do you really think so?"

Cathy nodded. "He's trying as hard to look at you as Ben is trying *not* to look at Linda. It's a little ridiculous. If people would just talk to each other, a lot of heartache could be avoided."

Linda sighed. Communication wasn't her problem with Ben. It was trust and forgiveness and the fact that Ben had rejected her love. And then she had rejected his. Because she had to be practical.

Oy, anyhow.

Did she really want to be the practical girl who spurned sentiment and missed out on love?

The giggling girls on the other side of the yard drew Linda's attention yet again. Wasn't Ben supposed to be putting up Bateman's garage? Why was he lollygagging in the shade when there was work to be done? He was wasting daylight.

"Linda." Freeman strode across the lawn with a wide smile on his face. "If I'd known you were going to be here, I would have come sooner."

"*Hallo*, Freeman," Linda said, not even standing up.

She liked Freeman, she really did, but she just couldn't muster any enthusiasm for him today. "Did you just get here?"

"*Jah*. I had to help my *dat* bring in some hay this morning."

Linda wouldn't have thought it possible, but Ben suddenly appeared next to Freeman. He must have sprinted from that side of the yard to this one. "*Vie gehts*, Freeman? I'm glad you're here. We could use your help with these support beams."

Freeman glanced at Linda and back to Ben. "*Ach*. Okay. Right now?"

"*Jah*. We want to get the skeleton up before dark."

Freeman seemed puzzled about why Ben was in such a hurry. Linda felt the same puzzlement. Not fifteen seconds ago, Ben was surrounded by a group of girls and didn't seem in a rush to get back to work at all. "Okay. I'll come." Freeman smiled at Linda. "Do you need me to drive you home later?"

Cathy picked up her ill-used sandwich and pointed it in Freeman's direction. "I can drive her home. She's not going to stay that long, and"—she glared at Ben—"she shouldn't have to wait."

Ben's confidence seemed to falter. He glanced at Freeman, eyed Cathy, then stared at Linda with a positively miserable look on his face. Ben placed a hand on Freeman's shoulder and firmly nudged him in the direction of the garage. "Let's go. I don't want the older men up on the ladders." He led Freeman away, and Freeman kept glancing back doubtfully at Linda as if he wasn't sure what he was getting himself into.

Cathy chuckled. "I love hanging out with you, Linda. There's always some sort of drama going on."

Linda watched as Ben pointed out the beams to Freeman. Then the two of them stood there and had some sort of a friendly chat as if they were the best of friends. They were either talking about construction or how fun it was to irritate practical, sensible Amish girls.

Either way, Linda had no interest in their conversation.

Chapter Eighteen

Esther slid the plate back into the dishwater. "You missed a spot."

Ben gave her the stink eye. "I did not."

"You're not paying attention, and there is a big glob of spaghetti sauce on the bottom."

Ben glanced at Esther. "Speaking of spaghetti, you have an uncooked spaghetti noodle behind your ear."

Esther pressed her hand to the side of her head. "Don't change the subject." She pulled a glass from the dish drainer. "Look at this. It's filmy. You've got to rinse better."

Ben examined the glass. "Now you're just being picky."

Esther giggled. "Don't you want a picky person inspecting the dishes you eat off of?"

Ben smiled. "If you don't like how I do the dishes, you can do them yourself."

Levi walked into the kitchen. He'd just put Winnie to bed. "You're not going to get out of dish duty that way."

"That's right," Esther said. "I'm sure you were hoping I'd just throw up my hands and decide it was easier to do it myself."

"That's exactly what I was hoping."

Levi shook his head. "None of those tricks work on Esther."

Esther laughed and gave Ben a side hug. "I've seen them all."

Ben shrugged and grinned playfully at his sister-in-law. "But don't you feel sorry for me? I'm getting dishpan hands." He pulled his hands out of the water and held them up for Esther and Levi to see.

"You're dripping on my clean floor, and is that a new blister?"

Ben studied the three blisters and two cuts on his hands. "This one is from pulling up that floor at the Mangums' house."

Levi nodded. "You should have seen him, Esther. He ripped out that floor so fast, dust was flying everywhere."

Esther wrapped her fingers around his wrist and pulled his hand toward her to get a closer look. "Chappy hands are the least of your problems. You've got three blisters, a purple fingernail, and calluses on your calluses."

Compassion traveled across Levi's face. "You've been working too hard, *bruder.*"

Ben didn't really want Levi's sympathy right now. He was trying very hard not to wallow in his own self-pity. "Well, if Esther didn't make me do the dishes, my life would be a lot easier."

Esther patted his cheek. That small sign of affection made Ben's heart hurt. "All for the love of Linda Eicher," she said. "I'm sorry."

Ben held his breath and let the pain wash over him. He refused to break down in front of Esther or Levi ever again. They felt sorry enough for him as it was. So he pretended it didn't hurt. Making a face, he pulled his hand from Esther's grasp and fished in the water for his dishrag. "Do you have to just blurt her name out like that?"

Esther laughed softly then gave him a sad smile. "I'm sorry. I know it's a sore subject."

Sore? Esther had no idea how sore it was. She had no idea how little sleep he got or how the heartache only got worse with each passing day. She had no idea how much it hurt or how often his regrets nearly suffocated him. "I just keep praying for Gotte to guide me. He seems to be giving me the silent treatment, but with the way I've lived my life thus far, I can't blame Gotte one bit."

Esther rinsed a plate under the water and set it in the dish drainer. "Ben, I have never seen anyone so determined to make up for his mistakes. You took charge of Mr. Bateman's garage. You apologized to everyone you've offended since you were seven. You have humbled yourself with your parents. You've helped in a community cleaning project, chopped wood for just about every family in the *gmayna*, and Cathy says you fixed her husband's walker."

"It just needed new tennis balls."

Levi squeezed himself between Esther and Ben. "Gotte doesn't withhold His love. The minute a sinner turns to Him for help, He will come running. He's not ignoring you. You simply can't see how He is working things out for your good."

Esther slid another plate into the cupboard. "Linda has a *gute* heart. I know she'll forgive you."

"*Ach*. She's forgiven me, but that doesn't mean she can love me."

Esther pulled the spaghetti noodle from behind her ear and snapped it in two. "You're very lovable, Ben. Once

Linda gets over feeling so hurt, she won't be able to resist you. I mean, you love children, you know how to chase away a bear, and you wash dishes. You're a catch."

"Linda doesn't think so."

"Just give it time, *bruder*."

Somebody rapped loudly on the door, and Levi went down the hall to answer it. The voice of the person on the porch was breathy and sharp. "Is Ben here?"

Esther glanced at Ben. Ben drew his brows together. Was that Zoe? And why did she sound so upset? He'd broken up with her weeks ago, and while she hadn't been happy about it, she'd only been drawn to Ben in the first place because dating an Amish boy had seemed exciting and unusual. In truth, she had found Ben interesting for a few weeks, but an Amish boy and an *Englisch* girl weren't likely to have any sort of long-term relationship. Besides, he'd kind of been using Zoe to upset Linda, and in very colorful language, Zoe had told him what a terrible thing that was to do to a girl.

Ben dried his hands and went to the front door. Zoe stood on the porch with a slightly wild, slightly panicked look in her eyes. "Ben, Linda's in trouble."

Linda's house was almost a twenty-minute drive from Esther and Levi's place, and Ben had never been so grateful that Cathy drove like her hair was on fire. Even then, by the time Cathy turned down Linda's road, Ben was frantic.

"This is what comes from too much alcohol and not enough brains," Cathy said, paying as much attention to Zoe as she did to the road. Ben would never complain about Cathy's driving, not when she drove him all over the valley without asking a cent, but he did clutch the door handle and pray he'd live long enough to stop whatever Wally was going to do.

Zoe's gaze flicked to the back seat. "I promise, Ben, I didn't give him any alcohol. Wally showed up at my house drunk, talking about how he was going to get back at Linda for stealing his best friend. I'm grounded from using my truck, so I called Cathy to come get me."

Ben's throat was so dry, it hurt to talk. "Didn't you try to talk him out of it? Calm him down?"

"You know how he gets, especially when he's been drinking. He loses all sense of reason. He doesn't have very much to begin with."

Ben shuddered. Wally was loyal, smart, and fun to be around when he was in a *gute* mood. Wally could make Ben laugh without even trying, and he had the uncanny ability to help Ben feel good about himself, even when Ben acted like an idiot. But Wally was also angry, troubled, and determined to hold a grudge. He took everything personally, like Mr. Bateman's spraying him with a hose or Linda's accusing him of being afraid to play volleyball. Wally also had a very stern and unyielding *fater*. There had been so much heartache in his life.

"All I know is that he better not touch a hair on Linda's head, or he'll have to answer to me," Cathy said.

"He still considers you his best friend, Ben," Zoe said. "And in his mind, his best friend would never abandon him like this unless someone put him up to it. You're trying to turn your life around for Linda. Wally sees Linda as a threat."

Ben buried his face in his hands. "I should have been

a better friend. I shouldn't have just cut him off like I did. I should have . . ."

Zoe sighed. "Ben, you asked him to help you build Bateman's garage. You encouraged him to stop smoking. You know that's not the way to persuade him. Wally sees you as one of them now. You did your best, but to Wally, it feels like a betrayal, a rejection. He's hurt."

"That's what I mean. I should have been a better friend. I know how I would have reacted if Wally had been the one to change. I would have resented it."

"Well, maybe it's not too late."

Dear Father in Heaven, please let it not be too late.

It wasn't quite dark when they pulled up in front of Linda's house. There was no sign of Wally, but that didn't mean he wasn't here. "Would you two knock on the front door and see if Linda's inside?" Ben said. "I'll go around to the barn."

Zoe made a face. "I don't see them giving me a warm welcome."

Cathy opened her door. "There's nothing to worry about. Amish are good folks, except Wally, and before two months ago, Ben."

Zoe got out of the car and slammed the door. "Okay, but you owe me one."

Zoe and Cathy crossed the lawn to the house, but it was slow going because Cathy had a bunion. Ben's heart was in his throat as he ran around to the back to look in the barn. Lord willing, Wally wasn't even here. Lord willing, he'd made threats that he never meant to carry out. Ben prayed harder than he ever had in his life. *Please, dear Lord, let Linda be okay.*

Both the front and back doors to the barn were wide

open, leaving plenty of light inside. Ben ran into the barn and stopped. He nearly jumped out of his skin when he heard Wally's voice coming from one of the stalls. "Ben was my friend until you turned him against me."

"What a silly thing to say."

Ben looked in two stalls before he found the right one. Linda stood with her back plastered against the far wall, her *kapp* gone, her hair falling out of her bun in a dozen different places. She looked more irritated than afraid. Ben should have expected that. A lot of things annoyed Linda, but very few things frightened her. His heart swelled as big as the sky. *Ach*, he loved her so much!

Wally's back was to Ben, his posture rigid, with Linda's *kapp* clutched in his hand like some prize he had won for being a bully. Ben yanked open the door and rushed into the stall.

Even though Linda hadn't seemed especially scared, she was definitely relieved to see Ben. The look she gave him only made his heart race faster. Fixing himself directly in front of Linda, he faced Wally and scowled like a badger. Wally was nearly as tall as Ben, but Ben was thicker. Wally would think twice about starting a fight. "What do you think you're doing?" Ben said.

Wally scowled back. "Teaching her a lesson."

"By scaring her?"

"I'm not scared," Linda said behind him.

Ben clenched his teeth until they squeaked. Was she deliberately trying to provoke Wally? Probably. He turned and pinned Linda with a stern look. "Could you just give up the need to be right for one minute?"

"I'm just telling you, bullies like Wally don't scare me. And he ripped off my *kapp*."

Ben gave up trying to get her to be quiet and looked at Wally. It was probably better to ignore the problem behind him while dealing with the problem in front of him.

Wally's nostrils flared. "See what I mean? Self-righteous girls don't care about boys like you and me, Ben. You'll never be one of them, no matter how hard you try. I'm your real friend, and I was long before Linda started paying attention to you."

"You have been a true friend to me, Wally. And you still are. You were my friend when no one else would be."

Wally seemed to get more agitated even as Ben tried to calm him down. Wally clutched a tuft of his hair in his fist and paced back and forth in the small space. "But now you've found new friends, and you treat me like dirt. I'm nothing to you. A nobody. You were my only friend, and Linda ruined it. She ruined you."

"She didn't ruin me, Wally. We both know that the way we were carrying on couldn't last. We were either going to get ourselves killed in some prank or get arrested. We very nearly got arrested. But Linda made me want to be a better man." He placed a firm hand on Wally's shoulder. "You don't have to keep living like this. You have it in you to be a better person."

Wally shoved Ben's hand away. "Don't preach to me. You've got nothing to say. I know who you really are. You can pretend to be righteous, but you're the biggest hypocrite in the world."

Wally's words hit their mark like buckshot from a shotgun. Ben *was* a hypocrite. Who was he fooling, trying to be a *gute* man, trying to be something he wasn't? Who was he to lecture Wally on changing his ways?

"That's not true," Linda said, her voice soft and soothing,

like a ribbon of water trickling over the rocks. "Gotte sees Ben's heart. The minute we repent and choose Gotte instead of our own selfishness is the minute we are changed. Ben always had a *gute* heart. He just didn't believe it. Gotte sees your heart too, Wally. He knows the pain and heartache you've borne in your life. He knows your sorrow and your fear. He knows your heart, and He loves you."

Ben kept his gaze focused on Wally, though he longed to see Linda's face. It was the most sensitive, sympathetic thing he'd ever heard her say. And he believed it. She was right. Gotte loved Ben for doing his best. Gotte loved him for trying and failing and trying again. Gotte saw his broken heart, and that was enough.

Wally threw Linda's *kapp* on the floor of the stall. "Save your breath. I'm not listening."

Ben expelled a long puff of air. "This is not Linda's fault. You're upset with me. This is between the two of us." He spread his arms. "If you want to punish me, punish me. Take out your anger on me. Hit me. Beat me up, but leave Linda alone."

Before Ben could draw another breath, Wally's fist shot out and caught Ben squarely in the nose. Searing pain accompanied a bright flash of light and the metallic taste of blood on his tongue.

"Wally!" Linda shouted.

Ben blinked to bring his eyes into focus as Wally stormed out of the stall and slammed the door behind him. He felt the warm trickle of blood from his nose as Linda pressed down on his shoulders. "Oh, *sis yuscht*, Ben. Sit down. You look like you're going to pass out."

That sounded like a *gute* idea since his legs felt like

jelly, and from the dark spots dotting the floor of the stall, he looked to be losing a lot of blood. Linda sat down next to him, pulled a tissue from her sleeve, and handed it to him. "You keep a tissue in your sleeve?" he said.

Linda pursed her lips. "For the times when I'm out milking, and I burst into tears for no reason."

Ben didn't even ask what those reasons might be. He was pretty sure he knew. He pressed the tissue to his nose, but it was soaked through in a matter of seconds. "I didn't think he'd actually do it."

Linda rolled her eyes. "It's the consequence of practically begging Wally to hit you."

Her unemotional common sense made him smile. "*Ach, vell.* I made the choice. I have to live with the consequences, right?"

Her lips twitched upward slightly. "It's what I always say." She pulled another tissue from her sleeve and gave it to him. Peering at him with those stunning blue eyes, she brushed her thumb gently across his cheekbone. The touch stole his breath and most of what was left of his reason. "I think your nose is broken."

"I don't know, but my ears are ringing."

The second tissue was soon saturated with blood. Linda grabbed his arm and pulled him toward her. "Here. Kneel up and lean your head forward. Pinch the bridge of your nose." She took off her apron, left the stall, and came back with a bucket of water. After dipping the apron in the water to get it wet, she rolled it up and placed it on the back of his neck. "This is supposed to help. I'm not sure if it really works, but it couldn't hurt."

Ben smiled to himself even though his head was already pounding. Every brush of her skin against his made his heart skip a beat. Having Linda fuss over him was worth every drop of blood. Of course, Linda's version of fussing over someone was giving them a lecture about how Gotte helps those who help themselves or finding the fastest and least fussy way to fix a problem. No fretting or sympathy from her.

Everything she did was so endearing.

He wanted to see that smile of hers. "I've been waiting and waiting for you to bring it up, but since you seem determined not to, I guess I'll have to ask."

She furrowed her brow. "What?"

"There must be an essential oil for broken noses."

There was that brilliant, blinding smile. *Ach*, he would hike a hundred mountains to see it. A thousand mountains to hear her laugh. She cuffed him on the shoulder. He winced. "I'm sure there is an essential oil for broken noses, but if you keep teasing me about it, I won't let you have any."

"Probably a *gute* thing. I would rather not smell like a rose bush."

She giggled, pressing the apron to the back of his neck and laying her hand on his arm. Ben just about went crazy at her touch. "How is the bleeding?"

Though he wanted to sit like this forever with Linda by his side and her hand on his arm, his knees were getting sore and the bleeding had slowed. "It's better," he said.

She took the apron off his neck and nudged his chin up with her finger. "Let me see." He shifted from his knees to a sitting position. "*Jah*," she said. "It has stopped, but your face is a mess." She dipped the apron in the bucket of water and dabbed at his face with the fabric.

"You're going to get blood stains on your apron."

"Blood stains are easy to get off." He winced when she pressed too hard near his nose. "Don't be a baby. I've got to clean your face."

"I'm not being a baby. Wally just broke my nose. Do you have any idea how bad that hurts?"

Her lips twitched in amusement. "All you do is whine." Ben growled at her, and her smile widened. "I'm joking. I'm sure it hurts something wonderful." Linda's smile faded, and the lines around her eyes softened. "*Denki* for saving me from Wally."

Remembering how frantic he was just a few minutes earlier, Ben took her hand and pressed it to his lips. "That was terrifying."

She glued her gaze to their hands. "I . . . I wasn't scared."

He couldn't help but chuckle. Linda was plenty stubborn in her own way. "Then I was scared enough for both of us."

"I was annoyed, and it was only a matter of time before I said something I'd regret, or worse, conked him on the head with the stall fork. He ripped off my *kapp* along with all the pins and a *gute* amount of hair. I probably have a bald spot."

Ben touched his thumb and finger to her chin and nudged her head to one side. "I don't see any bald spots."

"*Ach, vell*, the light is bad in here."

He smiled. "I'm *froh* he didn't hurt you."

Linda paused and studied his face. "I am too. I mean, I exercise regularly, and I'm in much better shape than he is, so I would have given him a *gute* fight, but I'm *froh* it didn't come to that. I didn't want to hurt him." She stood and held out her hand to help him up. "How did you know Wally was going to be here?"

"He went to Zoe's earlier. Zoe called Cathy, and Cathy drove us over."

Linda smiled. "We girls have to stick together." She sighed. "*Cum.* I'll take you into the house and see what essential oils Mamm suggests."

Ben laughed. "I was teasing."

Linda pumped her eyebrows up and down. "I don't tease about essential oils."

Ben looked down. Blood dotted the floor of the stall, and there were red smears everywhere on his shirt.

Linda touched a spot of blood on his collar. "For an Amish man, you sure get into a lot of fights."

"Does it make a difference that I don't hit back?"

Something important seemed to shift in Linda's expression. "*Jah.* It makes you more honorable than I could ever be."

The intense emotion on her face made his stomach do a cartwheel. "I'm not more honorable than anybody."

"You're wrong, Ben. You stick by your friends, forgive your enemies, and love with your whole heart. You're everything I want to be." She swallowed hard. "That's why I love you. I always will."

To his surprise, she threw herself into his arms and buried her face in his neck, even though she was bound to get blood on her dress. Something raw and visceral squeezed at his heart. This was where he belonged, right here, holding tight to the woman he loved. He wanted nothing more than to be the one to protect and care for her the rest of her life. They held onto each other like that for a full minute, savoring the pleasure of just being to-gether. "Please don't marry Freeman," he whispered.

Her body shook with silent laughter. "Isn't it obvious that's not going to happen?" She raised her head and eyed him in mock wariness. "Unless you aren't planning on asking."

Ben wasn't a fool. He seized the opportunity before Linda changed her mind. "Will you marry me?"

Her eyes glowed with delight. "Phew. I thought I was going to have to ask."

He squeezed her tighter. "You would have had to. I was determined not to push you into anything."

"You were trying to be noble. It was frustrating."

Ben laughed with unbridled joy. "You still haven't said yes."

Linda threw her arms around his neck and kissed him on the cheek. "Yes. Of course I'll marry you. Now, will you please stop looking so worried?"

He lifted her off her feet and twirled her around. After setting her down, he said, "No take backs."

She rolled her eyes. "No take backs? What, are we seven?" She frowned. "*Ach*, your nose is bleeding again. No lifting anything heavier than a loaf of bread until it heals."

"I don't think that's a real rule." Unable to resist, he gathered her into his arms and whispered tenderly in her ear. "I love you, Linda. I will always do my best to be the man you deserve."

"You always were," she whispered back. "You're the one who didn't believe it."

Her lips were temptingly close to his. He bent his head and drew her closer.

"Don't kiss me," she said.

"Don't kiss you?" Ben could almost taste his disappointment. The bishop—Dat—had made it clear that *die youngie* were not allowed to kiss before they got married, but surely Linda wasn't that much of a stickler for the rules. He'd go insane.

She pointed to his upper lip and grimaced. "There's too much blood." She handed him her damp apron, and he dabbed up the new blood from his nose. "Much better," she said. "Nobody wants to kiss somebody with a bloody nose."

"Do you want to kiss me at all?"

In answer to his question, she snaked her hands around his neck and pulled him close. Her lips met his, and fireworks went off in his head and they had nothing to do with his broken nose. His pulse raced, his breathing stopped, and his heart exploded. This was how it felt to be totally, completely, profoundly happy.

"Ben? Linda?"

With great effort, Ben pulled away from Linda. It felt like ripping out part of his hair. "Over here, Cathy," he called.

Zoe and Cathy appeared at the door to the stall. Zoe hooked her fingers over the top of the door. "Oh, shoot, Ben, your nose."

Ben huffed out a breath. "Wally punched me."

"Is it broken?"

"Probably."

Cathy didn't look impressed. "If you think a broken nose is bad, you should try childbirth."

Linda picked up her *kapp* from the floor. "Thank you for bringing Ben here, Cathy. Wally was pretty mad."

"Don't thank me," Cathy said. "Thank Zoe. She didn't have to get involved. She's not Amish. But she has the courage to do the right thing."

Zoe seemed quite touched by Cathy's praise. She lowered her head as the color traveled up her neck. "No problem. Wally can be a real jerk sometimes. I didn't want anyone to get hurt, and I knew Ben could take care of it."

Cathy nodded. "Wally can be a real jerk, but we've all been there. One time I hid the remote from my husband because I was sick of *The Bachelor*. I'm not proud of it, but I can understand where Wally is coming from."

Zoe glanced outside. "After we talked to your parents, we saw Wally coming out of the barn. I don't know how, but Cathy talked him into getting into her car. He's waiting for us."

Cathy sighed and looked at Ben. "I'll have to come back and get you after I drop Wally off at home. I don't think you and Wally should be in my car at the same time, and I don't want blood on the vinyl."

Linda sidled closer to Ben and took his hand. "I can take him home in the buggy."

"It's getting dark. I don't want you out on the roads by yourself."

Linda grinned. "That's very sweet. Annoying, but sweet."

Cathy's gaze shifted from Linda to Ben and back again. "So. Did you two work out your issues yet? The drama has been very entertaining, but it can only go on for so long before it gets tedious."

"Ben can be a total moron," Zoe said. "But you two belong together."

Ben put his arm around Linda. Even though an Amish engagement was supposed to be a secret, he didn't have the heart to keep it from Cathy or Zoe. In truth, he wanted to shout it to the world. "We've worked things out. We're getting married."

Cathy's expression didn't change. "Good, because I was about to recommend therapy."

Zoe grimaced. "Well. That was fast. But I'm not going to judge. I think you Amish are weird, and you probably think I'm weird. I guess we can just live with the weirdness and still be friends."

"For sure and certain," Ben said.

Cathy patted Zoe on the shoulder. "You're not weird. You're odd. There's a big difference."

Hand in hand, Ben and Linda followed Zoe and Cathy out of the stall, Linda resting her head on Ben's shoulder, a gesture that made him feel like he could face anything as long as Linda believed in him.

Cathy glanced over her shoulder. "I'm throwing you an engagement party."

Linda lifted her head and gave Ben a panicked look. "You don't have to do that."

"I know I don't have to. After all the fun times we've had together, I'm probably the closest thing to a maid of honor you have."

"I want to help," Zoe said.

Cathy nodded. "You can be a bridesmaid. Let's go to my house and look at Pinterest. They have party games and decoration ideas. I could make a balloon arch, or they have those balloons shaped like letters. We could spell out Linda's name and let them go into the sky."

"Fun," Zoe said. "My aunt had sparklers at her wedding."

Cathy had obviously never been to an Amish wedding. Unless she wanted to get baptized, she wouldn't be able to do much more than attend. Linda nudged Ben with her elbow. "Should I break the news, or do you want to?" she whispered.

Ben grinned. "*Ach*, Cathy doesn't get much excitement in her life. Let her dream a little."

Linda giggled. "We might regret that."

"For sure and certain."

Chapter Nineteen

The first *gute* snowfall of the year came at the perfect time. It snowed all day on Friday and into the early hours of Saturday morning, so that by Saturday afternoon, the snow was just right for snowshoeing.

Linda and Ben decided it would be best to do their first snowshoe outing at the golf course. There was no danger of getting caught in an avalanche, and the course would be easier on Cathy, who had just had an ingrown toenail ripped out and didn't want to strain herself.

They pulled up to the golf course in Cathy's new van. "If I'm going to be driving all these Amish people around, I need a bigger car," she had said. Esther, Levi, and Winnie had come with them, so the van definitely came in handy. Linda wasn't sure why Cathy had designated herself as the Amish chauffeur, except that she had a *gute* heart and she liked to stick her nose into other people's business.

As far as Cathy knew, Amish people led very exciting lives. Linda didn't want to disappoint her, but Ben and Linda's recent experiences were definitely not the normal Amish happenings. Most Amish just needed to be driven to the store or a relative's house once in a while. There was rarely a need for someone to intercept the police or stop a fistfight. Now that Ben had stopped smoking and drinking and making trouble, Cathy's life was going to get very boring. Unless Wally started asking her for rides.

Wally was likely to disappoint Cathy too. He had moved in with Simeon's family and had started meeting with a recovery group in Monte Vista. Lord willing, his wild, rebellious days were at an end.

They piled out of the van and grabbed their snowshoes from the back. Linda helped Cathy on with her snowshoes first. "I still don't understand why you're waiting almost a whole year to get married," Cathy said. "I had such plans."

"I know." Linda glanced at Ben who was holding Winnie so Esther could put on her shoes. "I hate waiting that long too. But we have to be baptized before we're married, and Ben and I are taking baptism classes."

"Well, how long do these baptism classes take? It doesn't seem like you're in a big hurry to get married."

Linda smiled to herself. It was something she and Ben had discussed many, many times. They were in a wonderful hurry to get married, but they wanted to do it right, so they needed to wait. Ben worked extra-long hours with his *dat* and Levi to earn money for the down payment on a house. Linda had taken on another job cleaning houses for *Englischers* in the area for the same reason. And then there was the wedding itself, which took a lot of planning and sewing and recipe collecting. Mamm could be overbearing, but she was ecstatic about planning a wedding. Linda certainly wouldn't rob Mamm of that joy by rushing things.

Linda tightened the strap on Cathy's snowshoe and

helped her stand up, then put her own snowshoes on. Levi got into his snowshoes and strapped a child carrier back-pack onto his back. Ben lifted Winnie into the backpack. Winnie giggled and kicked her legs as Ben secured her into the carrier. "Snow, Ben," Winnie said, pointing to the vast field of white on the golf course.

Ben winked at Linda and came close enough to whisper. "Esther says she will stay with Cathy so we can finally have our race."

Linda's heart pounded with anticipation. How many times had she challenged Ben to a race? How many times had she laughed at him and made him mad, so mad she hadn't expected him to keep coming back for more. She was glad he hadn't given up on her. His persistence was a testament to his *gute* heart and sweet disposition. It was why she had fallen in love with him. "You know you're going to lose."

His smile was wider than the sky. "We'll see about that." They shuffled into the deeper snow. Ben glanced at the others before slipping his gloved hand into Linda's. "I'm going to win, but it doesn't really matter if I finish before or after you. It's not possible for me to lose. I've already won the greatest treasure in the world."

Linda arched her eyebrow. "Hmm. You're already making excuses for losing. It's a *gute* strategy, but it won't work on me. Love is not an acceptable reason for losing the race. I won't go easy on you even though I love you to distraction."

His eyes lit up with amusement. "I wouldn't expect anything less from you."

"Okay then." Linda scanned the golf course. "I'll race you to the other side of that pine tree." It was the perfect place, away from prying eyes. "If I win, you have to give me a kiss."

Ben chuckled. "And if I win?"

Linda's heart danced like a leaf in the wind. "I have to give you a kiss."

"Sounds like a *gute* plan."

On the day she had caught Ben Kiem skiing behind her buggy, Linda never would have guessed that a practical girl like her would be wildly, irrationally, insistently in love with him. She didn't know what the future would bring, but she knew that Gotte had a plan. How else would she and Ben have gotten together in the first place? Lord willing, they would have many years together, growing older but never growing stale. Who knew, maybe they'd be like Cathy, snowshoeing in their eighties, going gluten free, and telling people about their health problems whether they wanted to hear or not. One thing was for sure and certain, every day she spent with Ben would be filled with adventure, joy, and lots of love. Love was the greatest adventure of all.

Ben smiled at her. "You know I love you, right?"

Her heart swelled to overflowing. "*Jah*. I do."

"*Gute*," he said. "Because there is no way I'm losing this race. Ready. Set. Go!"